DEEP BELLY OF THE EARTH

a novel by

Stephanie Whetstone

RABBIT HOUSE PRESS
Versailles, KY 40383

Published in the United States of America by Rabbit House Press, March 2026

For inquiries about author appearances and/or volume orders contact us at rabbithousepress.com.

ISBN: 979-8-9948202-0-9 (Print)
ISBN: 979-8-9948202-2-3 (eBook)

Editor: Erin Chandler
Copy Editor: Brooke Lee
Cover Photograph: Jeff Whetstone
Cover design: Laurie Smithwick
Interior design and formatting: Daphne Vorel

For Jeff, Cole, and
Jack Henry

DEEP BELLY OF THE EARTH

1

I've spent my whole life following Micah down one twisting trail or another, exploring the mountains inside and out until they took hold of me, until I felt exposed on any flat horizon. I learned to hold on to the shade and shadows of rock walls for comfort, like she did. We didn't know the swell of a mountain could be wiped away, make it look like nothing good was ever there, no people worth saving.

Micah convinced me to skip school again and hike up toward the high ridge above her house where the old Watco mine was so we could smoke pot and talk about everybody. We stopped on a switchback to catch our breath and smell the sweet, almost minty laurel and the faint must of the mossy trail. The yellowing leaves gave off a warm light. I took off my jacket and tied it around my waist. "Maybe we should go back," I said. "I'm missing a history quiz."

"You really think you're missing something from Mr. Mark's quiz? You'd miss this if you went back." She had a point. We hiked higher up the mountain. At first, I followed the horsetail swish of her long brown braid, then I passed her. She was taller than me, had longer legs, but I could still out-hike her. "Let's stop here and take another break," Micah said. Her cheeks were pink, her dark braid had come loose. We sat on a big, flat-topped rock and she took a joint out of her pocket and lit it. Inhaling first, she handed it to me then leaned back on the soft moss covering the rock, exhaling a thin column of smoke. She pointed to the mouth of the mine a few hundred feet away. The top of the mountain was covered by pine trees and laurel, a soft green blanket, except for the mine opening, a belly button of gray rock leading to the bowels of the earth.

"Let's go in there, Ava. We could go down into the places no one ever sees anymore."

I shook my head. I was scared, but I couldn't let her know. "In the pitch-black dark? What's the point of that? What exactly could we see then?" I took a tiny hit, held my breath, handed the smoldering joint back to her. I exhaled the smoke hard and blew my bangs out of my eyes.

"A lot," she said. "Your eyes adjust. Everything gets lighter. It's a world nobody gets to see."

"Plenty of people have been down there before it was shut down," I said. "We wouldn't be the first at anything." The mine had been inactive for years. My Uncle Gil, my mother's brother, had worked there. He never said much about it, just that they should have shut it down long before they did. Uncle Gil liked talking about the crazy times they had wildcatting, making money hand over fist, cheating death so often it felt like a regular day's work.

Micah kept pressing me, even after I told her that story. She liked to make me feel braver, but just a little weaker than her still, "They just worked there and got out quick as they could. We'd be sneaking in, investigating. You know, like archaeologists or something. We'd be on the mountain's side. Those guys just went in there to blast and dig the coal out. We'll be the only ones on earth to see it how it really was without all that equipment and dust. How it was meant to be. It's abandoned. We kind of have to go check on it."

Nothing was stable—not air, or mountains, or life above ground. At least not in Hensley County. The Earth might buckle. Maybe it was just a thin, hard shell, covering up a world of empty tunnels inside. What if it was hungry and wanted to swallow us up, keep us hidden until we rotted into dirt? Micah saw it differently. She claimed the mountains as her own.

"There's nothing to see down there," I said, but I knew this wouldn't stop her.

"There are ghosts," she whispered. "You know how all those miners died when we were in elementary school, when the gas blew?"

"Which time?" I said, but of course I knew. It was what made my heart chill when the wind got cold. Something about the cold air making the methane more volatile was all the science I knew about it. We studied it in chemistry, and I was the only one who refused to draw the structure of the gas molecules and tell how they bonded. I was the only one who thought it was morbid, how all those young men died. I didn't care that Mr. Lowry gave me a D.

"That first time, in second grade," Micah said. She was irritated with me for forgetting, but I hadn't. I tried to push things like that out of my mind; Micah liked to remember. "We were in Mrs. Kinder's class, and I sat right behind you the whole year. Jeremy Calvert sat behind me," she said, describing the whole classroom, what everybody wore, who came to school clean or dirty. She didn't know these were whole swaths of memories I tried to sweep out of my head. "Mrs. Kinder's husband was trapped in the mine, and she made us all pray for him. We laid our heads on our desks and prayed until another teacher came in and Mrs. Kinder could go sit outside the mines with the rest of the wives and mothers and girlfriends." Micah recalled every detail, down to the color of Mrs. Kinder's fingernail polish that day. It was hot pink, not quite fuchsia. According to Micah, it contrasted nicely with Mrs. Kinder's strawberry blonde hair and pale skin, which flushed when she got upset. Her face was bright red in my memory.

We watched that disaster from our small desks in room twelve, me huddled next to Micah, all of us children quiet, the widows on TV hugging and weeping into each other's long hair. I know now the miners were very young, not long past high school themselves, maybe leaving babies at home with their long-haired girls, never getting to watch them grow. "What if those spirits come after us?" I asked. "What if they decide to haunt us, Micah?"

"That is the most ridiculous thing I ever heard," she said. Then mimicking Father Matthew's nasal voice, "God will always look after the innocent. Hell, that's us, right?" Micah was always looking after me, especially since I started dating Collis Maynard. She didn't think much of him and worried he would pull me away. Maybe he would, but I wouldn't tell her that. "Well?" she stared at me. I nodded. "We'll be fine. Maybe you shouldn't be smoking pot. Some people are too sensitive. Maybe you're not developed enough."

"I'm not too sensitive," I said. "It's called self-preservation. You should try it."

"Come on, Ava. Don't be a pussy. Nothing's gonna happen to you." Micah could say words like pussy without flinching. She could say it to a grown man or a teacher. I had even heard her say it to her mom. She wasn't afraid to let anyone know she knew how the world worked. She got up from the mossy rock, brushed dirt off the seat of her jeans, and walked toward the mouth of the mine, steady and strong as a cop. I followed her, brushing my own pants, copying her walk, her fearlessness. She had a pull on me and could make me do things I'd never do alone. All she had to do was shame me, bring out the truth of my fear. She knew that existed in me before anyone else did. She could tell I was afraid of being called a coward, but she was going to fix me, make me strong and fearless as she was.

Once Micah could feel me following behind her, she turned around and threw me a small red flashlight. "Heads up," she said. Her mother, a complete neurotic, but one I was finally grateful for, put it in her backpack, *just in case*. I was never good at catching anything, but this was something I might need to get out of here. I caught it with both hands and slipped it in the pocket of my brown corduroys.

The opening of the mine was plenty for me. I could stay there all day while she went in and looked around, but I knew she'd never stand for that. Micah needed an audience. She shone in a spotlight. "Come in here, Ava! It's un-fucking-believable!"

I shook my head, "I'm alright here. You go ahead on."

The light outside the mine was fading. Micah ran into the mineshaft and yelled back, "You got to see this!" I couldn't see her, but her voice echoed in the rock. She sounded so much bigger than she was.

"So cool!" her words faded away and sank inside. I didn't want the mine to swallow her. I didn't want to be left at the mouth alone. Weeds vined around the ragged opening, green around gray rock around the darkest black. Warm air came out, it was always fifty-four degrees inside, warm from the fires in the earth's core, protected from all the water and wind and sun that beat the mountain down. Rock wore just like a face, or a body. I poked my head in first then stepped in on the path Micah had taken, "Wait up!"

"Come on!" she said. "Why are you always so slow?"

"Slow and steady wins the race."

"Bullshit. Here, stay close to me, so you can move a little faster." I didn't want to lose her before we lost all the light. Collis told me women going into the mines was bad luck. Who knew how our adventure might curse this place, or if the bad luck we spread might come home to roost? I held onto the elbow of her jean jacket until she shook me loose. "Let go," she said. "Just walk directly behind me. Do what I do." We'd studied myths in English class. She was my guide through this spirit world, Persephone. She stepped up onto a narrow raised ledge. There was a drop off to the right of it. Falling was my greatest fear.

"Oh, hell no, Micah. No way am I doing that."

"Stay here and suit yourself then," Micah shrugged, keeping one hand on the rocky wall, even as water trickled down and wet her fingers. She crouched to get through a small hole that led to an enormous room. I didn't want to stay back alone. I had no choice but to follow. "We should call this one 'The Mall.' It's that fucking big." She shined her flashlight around the room. In some places, the quartz embedded in the walls sparkled. "Look at this, Ava! It's like a million stars on fire!" She stopped so abruptly I slammed into the back of her. "Watch it! You don't have to be that close."

"All stars are on fire," I said.

"Just go with it. It's the most beautiful thing either of us has ever seen and you know it." She was right. We stood still and stared, shining the flashlight back and forth on the quartz to see it sparkle. "We could sell tickets to this," Micah said. "No one would believe it."

"No, they wouldn't," I said. It was our brand-new constellation. Closed in, in the dark space of the mine, it felt like a miracle.

"Let's just keep it to ourselves."

It wasn't too long after that day, maybe two months, in December, when a mine blew again, this time in West Virginia. I called Micah when I heard the news. She was getting ready to go to her uncle's house over the mountain in Tennessee. We were already on break from school. We had nothing to do but sit around and watch TV and eat Gammy's homemade fudge and divinity.

I had been hoping Collis would give me some sort of promise ring, at least a pretty necklace, so people could tell we were together even when we were apart. I wanted to belong to him. Collis was good for me, seemed so big and strong, even though he was just a few inches taller than me. Most people thought he was shy, but he was really thoughtful, always listening, saving his best words for me. Micah suspected he was a pothead and good for nothing.

The leaves were off the trees, and it might be cold, or it could be 65 degrees. It was hard to predict. Little kids believed in snow. Micah and I were seniors; we knew better. "Did you hear?" I asked her, the long telephone cord stretched from the old wall phone down the hall, into my room. I lay on my back on the pink carpet, staring at the square patterns of ceiling tiles as we talked.

"Hear what?"

"The West Virginia miners," I said. "How they're trapped. Fourteen, but they think three are already dead."

"How many widows?"

"Well, ten, if they don't make it. Plus girlfriends."

"Girlfriends don't count," Micah said. "They can find somebody else. No kids, you know."

"Well, ten then."

"Damn," she said. "That's a lot." We stayed on the line together in silence for a few minutes until her mother called her for dinner.

Ever since we were kids, we kept a tally of who lived and died underground and how many widows they left. When the air outside cooled, but the earth didn't, mines blew up and buried men in their depths. The mountains held power. All we could do was keep count and wait for spring when the air would settle.

2

Volunteers

The June after we finished college, Micah and I sat at our usual booth by the front window in Cullen's Cafe, eating lunch and watching cars go by. The place was packed, of course. There were six chrome and vinyl stools at the counter and six booths along the back wall. The green and white checkerboard floor was clean but worn down the middle in between the booths. So many feet had walked over it again and again. I stole a few of Micah's Doritos. She didn't mention it, even as I licked the orange cheese powder off my fingers.

"I can't believe you've done this to me, Ava," she said miserably, stuffing food into her mouth, but I was happier than I'd ever been. Collis and I eloped the weekend before, just over the state line in Tennessee. We were planning a big wedding for later, but it got too complicated with my parents, like everything did. They wanted a huge, prissy event. Collis and I just wanted to be married. So we did it.

"I'm still the same person, Micah. Plus, I'm twenty-two. That's plenty old enough to get married. We've been promised to each other for years. What would I wait for?"

"Me, maybe?" She stared straight ahead. "What am I supposed to do while you play house? "Micah always needed somebody around, and I was happy to join her, but that's the way it went, she called out the adventure and I responded. This was new, me taking on an adventure without her.

"I don't know," I sipped my Coke. "You seem pretty happy with the Vistas." Micah shook her head and took another bite of her sandwich. She had started hanging out with the young volunteers in town, but they were just here for the thrill of something different from their real urban lives. I heard through the grapevine Micah was sleeping around with them, maybe more than one, maybe both boys and girls, dirty and hairy as they seemed to me. She wanted something exotic too.

"Ava, you ought to meet these kids," she said. "They're good people. They're talking about shaking things up. You know, making something from the culture here, organizing."

"I don't have time for that." I had plenty of time, but if Micah had her way, I'd be protesting Collis's company up and down Main Street, and I'd be divorced by the end of the year. She'd kill two birds with one stone that way, I guess.

"What are you talking about?" She stood up. "You don't even have a job, and you're not going to unless somebody comes in to change things."

"There's nothing but mining here, Micah. What's left to save after that's gone?"

"Whatever came before that. The mountains. You and me. You think Collis is gonna have that job forever? You think you'll raise your family on coal? The king is dead." She shook her head. "All those executives are just trying to revive a corpse."

Micah could never accept the way things were or try to keep things stable. That's what I wanted most of all, a life that didn't wobble or move around. Change shook me. I wanted a life as unmoving and solid as a mountain. I had become Collis's lifelong love, the wife of a miner. I couldn't fight against that, didn't want to. I wanted the town I grew up in to stay the town I grew up in, with all the people I always loved. Micah wanted to tear it all to the ground and build something shiny, brand new, something completely unrecognizable.

These didn't even sound like Micah's words. She'd borrowed them from her new friends. She was "exploring her identity," as she put it. She was exploring a lot more than that, I thought.

She was becoming something separate from who we had always been, someone I didn't really understand. But she was still my best friend.

"Take me on home," I said. "I promised Collis I'd make dinner." Collis wouldn't be home for a while, but I didn't know what else to say to Micah. I wanted more time to think before I said too much.

"Ok, June Cleaver, but think about it," she said.

She could make fun of me, but all I cared about was Collis and making a family. I cared about a kind of love that Micah didn't know anything about. I wanted to belong to someone and have someone belong to me. I wanted to go through my whole life with someone who would know me inside and out, as well as or even better than he knew himself. The mountains would wait patiently, solidly. Hadn't they been there our whole lives? I couldn't imagine coal mining just going away, not completely. Since the first person had burnt a shiny black rock and felt its heat, this place and the people in it had felt useful, necessary, a part of the actual Earth. Coal was why this place was. It was this place.

Micah didn't know what she was talking about. She drove me home, curving along Zion Creek. Each time cars met ahead of us on the road along the creek, neighbors would stop and chat for a minute. We waited each time, three times if you were counting, listening intently to the music on the radio, not wanting to talk about how we were changing. This waiting for people to say hello to each other, to connect face-to-face through their rolled down car windows, this picking up the threads of a story or a conversation that had been going on as long as there had been a road, this tying tightly to each other was what I loved most about the creek. The narrow road required cooperation. Wide, lush green garden spots lined the creek on either side as it twisted and turned, rose and fell. Something was always growing and being tended. Collis and I had even put some tomatoes, peppers, and cucumbers in our own wide, flat plot. Like all of our neighbors, we nurtured them like children. The drivers ahead of Micah and me waved and drove off in opposite directions, so we could move again.

Finally, we reached the house. "See you soon," Micah said as I shut the car door.

"Sure," I said and gave her a half-wave. I didn't know when I would see her next or what we might have to say to each other, but I couldn't worry too much about it. I had Collis to take care of, and he had me.

My mother called me on Sunday, as she had every Sunday since she and Daddy moved to Indiana, to check in and chip away at my determination. She wanted to keep Collis and me from setting up house on Zion Creek and putting down roots that might keep us there forever. She still wanted us to move to Indiana, find a soulless cheap apartment near a big box shopping center. She wanted us to have dinner in her eat-in kitchen every Sunday at the long, oval wooden table I grew up around. My mother was like some kind of religious convert, praising asphalt and high rises. I wanted nothing to do with dry, flat Indiana. I worshipped creeks and hills, the mayapples and Indian paintbrush.

"Daddy can get Collis something in office supply sales at the company," she said. "He'll have room for promotion, and you'll find a job up here with your degree. You could work as a receptionist. You could work at a store. You could do anything, Ava! My grandchildren could grow up knowing me. That's the most important thing, don't you think? Being close to family?" Mom never thought this town was worth saving or that Collis was good enough. She told me so directly when we were first engaged. Still, she was happy I was married and settled now. That's one thing she expected for me, and I was happy to give it to her.

Mom had different ideas of what family meant than I did. It meant blood, we agreed, and shared history, of course, but it was more than that to me. It was the people you belonged to, the ones who saw the world the same as you did, wanted the same things. I didn't see anything the way Mother or Daddy saw it. I had always been the odd one, not the black sheep, maybe not even a sheep at all. I was more like a deer, running into the woods for protection and solitude. Collis and Micah understood me. Iona understood me. The mountains understood me; at least I imagined they did.

"Don't you miss being home?" I asked her. "There aren't any grandchildren yet, anyway. But when there are, this will be their home too."

"There's so much opportunity here, Ava. What kind of living can you make there? You've got to move on sometimes. You know, bloom where you're planted! You should see your brother's high school. The band just got asked to march in a parade in Chicago, and Travis is going on the trip! They got brand new blue uniforms. You ought to see them. I don't think they've had new uniforms in Iona since I was in school."

Travis spent the first years of his life as my baby doll, perched on my hip. He followed me and my friends around like a puppy. We shooed him away like one. He was fourteen when my parents moved. I was nineteen. Our lives had diverged there.

"You ought to at least give it a try," Mother said. "We miss you, Baby."

"I miss you too," I said. It was the truth. I mean, everybody misses their mother in some way, don't they? But it was a muddled truth. I didn't miss seeing my mom every day, having to manage my life entwined with hers. I had never been drawn to shopping centers or chain restaurants or suburbs with houses painted in palatable colors. What I did miss was the feeling of knowing my mama was right there, minutes away in Iona, in case I needed her.

Travis was an indoor kid, always playing computer games or watching TV. He was easy to manage. I was the one who constantly wandered off outdoors. They couldn't keep me inside. Gammy used to say the smell of the live woods hit some people deep in the heart, while others didn't even notice it. My nose and heart were full of it, but Travis never caught the scent. He hadn't left much in Kentucky but me.

On the edge of Indiana, where my parents lived, to be hillbilly meant to live in the poor neighborhoods. Hillbilly meant to have too many children too young, to search for scraps of jobs to piece together to make some kind of money quilt. Mother and Daddy wanted to prove that wasn't who they were. Or who I was. But I was proud to be a hillbilly and would call myself one to friends. To me, it meant I was part of the unruly land and stubborn mountains, and that I was just as strong.

We still had real places like Zion Creek in Hensley County and real people. My parents had been town people, even in Iona. They sure couldn't see the beauty in a place as remote as this, miles from the nearest grocery store. "What if you run out of milk, or bread, or eggs?" Mom asked.

"We'll drive into town. Or I guess we could borrow from the neighbors if we had to make emergency French toast or something. Everybody knows us."

"You're at the edge of the world," she feared.

I was, but not on an edge I could fall off. The tiny clear creek curved through rich bottomland, pocked with small, neat houses and trailers. Families lived together, intertwined. This life was richer than anything Indiana had to offer.

Each evening after work, Collis and I tended our garden in the fading summer light, filtered through the hickory and oak leaves. He'd haul white five-gallon buckets full from the creek to water everything. I'd hoe clean, straight lines down the middle of each row and push a seed down into the furrow every six or so inches. We made a pretty little entrance to the garden with flat rocks from the creek bed. The soil was rich and brown, not the hard-packed orange clay you'd find in other parts of the county. As the tiny light green sprouts emerged, they made my heart flutter. The garden was proof that life could be beautiful and abundant, even on Zion Creek. I could make it happen.

When night fell, we sat on the porch and Collis played Neil Young songs on his guitar, mimicking Neil's quiet falsetto. "Aurora Borealis, the icy skies at night / Paddles cut the water / In a long and hurried flight." It seemed like we could feel the roundness of each moment that summer, even as my mother talked on and on about her busyness and about feeling tired. Collis and I felt full of love, happiness, life itself.

We were on the porch watching the night fall, when Micah came barreling down the road toward the house. "Why the hell is she driving like that?" Collis said. "There's kids playing around here."

She parked in front of the house, got out and called to us, "Hey!"

"Hey!" I called back. "What are you doing out here?" I hadn't seen her since our lunch a month before.

"Ava, you're not going to believe this!" She made a beeline for the empty chair next to me, then looked toward Collis. "Hi, Collis," she said. Collis nodded and went into the house. He knew she was just there to see me.

"I got a job interview with Save the Mountains! If I get it, they'll send me to Knoxville for a week for organizer school. Then I get to speak before the legislature and lead meetings and stop strip mining!" Micah was on fire. I had never seen her so lit up about anything. She really believed she could stop strip mining, and maybe she could. She could do anything.

"That's great," I said, "but you gotta be careful organizing around here. People are protective. Collis isn't allowed to join any groups like that; none of the miners are. The company keeps tabs on them." I heard about men being demoted or fired, of course, but that wasn't what worried me most. It was the accidents on the road or in the mines that didn't seem like accidents that worried me. I knew people whose wives and children had been harassed because they tried to organize.

"Well, that's exactly what I'll be fighting against. They can't keep us down forever." Micah leaned forward to emphasize her impatience with the system. She smiled wide enough to show the dimple on her right cheek I always envied.

"I'm proud of you," I said. I was, but I could feel our lives pulling away from each other. I was too concerned about my happy little married life to care about what the legislature did. They never cared about us in the mountains, as far as I could tell, so why should we care about them? As long as Collis and I could live here where we felt at home; as long as Collis had a job and I could eventually find one; as long as we could build a life here, I didn't want to think about coal companies. I knew how miners had suffered. I knew about the mine wars. I could see what the strip-mining had done to the mountains. Still, I was focused on now because now was good, and now meant Collis having a job, keeping the peace, and starting our family. I got Micah a beer and we celebrated, then she went home before the night got too dark.

Those long summer days stretched into fall and I pretended to hunt for jobs that didn't exist. While Micah spent her days with twenty-year-old organizers, in love with each other's youth and beauty, I spent my days with elderly neighbors. The young ones on the creek were somewhere at work or school and the old folks were more interesting anyway.

Walker Whitaker lived three houses down the creek from Collis and me, toward the main road. He lived in the home place, and his sisters Lou and Ida lived in a double-wide he'd bought for them and put right beside the old farmhouse. The siblings were in their eighties and had lived on the creek most of their lives. They knew how to find ginseng plants in the hills, dry-land fish, or morels, in summer, and ramps in the spring. Walker taught us how to hill up our squash, to plant the corn and beans together. Lou and Ida shared their pickle recipe and taught me to can. The three of us were a sepia picture in their 1950s kitchen, sunlight lighting up the jars of tomatoes cooling by the window, steam coming out of the old pressure cooker, me in my torn jeans and UK T-shirt, Lou and Ida from another era in faded housedresses and aprons, a stray gray strand of hair falling down a wrinkled cheek. They were somehow both of their time and timeless. I wanted to enter that slipstream, where past and present could be layered on top of each other, taking turns at being up front.

Walker taught school to almost all the children on the creek until the old schoolhouses were consolidated and sprawling brick schools were built in town. He taught over sixty children to read and write. All of his own children had moved to Knoxville, a few hours south. The creek was too small for them, they said, too dark.

Walker grew about an acre of corn, on down the creek past any houses, before it met up with Flat Rock. He drove his ancient tractor down the narrow road, through a part of the low flowing creek, to get to that other land. I'd walk down there every morning, through the mystical tunnel of water, creek rocks, and trees, just to see Walker's cornfield, looking like some sort of green and gold gift God had left for only me to find.

Our tiny white clapboard house was built on narrow pillars of river rocks for support. Sometimes, I thought I could feel the house move a little with each strong breeze. One night in the fall, when Collis was long asleep, I heard somebody knocking on the window. I don't mean I think I heard it. That's what it was. A fist rapping on glass. There was no tree nearby, no limbs loose, not even a stray dog out.

"Wake up," I said.

"Good Lord, Ava. What time is it?"

"Shh, listen!"

"I don't hear nothing." He pulled the covers up over his head. "Please let me sleep, Ava. Please."

That's when the knocking came again. "See?" I nudged him.

Collis sat up against the headboard, "Could be the wind."

"There's no wind out there. You know plain as day, that was a knock." We clung to each other, waiting for the next knock, but it never came. Collis drifted off, but I couldn't. I wasn't scared, just excited at the possibility of meeting a ghost. I thought about calling Micah, but it was 3:19am. We hadn't talked since she went to Knoxville to train for her job. Still, I wanted her to love the creek and its spirits like I did. She was the person who had known me the longest, held my childhood as I held hers. I missed her.

I was hoping to hear the knock again, and maybe to answer it. I could see why whoever it was didn't want to leave. Maybe we could buy some land on the creek, eventually. We'd build a house, and when our kids were grown, we'd build them a place. We'd be here for generations, just like my ghost.

Micah didn't have anyone like I had—Collis with his broad smile and the tiniest dip of a cleft in his chin. When we were snowed in with the power out, keeping each other naked warm, feeling the heaven of that place, we made a family. Our Joshua was conceived in that ramshackle house that winter. Our landlady, Mary, couldn't help acting like a mama. She came over and brought us some soup beans she'd cooked all day on her gas stove.

"I don't want you all to starve," she said unpacking beans, cornbread, and some chocolate chip cookies. There was enough food for ten people.

"See," Collis told me later, "this place takes care of its own." He was right. My mother and daddy were foolish to have gone to a place that would just as soon not have them.

Every morning until the snow melted, we huddled together in a cocoon under the down comforter. Collis's body became as familiar to me as my own. I touched the tiny beige birthmark to the left of his belly button, shaped like the state of Tennessee. I held on to his broad shoulders. We made love until we were in a full slick sweat under the covers, then made deals about who would get out of bed in the cold room to get the fire going again in the wood stove. I usually talked Collis into tending it, then the fire would come back to life and burn, the black iron of the stove glowing red.

———

By February though, they'd stripped all the coal in Buxley, ten miles away. Collis's work moved toward Hubbard, fifty miles away, so he came home later and later each night, driving from little town to little town dotting the hillsides. When he got home one night at eight, I was having Braxton-Hicks contractions.

"We might have to move in closer to town," Collis said. "This is getting scary."

"No, it's alright," I shook my head in between a few quick breaths and a long one. "I want to stay here."

"And who's going to deliver our baby when it comes? I may not be able to make it home in time to drive you to the hospital. I don't think old Walker is up to the task, and Mary doesn't drive."

"I'll be fine." But the contractions made us both nervous as they got closer and closer to the real thing. For once, he and Micah were on the same side. She checked in on me every few weeks, and she wanted me closer to the hospital too. There was no use fighting them when they were united.

We moved to town that month, to a house with a small room for a nursery, just a few blocks from the hospital, but I missed the creek, the swaying house, and Walker driving his tractor through the water to tend his fertile field. I'd whisper stories about the place's magic to Joshua as I rocked him to sleep a few months later. "I'll take you there when you're big enough. I'll teach you every bend of that creek someday."

I never found a way to keep my promise, though. Not so Joshua could grow up there and make it his. When I finally took him out to visit old Walker, let Walker bounce him on his knee and sing to him, my dream seemed further and further away. Sometimes I thought I'd made our time there up, like it was more imagination than memory.

3

Wallace's Bend

Each time Collis's job was at risk, and it seemed perpetually at risk, he followed the work to a new mine. He worked the hardest and longest to make sure they'd keep him on, though in the end it didn't do any good. Like everyone else, from the slackers to the overtimers, he was laid off. If a site was mined out, there was no way to stay there and nothing to stay for. A couple of Collis's friends moved to Knoxville to work on a construction site, but he wanted no part of that. He wanted to stay in Iona, not to come home on odd weekends and get pulled gradually into the fabric of a city. Collis had a friend, Johnny Roberts, who always made sure he made the cut at whatever job he was aiming for. Collis never asked how or why, and neither did I, even though I wondered. I wouldn't want a friend if they had to hide things from me. Favors like that came due quickly and painfully.

"Let's just be grateful, Ava. Friends look out for each other," Collis said.

I never trusted Johnny though. His face was the made-up story he showed the world. He didn't bother with taking care of people that I could see. He didn't even care about hellos or thank yous. I'd answer a knock at the door, and he'd greet me with, "Where's Collis?" Only sizing me up to see if I could be worth something to him. Johnny was the kind of man who took what he wanted, whenever he wanted, and didn't care if somebody called it stealing.

"I don't like you working with that man," I told Collis. I heard more and more stories that set me on edge; Johnny beating up Clyde Davis so bad he couldn't be recognized and was laid up in the hospital for weeks; Johnny recruiting high school kids to sell drugs for him; men who worked for Johnny getting arrested and going away for years. Collis brushed them all off, and my words hit him the wrong way.

"Oh, you don't like it? Well, if you like me working, Ava, it might have to be with him."

"You can't trust him, Collis. You've heard what people say. I don't want you involved with a criminal."

"Rumors, Ava. Johnny's no criminal. That's all just small-town talk. He's good to me. To us. What else would you have me do? Flip burgers? Do you want a man with a job or no man at all?"

I bit my tongue and kept my worries to myself. I'd go to bed thinking about them and wake up with those same worries hovering over me in the morning. I was glad Collis had work, I was, and I hated when he hinted he'd leave. But what he didn't know about Johnny might hurt us. So would what he did know and would never tell.

＝

Micah stopped by the house Thursday night, wanting to hang out, go somewhere, do something. She was restless. I was exhausted. Her life was completely different from mine, but I was somehow still a part of it. The Vistas came and went, loved her and left, but I had been here her whole life.

Joshua was three, and "no" was his favorite word. He was covered in spaghetti, the orange residue of tomato sauce around his tiny mouth, fighting me about taking a bath. He slipped out of my arms and ran, as fast as his little legs would go, down the hall, into the living room. "You get back in here right now!" I yelled.

"No!" he screamed.

"What in the world is going on?" Micah had let herself in the front door, just like she used to. She could see Collis's truck was missing from the driveway.

"Joshua Maynard!" I was in the bathroom, kneeling by the full tub. Joshua was running around naked, laughing. Micah grabbed him and lifted him up into the air, then carried him into the bathroom and plopped him gently into the tub.

"Thanks," I said. I was about to kill him."

In the tub, Joshua splashed and played. He wanted to play a game of chase, but I was too tired, so he let me give him a bath. Micah sat on the edge of the tub and kept me company.

"Collis still at work?" she asked.

"If you call what he does for Johnny Roberts work."

"What's he doing?"

"I'm not sure exactly… errands, he says. It's not fixing things or doing yard work because he comes home clean, his truck is clean. I'm not so sure about his conscience. He hasn't been home to put Joshua to bed in two weeks."

"Johnny Roberts has done time, Ava."

"I know, but Collis says Johnny was set up, that they're mining buddies, and that if you can't trust old friends, you can't trust anybody. He says the stories are just from busybodies with too much time on their hands.

"You look like hell."

"Thanks, you're a true friend. And an old one for sure." I swatted Micah's leg with the washcloth before turning serious. "It's worrying me to death."

"Well, you can't change anything by worrying," she said. "You need a break, is what I'm saying. When are you going to come to one of my meetings?"

"Uplift myself with thoughts of strip mining?"

"No, with plans to fight it. There's a meeting at the VFW Tuesday night. We're trying to get a big group to sit in at Calvary Rock, where they're strip mining on the mountain behind the houses. You should see all the run-off and slag sliding down the hill."

"One of your protest meetings is a break?"

"From this glamorous life of intrigue?" She swept her hand in the air to show me what she was seeing, a messy, pink-tiled bathroom, a soapy toddler splashing, a woman on her knees by the tub, wrung out. "Yes," Micah said. "Most definitely." I missed our teasing, our back and forth, keeping each other honest, making each other smile.

"I'm lucky to get out to the grocery by myself these days, Micah. Besides, I can't stir things up. Collis needs this job." I pulled the drain plug out of the bath and Joshua tried to catch the water from slipping away.

"No, Mama!" he said. I pulled him out of the tub and wrapped him in a towel, kissing the top of his wet head as he howled.

I signed up for this life when I signed my marriage license. I wanted to be known as somebody's wife. Mining was part of it too. I loved the idea that Collis and I both went back generations here. The mountains had a long memory. People remembered who was for and who was against. Besides, everybody knew that Bud Jacobs had been canned because his sister, Eileen, had put up signs in her yard against Big Coal. Bud hadn't even talked to Eileen in years, but this was a small town. She was known as an environmentalist, which to some people meant anti-job, anti-community. It was easy to make examples of people. Micah and her protestors might be right. Anybody could see by looking out the window what the coal companies had done to destroy the mountains. You could taste it in the water coming out of the tap too, the water Joshua splashed in, but what good would it do to protest when those were the only living wages around?

"There aren't going to be jobs for long, Ava. I keep telling everybody, but they don't believe me. Soon enough, if they keep blasting for the last little bits, there won't be any mountains either. What's Collis gonna think then? Will you still listen to him?" Micah didn't care what anybody had to say about not getting on the coal company's bad side, or about trying to keep jobs. She didn't have to care. She'd probably still get a paycheck from Save the Mountains when the mines shut down, might even get a bonus. Micah could be brave and free. I couldn't.

Micah stayed and cleaned the bathroom for me while I got Joshua into his pajamas and into bed. Once he was down and fading off to sleep, we sat in the living room and talked about safe things, the past, our families, our love lives or lack thereof, until Collis came home an hour later, slipping in the back door and poking around in the kitchen for something to eat.

"Come on in and talk to us," I said. He came in with his plateful of leftover chicken and mac and cheese and sat next to me on the old brown couch. Micah scooted down to the end to make room for him.

"They sure are working you hard," she said.

"They are," he nodded. "I'm doing a little work on the side too."

"I thought you were gonna quit that," I said. It worried me he would bring that out to impress Micah. I thought of all the things a person might do around here to make extra cash. None were good.

"It's no big deal, Ava. It helps."

I didn't want to start a fight in front of Micah. I didn't want to give her another reason to tell me I'd messed up by getting married. "Collis, I'm gonna steal your wife away on Tuesday night," she interrupted, saving me. "Can your mom babysit? Ava says she's asked her too many times already, but I say that's what every grandmother wants."

"I'm sure she'd do it," Collis slid an arm around me, a peace offering. "You know she would, Ava."

I knew Alice would watch Joshua, but I was tired of her telling me how to raise him, how to feed him. Last time had been a battle. I'd brought him snacks in tiny Tupperware boxes, carrots, goldfish crackers, a couple of cheese sticks. When I came to pick him up, he ran to the door and hugged me at my knees, "Look, Mama," he said, "Cheetos!" His little pink mouth was encircled by an orange smear of Cheeto dust.

"I left him snacks in his bag, Alice," I said.

She picked him up and put him on her hip, "Oh, Nana has to give her baby treats!" This was another thing I thought she shouldn't do, now that he was bigger. She finally put Joshua down and he ran to the table, then back to me.

"Look, Mama. I have a hotdog!" Joshua said. He had a whole hotdog in his fist and was about to take a bite.

"No!" I grabbed his hand and squeezed until he let go of the hotdog. "He could choke on that!" Joshua began to cry.

"He's fine," Alice said. "All kids like hotdogs. And I have an eye on him. All the time." She looked at me as if to insinuate that I didn't keep a good eye on him, but I didn't have the heart for another argument about how Collis ate this or that and grew up just fine. There was a lot about him that wasn't fine.

——

I had my own way of doing things with Joshua. And most of the time, it was easier to do it myself, but this time, with the odd force of both Collis and Micah pushing in the same direction, I gave in. I'd let Alice watch Joshua again. But definitely no more hotdogs. "Okay, okay. I'll go out, but it's not going to be for some hellraisers' meeting."

"Fine, as long as you'll get out of the house." Micah grinned. "We'll go out in Hubbard Wednesday to the new Chinese place and I'll give you the play by play of how the meeting went."

Collis gave me a look that told me what he thought of Micah's meetings.

"Ok. Who knows, at this rate, Collis and I might even get a date soon," I said.

He pulled me close and surprised me with a kiss. "It could happen. Matter of fact, you pick out the movie, and we'll go Friday night, at the old theater over the mountain in Virginia. I may even spring for dinner."

"Better make him pinky promise," Micah said.

"I still got it, don't I?" He smiled and winked at me with those big brown eyes, the thick dark lashes "wasted on a boy." At that moment, I'd have forgiven him of anything. He might be working more, but it made him happier. He got down when he had too much time to think and not enough work, sleeping and drinking too much. He was short with me and Joshua, ready to bite at any perceived slight. It was a tradeoff, his working for Johnny. He came home from work in a good mood, relaxed, even if I felt on edge. That was enough. I made it enough.

—

Tuesday night at seven, Micah came by to pick me up. Collis was still at work, but Alice was already there. From the minute she had gotten to our house, she had Joshua on her hip, letting him pull her hair and play with her necklace.

"Stop pulling on your Nana!" I told him.

"Oh, he's fine," she said. He was big for a three-year-old, but she wouldn't put him down. "You girls stay out just as long as you want. We'll have a big time here." Alice still babied Collis. She babied me when I let her. I wasn't used to so much attention and tried to shake it off. Since she had retired from teaching, she was like a border collie with nothing to herd, always trying to gather us around her.

—

After Collis's dad died when we were in middle school, Alice threw herself into her third-grade classroom. She was on every committee they could come up with. Still, when she had her thirty years and was eligible for retirement, they pushed her out. The mayor's daughter had just graduated with her teaching certificate, and he pressured the school board to find her a job. They found Alice's. That was just before Joshua was born.

Alice liked Micah, but she was wary now that Micah was an organizer. It was too dangerous for someone with a child to get into all that, she told me, just in case I had my own ideas. She was okay with the Chinese restaurant though.

"You want us to bring you something back, moo goo gai pan? Egg rolls? Anything?" I asked. She declined my offer, saying she had eaten before she came over. "Collis ought to be back by 8:30. They're trying to finish up at that site by the end of the month." I grabbed my jacket and headed toward the door.

"I wish he'd get out of there and find something regular." Alice frowned. "He's gonna regret missing this time." She kissed Joshua on his fat cheek. "Won't he, baby?"

"I'm not a baby, Nana!" he said. I blew him a kiss and left with Micah. Joshua was getting big, but we had our whole lives to watch him grow. I didn't think Collis was missing anything he couldn't catch up on in a few years. But that was when I thought we'd be there, in that little house on Wallace's bend, or one just like it, forever.

4

Hard Rock Falls

One Saturday morning, Collis was home and seemed restless, as if he didn't know quite what to do with himself when he wasn't working. I poured us each a cup of coffee, and we sat at the kitchen table, sipping.

"It's time to get this boy out in the woods," he said. "Let's take him to the falls!"

My first thought was it was too dangerous to take Joshua on a hike like that, but he was almost five, more a little boy than a baby. His sandy curls were gone to a spiky brown buzz cut, his big eyes constantly studied the world. He was a sturdy little hiker and listened when I told him to stop, so I said it was a great idea.

It was the first warm day we'd had, the snow all melted. Collis packed us peanut butter and jelly sandwiches, a couple of apples, and some water. Joshua ran the first two hundred feet, so happy to be set loose. When his legs tired, he sat down on the middle of the trail and refused to go any farther. Another time, he chased after a tiny peeper until it hopped into the trees.

Collis wanted to move straight ahead. "Come on, baby," he said. "Try and move a little faster." We hiked the rocky two-mile path that hugged the side of the mountain. Joshua trailed behind. Sometimes Collis got antsy and I couldn't tell if it was excitement or something else, more like agitation. He'd been spending more time with Johnny, but when I asked him what it was, he was vague. I wasn't brave enough to push him for details.

It was like Collis was holding something in and had to let a little of it out in the freedom of the woods. Lately, he was spending too much time on his phone texting I don't know who. He sure wouldn't talk to me about things that were bothering him. Didn't want to worry me, he said. To tell the truth, I really didn't want to know on beautiful days like this. Outside in the lush woods, I wanted things to stay light and easy.

Collis wasn't more than a few inches taller than me, his legs weren't much longer, but he moved up the steep, narrow trail like a deer. He dipped to avoid low branches and blackberry brambles without missing a beat. I followed the way his body curved through space.

"I'm coming," I said. "This little boy's taking his time."

Collis looked back at us.

"I don't think I can carry him the whole way," I said.

"I got him," Collis said, swooping Joshua up in his arms and sitting him on his shoulders.

"Come on, Daddy, faster!" Joshua said. Then we were really moving down the trail. It followed the creek, sometimes right at the water level, sometimes far above it. The sun filtered through the branches, the pines old and heavy, the oaks and maples fresh with tiny green leaves. There was a section, when we got close to the falls, where we could hear the water gushing, loud as a fire hose. Then we had to climb up a few big rocks. Collis put Joshua down for that and they each scrambled over.

"I see it, Daddy!" Joshua shouted and pointed toward the gushing white water.

There were a couple of teenagers in shorts and tank tops, sunning themselves on the huge rocks that fanned out at the bottom of the falls. "How cold is it today?" Collis asked.

"Pretty damn," the skinny boy stretched out on the rock nearest us said. "But it's worth it." He lay back on the rocks and stared at the clouds, unconcerned with us. The girl next to him looked like she had fallen asleep. I couldn't tell if they were high or just relaxed.

"Let's go!" Collis stripped off his shirt, even though there was still a chill in the air, and climbed the rocks straight up to the falls.

I got close enough to feel the freezing spray. Then he stuck his head straight under and let out a yell. "Woohoo! You coming?"

"What? You think I won't?"

"Oh, she's brave! Look at Mama now, Joshua!" Collis climbed down and sat with Joshua while I climbed up to the falls. There was no turning back now. I threw him my jacket, then stuck my head under the frigid water, much stronger than any shower or hose. This came off the top of the mountain, split the rock over time. It took my breath for a second, but after I let it out, I breathed in everything clean and fresh.

"That's my girl!"

I loved him best when he was free and light, when I could see how much he loved me back. We had our picnic and lay on the boulders like the teenagers, while Joshua waded in the shallows and threw pebbles into the water next to us. Later, sun-warmed and lazy, I followed Collis back down the trail to the car. He was a strange totem pole with a child growing from his shoulders, all of us free in the wild.

5

Air

Collis finished a dozer job an hour and a half away in Paintsville. He wouldn't start up on the new site for another ten days. To keep busy, he worked on things around the house, the bathroom sink that kept clogging, the shoe molding that had come loose in the living room, but he was tense, an electric current surrounded him, any odd word could spark it to a flame. We fought again about him working for Johnny. He said it was the only way we could make ends meet, but I knew there had to be better ways.

"You've got to decide what's more important to you, Collis," I demanded, "working for Johnny or keeping your family together." He didn't say anything for a few minutes, and I didn't either. He shook his head. The silence held our fragile love together.

Finally, he threw his hands up, "I love you and Joshua, Ava. You know that. I'll let Johnny know I've got to quit."

He tried to quit anyway, picking up odd jobs in the neighborhood, fixing leaks, painting somebody's living room, patching a hole in the neighbor's roof. He was a good handyman, but while there were lots of people who needed work done, there weren't enough people who could pay him to do it. You can't buy groceries with a trade. Alice was helping us with the fees for kindergarten, at least until Collis got something more stable. I applied for a counselor position at Stone Healthcare, and it looked like I might get it. I wanted to wait until after we had another baby to go back to work, after all, Joshua was five, but it didn't look like a new baby was in the cards. Lately, Collis hadn't been interested in getting close to me at all.

Stone Healthcare had a big five-year grant from the state for addiction counseling, and already they couldn't meet the demand. It seemed like more and more people were strung out, especially on Oxycontin. I didn't have my certificate in substance abuse, but I did have my bachelor's in social work and I had known Gabe Jacobs all my life, so he was willing to hire me. It was a good step toward something, even if I didn't know what that something would turn out to be.

Alice came over to the house early for Joshua's sixth birthday party. She made homemade party hats out of red and blue construction paper for the five kids we invited from his school. Once a third-grade teacher, always a third-grade teacher, I guess. I didn't have a crafty bone in my body, so I let her take over the details. decorating, making favors, planning games. The room was colorful as a carnival, with streamers twisted from the light fixture in the middle of the ceiling to points in every direction across the room.

Collis and I blew up the party balloons: red, green, blue, and yellow. Alice said we needed at least fifteen, but we were both running out of air. He tried to blow a blue one up, but it slipped away from him and fizzled to the ground. Neither one of us could stop laughing. "I think they'll have to live with an even dozen," he giggled. "I'm getting lightheaded."

"That'll be plenty," I said, taking a deep breath to calm my laughter. There was something so ridiculous, something so sweet about Collis and me trying to fulfill Joshua's tiny dreams and Alice's meticulous plans. Collis shot the last empty balloon across the room like a rubber band. I swatted at it and missed.

"You think you're gonna like that job?" he asked, getting us both back down to earth.

"I hope so." I pushed the filled balloons to one corner of the room and started tidying up.

"You know, I can get us by, Ava. You don't have to take it. Things'll pick up. Johnny says he has a few jobs for me."

I didn't want that. I admit, I checked Collis's phone every morning. I always got up before him, around six, so it was easy.

Johnny had left messages about a "delivery" job, and maybe a "security" job. I deleted the messages and didn't mention them. There was another number in missed calls I didn't recognize, but they never left a message.

"I know things will get better," I said. "But now that Joshua's in school, I need to do something. Gabe said he'll let me leave early to pick Joshua up, as long as I come back to the office for a few hours afterward. This will be good for all of us."

"Well, I am proud of you, Baby," Collis said. "Those are some lucky addicts. A man might want to get into all that mess if it got him an appointment with you."

I threw a balloon at him, "I wouldn't wish that on anybody."

At first, I went to work and since his mining site had shut down, Collis kept to the house, fixing every little thing he could think of, calling leads on jobs. Then, he started hanging out with a couple of guys from the mines, drinking a few beers, smoking a little pot, playing poker a few nights a week. Every now and then, one of the guys would ask Collis to help on a backhoe job or help move somebody to Lexington. Finally, he got back on at Macy Mines full time, stripping a highwall near the Virginia line. He even worked extra on the weekends to fill in for people on vacation.

"See, Ava," he said. "It was only a matter of time. When you got real friends, they help take care of you."

"Don't you think it's too far away?" I asked. "It'll take you two hours each way."

"Does it matter? I've got a real job again. Can't we celebrate that? I may even get the foreman spot next time."

"You're right," I kissed him gently. "It's great. Congratulations, Baby." I wanted to hold onto his good mood as long as I could. Still, I couldn't shake the feeling we'd crossed over some threshold. Our lives were beginning to stretch away from each other, only connected by Joshua each night.

6

Piecing

I held on to Micah. She kept me company, kept me busy with her schemes to save the mountains. I was just trying to save my own family. Her latest plan was ridiculous, as usual, but with her, you never knew. Micah believed in things hard enough to push other people through. She might actually make it work.

"I've got a great idea," she said. She always had a *great idea*. We were sitting in her kitchen, in the house that used to be her granny's on Cattle Island. She pulled out the boxes, "I'm gonna have a quilt-a-thon."

"Why?" I asked. "Who would want to go to something hokey like that? I don't think anybody our age actually quilts."

"Are you kidding? It's a great idea! I'll raise money for Save the Mountains. Those old ladies around town have nothing else to do, except gossip and get into trouble. We'll get them to compete making quilts all weekend, maybe in teams. Then, we can auction off the quilts in Lexington at some big party. People there always want something to remind them of home. Quilts make them feel good about the mountains. Reminds them of their grandparents. Makes them feel authentic."

Some people had to be made to feel good about this place they had come from; others of us couldn't imagine ourselves anywhere else. I think it had something to do with whether you were happy with who you were to begin with, whether you liked the fact you were a part of something, or whether you were ashamed of your people and the fact we didn't have things other people could buy.

I was proud of the mountain twang in my voice, like Dolly and Loretta. I wanted to be strong and beautiful, like them.

When Micah's granny died, she left boxes and boxes of scrap material that Micah had no use for but couldn't bring herself to get rid of. I couldn't picture Micah sitting still long enough to make a quilt. I couldn't even hem. But Micah always saw an opportunity in what was left behind, people, places, things.

Some boxes were full of old jeans, some were crammed with scraps of old pillowcases. Some were piled high with bright colored remnants that used to comprise fancy polyester suits in the '70s. Micah's granny never said no when somebody had something to give her, as if she could make enough colorful quilts to keep the whole world warm. I think that's where Micah got her instinct to try to save the world, at least our world.

"Might could work," I said.

"Didn't you say you had a client who was a real good quilter? You know, the one who was helping her grandkids sell pills and got hooked herself?"

"I could get in trouble for telling you that."

"But maybe I just happen to know it," she said. "The quilting part that is. Maybe you didn't tell me. I just heard it somewhere, but I don't remember where."

"No," I said.

"Well, I bet I can find fifty pill-head ladies to be in my quilt-a-thon, even without your help."

"You're a sight! Knock yourself out Ms. Quilting Bee. I've got to go pick up Joshua."

"Here, take him some quilting scraps. He might like to quilt too." She started filling a plastic grocery sack with different types of fabric. "We could get kids in on it!"

"You're nuts!" I laughed. "Unless you make it into some kind of video game." I wanted to steer clear of Micah's quilt-a-thon. She'd find a way to make the elderly and the elementary school set radical. She'd have them beating on bulldozers with their book bags and canes. I was trying to stay out of the big mess that was brewing between the landowners and people like Micah against the company Collis was working for. I understood, agreed with her even, but that wasn't something I could say out loud. Of course, I worried what would happen when the mountains were torn to rubble, the creeks full of sludge. I just thought it wouldn't happen as quickly as Micah said it would. I wanted everybody to have work, and water, and stay out of trouble. Was that too much to ask? Micah thought that was impossible. I held the bag of scraps out to her. "The ladies will do more with these than Joshua."

She snatched the bag back from me. "You'll see!"

I shook my head, but it made me smile, thinking of Micah and her quilt warriors.

Joshua was spending more time at his friend Jonah's house, doing seven-year-old things, looking for crawdads in the creek, racing each other down the hill and back, riding bikes around the neighborhood, and catching insects to put in mason jars with holes poked into the lid. I had known Jonah's mom, Anita, since she moved here as a Vista volunteer when I was in high school. She left for a few years to finish her medical degree in Johnson City and now was a doctor at the clinic. The boys had been in the same class since they started preschool.

I pulled up to their house at the top of Big Crest hill in town, and Joshua came running out to meet me. He stopped at my driver's side window. "Where's Daddy?"

"He had some work to do. He'll be home later."

Joshua considered his options and leaned in closer. "Can I stay again tonight then?"

"It's fine with me," Anita said.

"Please!" Jonah begged. He had come out to the car to stand beside Joshua, leaning in my car window too.

"Okay, okay! But just tonight, Jonah. Then you can come to our house."

I waved at Anita, who was watching us from the front door. "Thanks!" I called out. "I'll pick the boys up tomorrow."

"No problem!" She waved.

The dark circles under Collis's eyes had resurfaced and he ground his teeth in his sleep until I poked him in the side and made him roll over. Nothing made him smile these days. I didn't know why. All I knew was that something had shifted. "You okay, Sweetie?" I asked softly.

"Huh?" He looked up from the newspaper he was reading. "Just tired."

"Maybe you should cut your hours a little bit. We can get by. It'd be nice to have you home more."

"Then how would we pay for the house, Ava? Collecting money is easy, air-conditioned work. I drive around in my new truck that Johnny's money bought. I'm just tired is all."

"We could move if we had to," I offered, knowing I could find a better job.

Collis wouldn't hear of it. "I'll do what I need to, Ava," he said. "I'll do what I want."

He had been doing what he wanted, and I was beginning to wonder if all of it had to do with work. I had seen that number on his phone again, and sometimes, when we were out together, I thought he made too much eye contact with this cashier, or that waitress. I didn't say anything though. That would really set him off. When Collis got like this, Joshua and I tried to walk a little quieter and keep out of his way to keep from getting snapped at. I didn't know how to help. He'd been to Dr. Talbot, who gave him a prescription for an antidepressant, but Collis refused to get it filled. Said he was worried he'd get flattened out and wouldn't be able to feel anything. Instead, he tried to grit it out alone. He even turned down a hike I planned for us with Jonah and Anita on Pony's Ridge that weekend. Getting out in the hills usually set Collis right, but he wouldn't budge.

"Y'all go take the boys. I've got a few errands to run," he said.

"Oh, come on, it'll be fun," I said. "You need some fresh air."

"I get plenty of air, Ava. I work outside. Go on." And I did. Maybe Collis was medicating himself with pot, maybe something stronger. I noticed him slipping away sometimes, lost in thought, or maybe high, or both. I didn't worry too much as long as it got him to feeling better, to acting more like himself.

Anita and I took the boys on a three-mile loop hike. By the end we were triumphant, the boys chattering about all the animals we had seen, two black rat snakes, a chipmunk, a hawk, and a couple of finches. The mountain lion they marveled at was only imaginary. When we got home, Collis was sitting on the porch, waiting. "We saw two snakes, Daddy," Joshua said.

"How big?" Collis asked. He seemed calmer.

Joshua held his arms out wide, "at least this long, right Mama?"

"Just about," I said.

"I'm glad you all got out," Collis said. "I'll go with you next time." Was he softening toward me? Maybe. I'd take it.

There were rumors, like there always were, of Macy closing down the few remaining mines, moving to West Virginia, maybe even going out West. Maybe calling it quits altogether and taking a loss. It was keeping Collis up late. I woke up in the middle of the night to find him on the porch, smoking a cigarette.

"Come back to bed." I folded my arms around myself to keep warm.

"I will. I just need a few minutes to myself. Do I always have to go to bed when you do?" There was a time he wouldn't have ever wanted to ask that question. A time when he'd do anything to be in my bed.

He stayed outside most the night and was up and on his second cup of coffee by the time I got out of bed in the morning. Was he talking to someone else all night? Confiding in her? The only way I could tell he'd been to bed at all was the indention his head left on his pillow, the absence of him. I worried about my other problems all night on my side of the bed. Our clients used to smoke too much pot or drink too much of anything they could get their hands on in our dry county. Now, they were strung out on oxy, Vicodin, Xanax. Some were trying out meth or heroin, too. Whatever was cheapest and easiest to come by. Their teeth and bones rotted away. They held up grandmothers and uncles at gunpoint and stole from them, just for the chance of feeling good or feeling nothing, at least for a little while. It made me feel gutted.

It made me want out. Running away would be easier than looking at what had happened to so many people I cared about. The only person I told that to, though, was Micah.

═

There was a job in Lexington doing the same kind of counseling I did in Iona, but for a lot more money. There, I'd be working with strangers. Here, I knew everybody. In Lexington, I wouldn't have to look at the faces of people I'd gone to school and church with, now sunken in from meth, asking for one more hit. Here, I'd even seen Lizzie Mays, a little girl I used to babysit, now a teenager, fall in and out of rehab. I used to braid her long red hair when her parents went out to dinner or to a movie over the mountain. Now, I was sure she'd end up in jail, or worse.

The sheer numbers of people needing something was beginning to wear on me. Gabe held the whole place together somehow, but our five-year grant was running out. He might not be able to pay me much longer. And a job didn't make a life, did it?

Maybe if Joshua and I left Iona, we wouldn't have to watch Collis slip farther and farther away from us. The guys he was hanging around, Jim Pike, Tim Wilson, all of them worked for Johnny Roberts. None of them was any count, but Collis called them brothers. More than once, I answered the phone only to get hung up on, only to see Collis rush into the room, asking who it was. "Nobody," I said.

Talk got back to me that these friends were finding ways to make money that would put them in front of a judge soon enough, and they would push aside anyone who got in the way. Was Collis doing it too? Could he hurt somebody? Would he bring all that home to Joshua and me? Maybe in the city, Collis could find something that was growing instead of drying up. We might pull closer together. We might be safe.

═

"Collis is never going to move to Lexington, Ava," Micah said. "You're wasting your time."

"How would you know?" I asked her. "I might be able to persuade him."

"Doubtful," she said. I hated when Micah was so sure of herself. She thought she knew everything, especially when it came to my life. She'd never leave here, and while she told me I should do what I needed to do, I knew she was ashamed of me somehow for not staying and fighting. She thrived on battle. I had already surrendered my home, my family, maybe even my marriage. It was easy for Micah to stay. She only had the mountains to lose but that fight seemed impossible to win. Micah didn't have a partner, or son, or even parents. She could stand up for anything she didn't think was right. She didn't have to be afraid of what might be. I started quietly working on my resume when Collis wasn't around.

I knew something had already gone wrong in our marriage long ago, even though Collis and I never talked about it. I could tell by the subtle rise and fall of his voice when he was lying. Sometimes, I thought I could hear a woman's voice on the other end when Collis made a call; sometimes I thought that was my imagination. Sometimes I thought I smelled a spicy perfume on his clothes. There wasn't a dramatic shift in Collis, like it happens in the movies when somebody goes astray and walks out, but it was there. It was the way he wouldn't look straight at me, the way he'd grab Joshua up in a tight hug when I tried to get close. I could tell what it was, and I could tell it would pass. It wasn't the first time. Joshua was a toddler when it started, maybe three or four, when I'd go to bed with macaroni and cheese from his toddler hands in my hair and genuinely not care. I was the farthest from sexy I had ever been. The farthest from Collis too.

Somebody who's never been married might not understand why I didn't confront him, ask about the other woman I could feel slipping into in our space, ask at least for a separation. But not talking about it kept what we'd worked so hard to keep alive safe, held our family together.

"You okay?" was all I'd ask. I had a way of asking but not looking him in the eye. We were sitting on the couch, watching some sitcom, and I had finally gotten Joshua down to sleep after reading him four picture books, two of them twice, then tiptoed back down the hallway into the living room.

"Fine, why?" Collis said.

"Just wondering. You seem like you've got something weighing on you." I turned away from the TV and looked at him now, breathed and prepared myself to hear the truth, find out her name at least.

He sat back on the couch, leaning away from me a little more, "I do, I guess. More rumors of a shut down. Tim heard about it from somebody in the office. What would this town do without Macy?"

That was what was on his mind, a shut down? I felt relieved, lighter. I could keep us going. "We'd make it," I said. "Those company guys don't think twice about us." Neither does Johnny, I thought, but didn't say it out loud. The TV show had gone to commercial, so the sound had gotten louder, somebody was selling washing detergent. I reached for the remote to turn it off.

Collis was studying me, as if to figure out what I was, if I was real. He could blame all his troubles on Macy Mining Company, the trouble I already knew, instead of telling me the truth I was looking for. He needed me too much to do that. I had to go with him, past the rifts and tears between us, until his storm passed. I could feel his depression coming on cold, and I wanted to pull him up before he got bowled over by it. He wouldn't take the medication the doctor prescribed, said he'd tried it and it made him feel nothing, or worse. I worried the girl might be leading him to all kinds of evil temptations. I worried Johnny was leading him to oxy. Dangers popped up like mushrooms after rain around here.

"We could move," I said.

He looked at me like he didn't understand my words, "They don't need coal miners in cities, if that's what you mean."

"I know that Collis, but you'd find something different. Or I would. You have skills."

Collis knew how everything mechanical worked, as if it came to him in a dream. He thought everyone knew what he knew about the physical world, but I couldn't even fix the flusher in the toilet. He looked me in the eye, and I wanted to look away but didn't. "Some people, Ava, they can switch up, start a business, move around but not me. I guess you should have known that I was a miner, deep in the blood."

I moved closer to him, put my hand on his shoulder, "I do know you. I just don't know how long you'll be able to find that kind of work. We've got a little time to figure it out, though. My job will keep us for a while." I hugged him tight.

We held each other, and what began with a gentle kiss, Collis turned into real desire. He slipped his hands around my waist. I pulled his shirt off, and he kissed me so hard I had to hold my breath. He eased me onto the couch and we clung together, rocking into each other, grasping for love that kept trying to slip away. Times like this, when he was trying to outrun sadness, he held onto me like a boat to an anchor.

"I need you, Ava," he whispered, when we were spooned together on the couch, drifting into sleep. "I need you to believe in me."

"I do," I said, and kissed him on the arm he had wrapped around me. In this way, we worked around the real problems for a while, put our fears on other things that wouldn't mean we would split apart. We loved each other; we were each other's past. You don't know how valuable that is until whole sections of your life are scattered in ashes across a mountain.

This girl I imagined waiting in the wings, whatever her name was, really didn't matter to me. At least that's what I told myself. I didn't want all of Collis then anyway, as long as he still needed me sometimes. If it went on for too long, I'd find someone else, some other life. I told myself that too. But for now, I was sticking with this one.

7

Cassiopeia

I was washing dishes and heard a boom outside, then another—an explosion. I put the last pan in the drying rack and peered out the kitchen window. All I could see was tree limbs and black night. "What was that?" I called out. I'd be more worried if I was alone, not knowing where Collis was or what he was up to, but he had come home early. I'd made a roast chicken, a real family dinner, and we were about to settle in to watch a movie.

"I don't guess they'd be blasting the mountain this late," Collis turned off the TV, walked over and stood beside me at the window. "Maybe trespassers?"

Gunshots on late summer nights usually meant somebody had stumbled onto a hidden pot patch in the woods. You could get killed just for getting lost. But a gun only holds so many bullets. This sound kept exploding, over and over.

"Come on," Collis said. "That sounds like the fireworks show!" I had planned to tell Collis what I'd done but couldn't now. I followed him out the front door. Didn't bother to lock it. We took Joshua in his pajamas, his small hand gripping mine on one side and Collis's on the other. We pulled him up Sanders Street, through the Childress's back yard, through trees and laurel, to the path to the ridge. The sky lit up in glowing red flowers. The flowers exploded and spawned more flowers, silver this time, then sparkly blue, magic. A crowd had gathered at the ridgeline to get the best view.

The fireworks place in Jellico was having their big display night, where they showed the distributors what they had to sell for the whole year. The store's red neon sign was a marker for the Tennessee state line and had been there as long as I could remember. The slope of the mountain fed drivers toward the parking lot as they coasted down the highway into Kentucky.

"I thought they were closing down, moving to South Carolina," I said. Collis put his arm around my shoulder. We looked straight up, like everybody around us.

"They are," he said. "This'll be the last time."

Everybody kept quiet, except for an occasional ooh or aah, maybe a kid running down the hill and his Mama calling him back, her words fading into the cool night after him. Joshua stood in front of me, leaning his small head back into the soft of my belly. We could hear some man's voice warbling far away over the ridges on an intercom before each eruption, but we couldn't make out the words, just the rise and fall of his excitement. He must have announced the names of the fireworks, but Collis and I made up our own names for them.

"Big Dipper," he said.

"How about Cassiopeia?"

"Sure—Cassiopeia!" Joshua craned his neck to get a better view. He was a little taller now, and skinny, since he'd just gone through a growth spurt. "Mama, that one's on fire!"

Collis put his hands on Joshua's shoulders, pulled him gently back. "You think the noise will hurt him?" Collis asked.

"He hears blasts up on the mountain all day."

Joshua pointed to the sky, "Look at that one! It's golden!"

"We can stay as long as you like, Buddy," Collis said. We sat down in the grass, Joshua on Collis's lap, me leaned against his shoulder, watching the fireworks sparkle through the trees, surrounded by people we had known all our lives. I looked at all their faces in the firework glow. Our neighbors, Joe and Carol, stood near us. Their son was a client of mine, back in rehab, and I could see how his struggles had aged them. To the side of us, Carly Colgan held her baby in her arms. She was doing much better now that she had someone to take care of. Even Ralph Goforth, old enough to be my grandfather, was there. He had survived wars, booms, layoffs, and his whole family moving away. He was a fine man. There were still some people like him around, but I wondered how long they would last. I couldn't see anyone moving forward here, only standing in this exact same spot, years and years from now, the sky gone dark.

"We can't stay here," I said, watching another neon explosion.

"Andromeda," Collis said and pointed toward the green light shimmering through the clouds. "See that?" He ruffled Joshua's hair, which had grown too long over his eyes. I'd cut it short soon.

"Stop it, Daddy. I can't see!" Joshua wiggled loose and ran over to join a small pack of neighborhood boys he went to school with.

"We'll go home in a minute, Ava," Collis said.

"No, that's not what I mean. We can't stay here. In Iona. I've applied for a job in Lexington. They want to interview me. I'm gonna try for it. There's nothing here for us, Collis." I couldn't hold it in any longer.

Collis stared at me, fireworks bursting all around him. He thought everybody could live on bits and pieces of hope, but I could barely carve out a life here. I couldn't save him, us, from the trouble that waited here if he kept working for Johnny, kept sliding toward darkness, maybe drugs, jail, violence, all of it. How could I keep him from that? I'd meant to tell him right after I sent my resume, but there never seemed to be a right time.

"I can't go, Ava," he said, as if it was the final pronouncement. As if he had a real reason besides some girl, a pack of shady friends, and love for a place that might not ever be whole again. I was tired of holding on to what used to be, or what might never come. I was tired of sharing him. He turned his body away from mine enough to leave space between us. Some people couldn't be changed by words, so I quit talking. We watched the last fireworks sear through the sky and set it on fire, then walked slowly back home, where we could still smell the acrid smoke settling.

8

Homes

The last time I tried to pull Collis away was on the porch of our house in Iona. The air was warm and thick. I cleaned up after supper and followed the chords of his guitar outside. Could have been "Summertime" I heard him playing. I wasn't sure. He'd add and subtract around the melody until the ghost of a song was barely visible inside his own. He had been playing guitar since ninth grade but never had a band. He started playing: "In my mind, I still need a place to go / all my changes were there…" He had a place to go. If he would only listen! I stood in the door of the porch and listened. He put down his guitar and held his beer to the back of his neck. Sweat ran down the brown glass and his coppery skin. I sat next to him on the chipped brick steps of the porch. I wanted to be close enough to touch him, maybe save him. He put the bottle to the back of my neck and goose bumps ran down my spine. He studied the mountains; I watched how the muscles in his arms shifted as he put the bottle back to his lips.

"You alright?" I asked. I leaned toward him, and he put his arm around me. Whenever I felt him pulling away from me, I moved closer.

"It's real this time, Ava. Macy's pulling out of Kentucky completely. They're moving all operations to West Virginia."

I sat back up and looked directly at him. I was glad this time had come. Maybe he would see the sense of what I wanted. Maybe he would move on. I knew better than to say this out loud.

"Gave us notice today. We'll help them pack everything up for a week or two." He seemed more confused than sad, like this was something he couldn't really fathom. "Then I don't know what," he said. "I just don't know."

"What happened?"

"Nothing happened. We mined it out, the whole damn area. Insufficient yield, they said. They got plenty of miners out of work there. Why pay to move all us? Most of us wouldn't leave here anyway." He sipped his beer and looked straight at me. "What do you want to do, Ava?"

I shrugged. I had no idea what I could possibly say that would help. He knew what I wanted but didn't want to hear it. He just wanted a fight.

"No, really. What do you want?" he asked again. His voice deepened and grew louder as he talked. I looked around the yard to make sure no one else was listening.

"I don't know. Nothing." He had never asked me that directly before, at least not that I could remember, not when he really wanted to know the answer.

"You don't exist if you don't want nothing," he said, louder still, as if everybody allowed themselves to want. I came from a long line of people who only knew need.

"I want you," I said. "I want to be safe." I wanted to keep him close. If I said what I honestly wanted, he'd go a million miles away. I learned over the years how to work my own desires around his moods. It was a tricky balance I'd grown used to and even prided myself on in an odd way, how much I could absorb and still move forward. The evening sky was turning into streams of orange and blue. I wanted to wrap us up in that, protect our family. But all that beauty would be gone in less than an hour.

I wanted to get far away from Iona and the mountains that held us tight. The job I'd found in Lexington was meant to be. They wanted me. What I wanted had nothing to do with this crumbling place anymore, nothing to do with its sadness. Collis loved Iona, and all the people in it, good and bad. I loved the good, but the bad was pulling us under. I wanted to breathe.

Collis looked away from me, leaned toward the porch railing, drank his beer.

"I want to be a miner, to be a part of something," he said. Every man in Collis's family had gone into the mines. They'd made a good living in boom years; they got by in the busts. Collis was smart. He could have gone to college. He didn't have to rip off mountaintops with a dozer, breathing in rock and coal, centuries deep, but he couldn't imagine his life any other way. Miners suffocated. Tiny shards shredded their lungs over time. They were killed by the same mountains they tore apart.

"We can move on," I said. "It'll be better in Lexington." He stared at me for a minute until I was absolutely sure I'd said the wrong thing.

"Move on?"

People did move. Things changed. There was a future, or at least a hope of one.

"We don't know anybody in Lexington. Not any real friends, Ava. We've got people here. That's what matters. I bet you never knew anybody besides me who'd die for you," Collis said. "I got twenty or more men in Iona who'd risk their lives digging me out. They wouldn't stop to think about their own families. They'd just do it. They'll be with me till the end, regardless of whether any of us have a goddamn job." The night air was holding onto the heat. I knew the kind of men he was talking about, and I wanted nothing to do with them.

"But would you dig me out?" I asked.

Collis's eyes burned almost to black. He pounded the railing and leaned in toward me. "You can't love nobody but yourself, Ava. Nobody. Go on then!" He got up from the steps, grabbed his guitar by the neck, walked into the house and turned the TV up loud.

Late that night, when Collis had passed out on the couch, I called Micah, the only person I knew who would die trying to dig me out of anything.

"You've got to go," she said. "You've got to go for that job. Collis will come around."

"I don't know, Micah."

"Go find what you want. I'll come see you. I'm up there once a month for work." I wanted to leave, but I wanted the mountains to grant me permission. Micah spoke for them, "If Collis wants to stay in the past, let him. I won't let go of you."

"I'll miss you most, Micah," I said.

"Stop that."

"It's true."

"I know," she said. I'd dig her out too.

9

Subdivision

"Mama," Joshua said in the car on the way to the new school, "when can we go back home?" His reflection in the rearview mirror was calm, dead serious. His front teeth looked too big for his face. They stuck out at a slight angle; his lips barely closed around them. The sandy fringe of bangs I needed to cut hung across his right eye. I was too busy to answer, driving with my left hand and putting mascara on with my right.

"Mama?" he repeated.

I stopped at the light and turned to look at him, "This is home now, Joshua." I looked back toward the road. He punched the back of the passenger seat. "I want Daddy!" he said. In his tone, the way the anger narrowed his eyes, I felt Collis. I didn't want Joshua to turn into that. I'd keep a close eye on him, keep him safe.

"Stop that!" I said.

He looked out his window, eyes welling up. I felt sorry for everything but I couldn't go back. This was home now. It had to be.

The week before we left Iona, Collis blew up at me. We had gone over and over it.

"Collis," I said, "It might cheer you up to be in a new place. You might feel better." As soon as I saw the effect my words had, I wanted to take them back.

"Ava, you got no idea what I'm going through. No fucking clue!" he said.

"I do know."

"The worst part is, you don't even care. You won't even let me try to make it. You don't even want our family." Anger came off him like a scent. I was too stunned to try to answer. Collis had been up and down since I'd known him, but the past six months, he'd fallen into a low spot he didn't seem to be able to get out of. I let him say what he was going to say, but I couldn't look him in the eye.

"Who the hell are you, Ava? Do you even know? 'Cause from where I'm sitting, you look pretty lost." His eyes narrowed to dark slits, and he stood forward, ready for fight, flight, or both. "You're a fake, is what you are."

"Don't stay with someone you don't want. That'll kill you," I said. I heard some psychiatrist say that on a radio call-in show, and I was proud of how sure I sounded, even though it was the opposite of what I wanted. I didn't want to let him go. I felt my cheeks flush.

Some, like Collis, do all they can to hold on to a world that doesn't exist anymore. I wanted to raise our child in a place that was still alive, not a husk of something. Not just where we imagined we would be when we were Joshua's age, a place that may have never been.

I wanted Joshua to imagine more, to want the whole world. I convinced myself to move forward, be an adult, take the job in Lexington, file for separation. But the last three weeks had done nothing to convince eight-year-old Joshua that this was a better life. He missed Iona, where everyone would be where he expected them to be. He missed the mountains towering over him, even though he'd grown up almost to my shoulders now. He missed Collis. I did too, but I couldn't say that. I would not let Collis see me run back, settle for standing still, hoping for something or someone to swoop in and save us.

"I can't even tell which one is our house," Joshua said, as we drove into the subdivision. We passed rows and rows of new construction, beige, tan, brick. "There's no kids here."

He was right about the neighborhood. The brick and clapboard two-stories either had a front porch, the Mayfair, or a back deck, the Brighton. I had accidentally pulled into the neighbors' driveway three times already. Their house was a Mayfair, too.

"The kids will come out," I said, looking in my rearview mirror to see him sulking in the back seat. "Maybe we're just missing them."

"Yeah right, Mama," Joshua said. "They're all busy, all the time. They're mean at my school. I hate it. It's ugly here." He slid deeper down in his seat so I couldn't meet his eyes.

Lexington was rolling green hills, elegant horses behind endless white fences if you drove out the country roads. I imagined it was what England looked like, at least the parts that don't have coal in them. That's what people say anyway. Joshua and I drove around a lot, looking at the grand brick houses on Richmond Road, driving through the university. I showed him where I took classes. I showed him Rupp Arena. "I'll get us tickets to a basketball game," I said. "Would you like that?"

"Can we get T-shirts, too?" Joshua asked.

"Sure. T-shirts, too."

"I still want to go home," he said.

Things were different in our new life. At home, like every eight-year-old in Iona, Joshua knew the layout of town, the names of the doctors, the librarian, the woman who drove his school bus. The roots of the rock stuck deep into the dirt, down to the center of the earth. It was the most immoveable place in the world. Houses stacked up on hillsides, crammed into crevices along the side of the road, teetering on the edges of the mountain. The hills were cinched so tight, you could barely see the sun until eleven in the morning. People kept their lives close to the ground. Zion Creek, where we had lived when we were first married, was in another world, another lifetime. I couldn't even go back to the fantasy of that. If I did, I would get caught in the vortex of Collis and the pull of the people I had grown up with. Gravity seemed to have a stronger hold there.

"We are home, Baby," I said to Joshua, as we stopped at the light. "You'll see Daddy next weekend." He kicked the back of the seat hard as he could, daring me to turn around and do something. "Stop it! Use your words."

"This sucks," he said. "I want to go back to Iona."

"Not those words," I said.

When we got to the school, the car rider line was thick and solid. It moved slower than any creek I had ever waded through. I kept thinking of Wallace's Bend, Hard Rock Falls, of Collis and everything good we'd left behind. But this was the right thing. It had to be. If only the cars would move forward.

"I don't want to go to this stupid school," Joshua said.

"Well, you're going."

"I won't like it," he said. "Not ever."

The Honda in front of me pulled to the school entrance and let out two little girls with neon green backpacks almost as big as they were. We were next. The principal told me it was better not to walk in with Joshua. The teachers on bus duty would get him where he needed to go.

"Hop out," I said. "I love you, Baby." Joshua glared at me and slid out of the seat, tugging his backpack along behind him.

"Love you," he mumbled. A smiling teacher with neat rows of long braids, in a floral dress and pink flats, closed the car door after him. I pulled out onto the busy street and someone honked at me. "I'm going!" I yelled.

I took a wrong turn on Short Street, still learning my way, and ended up going around the block a few times before I found the right parking lot to pull into my slot. I could turn around and pick up Joshua, take him back to Iona where we knew how the world worked. Things didn't rent quickly in Hensley County anyway. Our house might still be there, familiar and warm, waiting. Collis would be there too, smug smile on his face, high on something Johnny Roberts gave him, but still, there for us. I sat in the car and took a few deep breaths. No. I couldn't quit yet.

The next morning, Joshua was up before me, sitting at the small wooden table, studying the back of the cereal box, the round yellow puffs overflowing from his bowl. I ignored his mess and made coffee. The kitchen was flooded with sunlight from the sliding glass door that led to the fenced backyard. I pulled the thick beige drapes to block the light. It was too much for me this early.

"I'm going exploring, Mama," he said.

"You are? Where?" I asked.

"In the neighborhood. There's a bunch of new houses. I bet I could find something there. Lucas said he found a snake under the front porch of one of them this summer."

"Who's Lucas, a new friend?"

"Kid at school. Not a friend. He brags a lot. He lives near the main entrance. If he can find a snake, I can find something cool for sure."

"Okay," I said. "Just be careful. And finish your breakfast first." Joshua began to cram his cereal in as fast as he could. I was happy to see him finally wanting to check out our new neighborhood. It wasn't Iona, but it had plenty of possibilities.

"Chew," I said.

When he left, pillowcase in hand, I watched him from the back porch. He crossed through two or three yards and onto a sidewalk before he disappeared from my view. I knew it was too late to find snakes in early October, but I wanted Joshua to explore, to find something to own about this new place.

When he came home half an hour later, the pillowcase was empty.

"No snakes?"

"Nothing. Not one living thing. Not even kids. Just an old man washing his car. I wish I could walk over to Nana's. I'd sure catch something there."

"Well, that would be a really long walk from here. Let's go on a hike. There's a good park near here."

"No," he slid onto the couch, turned on the TV, and stared at it. "I wish I could live with Nana instead of you."

I didn't let the hurt show in my face, just breathed deeply, "Maybe we'll go see her soon. She's wanting you to visit." I didn't think Alice would welcome me back. She'd take in Joshua in a heartbeat, but she had to choose a side and didn't choose mine. She'd been sticking to Joshua since he was small, just like she kept close to Collis. Truth was, I loved her, and I'd left her too.

10

Change

The man slumped on the steps of the courthouse held his hand out for change. The rest of his body was wrapped in a quilt, slick with use, eaten away at the edges. The arm stuck out, pale, covered with dark hair. Blurry tattoos fought for space on his forearm; his palm faced the sky. In my work, I was used to people in need. I tried to stay compassionate, but day after day, I saw the worst of people and heard of all their transgressions. The man leaned against the building, next to the heavy glass door I had to go through to get to my office at Child and Family Services. I tried to find a way around him but had to get close enough to touch him in order to get into the building, to my new office. I could smell his sweat. I had seen him every day for three weeks as I went to work, but we had yet to exchange words. He smiled at me, revealing a full set of solid teeth, where I was expecting empty space or a jagged row of gaps and blackened nubs, meth-mouth. But they were all there, whitish and rectangular, strong. His smile reminded me of Collis's, though not as beautiful, still a face-altering grin.

The summer I met Collis, between my junior and senior year at a party celebrating the end of the school year, he smiled at me. His white teeth almost glowed next to golden skin. Their order set off the soft swell of his lips. I stared at the man on the steps, trying to see if his teeth might be false. "You got some change?" he asked. When he talked, the man looked younger, maybe even my age. Maybe he had kids who went to school with Joshua. I gave him a dollar.

The waiting room outside my cubicle was thick with clients pressed up against the smudged beige walls. They were mostly women with babies wriggling in their arms and one or two children yo-yoing into the hallway, shoes slamming flat against the shiny linoleum as they ran, sprinting back to touch base. The city bus arrived at the courthouse ten minutes before I was supposed to be at work. The early birds had already laid claim to the chairs lining the room. They began to talk to me as I entered my gray cube, coffee in one hand, bag of files under my arm.

"Miss, if I could just talk to you for a minute, Miss," a thin young woman said, grabbing my arm.

"Give me a second," I said. The woman let go and sat down. So many people wanted me to fix something. I looked down toward my skirt and noticed a tiny glob of raspberry jelly, which I tried to brush discreetly to the floor.

"I was going to tell you about that," the woman closest to my desk said. She was twice my age, I guessed, probably somebody's grandma. She talked in a loud whisper that drew more attention than a normal voice would. People around her looked up.

"Only a true friend will tell you when you got something wrong with you," she said. I didn't have any true friends here. At home, I had Micah and Collis. At least I still had Micah. My new friend looked me up and down, took in the thrift store suit, the white blouse I hadn't had time to iron, the black shoulder bag overflowing with papers. I smoothed my hair back towards the ponytail, hoping my roots weren't showing. "How you doing?" She was looking for a real answer, full of concern if not for me, then for some friend I reminded her of.

"Can't complain," I said. She nodded her head, sat back in her seat to mind her own business. If I did air my troubles, I might never stop. I was better at fixing other people's lives. The only sure thing was that someone, a parent, a child, a foster family, my own family, would end up hating me before the day was out. I took the file from the top of the giant pile on my desk and opened it.

"Fowler?" I called. "Ms. Fowler?" A heavy, pale woman in a royal blue low-cut top and tight jeans walked toward me. The rolls of her stomach hung in tiers over her waistband. Her hair was dyed black, matching the eyeliner that rimmed the ice of her eyes. She held a little blonde girl by the wrist, toddling at her side in a matching top and jeans, miniature fingernails painted purple in patches like her mother's.

"Pleased to meet you," the woman said, and offered the hand without the toddler attached. "Destiny Fowler."

"Ava Maynard," I said. "Have a seat." As Destiny answered my questions about her family history, food stamps, childcare, monthly income, the waiting room filled and shifted. Audible sighs and conversations about how slow I was filtered from the waiting area. "You should go back for your GED," I told Destiny and gave her a flyer for the program at the community college. "You can do it!"

"When do I get my check?" she asked.

When the phone rang, I excused myself to take the call from Ms. Davies, the principal at Little River Elementary. I spoke in a calm voice. Inside, I was exploding. Joshua had been in school for three weeks and this was the third time I'd been called to come get him. The first was considered a misunderstanding about classroom rules. The second, I gave him the benefit of the doubt it was the other boy's fault. Now, I wanted to kill him with my bare hands for starting something again. What kind of mother feels that? I cancelled my appointments and ducked out through the crowded waiting room.

I didn't see anything I drove past. Taking a breath when I got inside the school, I smoothed my skirt and slowed my step. Joshua was sitting outside the principal's office, the skin underneath his right eye a grayish blue. The kid two chairs away from him, waiting against the painted white cinderblock wall, had a swollen lower lip with a small gash, exactly in the middle. Blood oozed out of it, and he licked it away. "He started it," the kid said. He was bigger than Joshua, buzzed hair, already thick around the middle.

"I ran out of words, Mom," Joshua said. "And I can't say the ones he called me." He let his head drop so his bangs covered his eyes. Times like this, he looked a lot like Collis.

"Mrs. Maynard?" Ms. Davies said. I nodded. She ushered us into her windowless office. Joshua sat in the chair next to me, across the desk from Ms. Davies. He looked at the floor and didn't say a word. His feet didn't quite touch the floor.

I tried to explain to Ms. Davies it really wasn't his fault after all he had been through, moving, the separation. Ms. Davies had seen plenty of kids who'd been through worse. "I know he can do better," I said. She held her ground and told me Joshua was suspended for two days. "Please give us one more chance," I pleaded. I needed a thousand chances, but maybe she'd start with one. Ms. Davies shook her head and sat up straighter.

Her face was set, "I have to be consistent. Joshua has to try to adjust and learn to respect other people. He can show me how he can do that when he returns to school next week." She stood up. The door creaked as she opened it.

I put my arm around Joshua's shoulders and herded him out the door. Ms. Davies' tall thin heels clicked away from us, as she walked down the tiled hallway to some other problem. Outside, Joshua kicked a piece of gravel across the parking lot, never looking up, and slammed the car door as he got in. I was too mad to talk, afraid of what I'd say that I wouldn't be able to take back. He didn't say a word all the way home.

———

That night, I had no choice but to call Collis. I closed the door to my bedroom and covered up on the double bed in my fluffy white comforter for protection before I dialed. "Hey, I need to ask you something," I said. I was trying to start things off nice, civil. I was trying to keep everything I really wanted to say, everything I felt, from coming out of my mouth.

"What? You ready to come home?" he said, like it was a fact, rather than a real question. I wondered if he could sense me tearing up, hear the deep inhale of my breath.

"Collis, please don't. Look, I need you to take Joshua for a few days. He got into a little trouble at school, nothing serious, he just needs to spend a couple of days with you. I don't have any vacation days yet." I didn't know anybody here, not enough to leave my child with for two days. At home, I had a lot of people. I never would have had to call Collis if we were still in Iona, but then again, he'd have known about this by the time I got to the school. Here, I was the only person who knew anything about our lives. My cousin Sonia and her family lived across town and she had sent a fruit basket when we moved in, but she had worked a long time to be accepted by the people who wanted to forget we had all come from the same tight mountains, the same huge county high schools. Her new friends were from families who owned mines instead of digging in them. They were men of khaki pants and blue blazers, women of platinum hair and red lipstick.

Collis knew I needed him but didn't want to need him. He held on to that powerful silence before he spoke. "Guess you aren't so much better off there, are you, Ava? Meet me at the Quick Stop in Camden at 7:30."

We hadn't had warm words, barely any words at all, in the weeks since I had filed for separation and left Iona. He hung up before I could say anything else.

—

It was a two-and-a-half hour drive from Lexington to Iona. The Quick Mart in Camden was half-way home, an equal burden for each of us to drive. Joshua and I rode without speaking, the fan of the heater filling the space between us. A chill came into the air as the sun fell. The leaves were beginning to turn. Soon the whole world would show through the tree limbs. The mountains began to push up from flat beige fields, stubbly where tobacco had been cut. The savory smell of it curing in barns thickened the air. Small hills swelled at first, then larger and tighter peaks emerged, steeper valleys fell. The tobacco faded away, pushed out by acres of pine. We were going into some kind of fortress. Finally, I couldn't see around each bend before I took it. I had to trust my memory of what was on the other side. Silver leaf maples waved us on. Joshua kept his face pressed to the window, drew pictures in the fog his breath left.

The roads began to curve and narrow, the pavement faded to a light gray, pocked with potholes. Houses marking different eras of poverty clung to the mountain's base, clumped at the banks of the river. Houses from the good times looked down from the hills. Whole families lived side by side, among wild spurts of kudzu and slides of dirt and rock. "We're getting close, aren't we?" Joshua asked. "I know this part," he sat forward in his seat.

"Yeah, we're closer," I said. The peaks cast heavy shadows. The towns under them pushed up against the mountainside. People had blown plenty of holes on the insides to pull out what they wanted, but the battered half-mountains still stood.

I pulled into the neon-lit Quick Stop. Inside, I got Joshua some chips and a soda, things I would never normally buy him, peace offerings. Maybe bribes. I'd do anything to get him to see that I was doing all of this for him. For all of us, really.

"Can I get some gum, too?" he asked, reaching a bright pink package toward me. I gave him a look and he put the gum back in the rack.

We got back in the car, with the engine running just for heat, and waited for Collis, leaning forward in our seats any time a black pickup passed. I searched the radio and found mostly country stations or talk. Joshua crunched his chips and wiped his small greasy hands on the back of my seat. I stared at him in the rearview mirror, but he wouldn't make eye contact. He looked small under the seat belt, uncertain. "What if Daddy doesn't come?" he said. "Will we turn around and go back? Will I have to go to school anyway?" He dug down into the chip bag, came up with nothing but crumbs and carefully licked his fingers.

"He'll come, baby," I said. "Don't worry. He wants to see you. He wants that more than anything."

"Me too," he said.

An old rusted sedan pulled up to the gas pump, and a new four-wheel drive pickup pulled up beside it, from the other side, window to window, so the drivers could talk. Joshua and I listened to a song about a girl keying her cheating boyfriend's car and watched the two drivers lean out of their windows to kiss. A minivan had to pull around them to get to a pump, but its driver didn't blow her horn, or yell anything at them out her window. She just watched them as she pumped her gas. They didn't stop, even to breathe.

"Why don't they get out of their cars, Mama?" Joshua said.

"Maybe they don't want to let go of each other." I still remembered how that felt.

"Gross," Joshua said. He drifted off in the heat of the car until I nudged him.

"I think that's Daddy coming there." Joshua sat up straight and spotted the truck down the road, coming toward the Quick Stop. It was the only vehicle on the road, and I felt it was Collis before I could really see it was. Joshua must have too. "Let's go," he said, "It's Daddy." He opened his door and slid out of the seat. I followed him.

The truck pulled into the parking lot, clean and shining like the first day Collis and I bought it at Hensley's Chevrolet on the bypass when he started his job at Macy. He smiled as he parked beside us. In the gloss of the black paint, I saw the reflection of my own face, a little distorted, clearly upset. I took a deep breath and tried to relax the tight stitch of my mouth.

Collis's eyes were glazed. He looked like he might start laughing any minute, like there was a giggle caught in his throat. He was high. This was the way he got through, chased away feelings he couldn't live with, had been as long as I had known him. But now, he'd have my baby, our baby without me. What else was he doing now? Selling? It wouldn't be the first time. He had sold pot in high school for Jim Pike, who was still into just about everything bad. I can't say I'd been totally innocent, but I thought those days were long gone. Collis insisted that Jim was a good man, that it wasn't a big deal. But it was to me now. "What?" he yelled out his open window, grinning at us like he won a prize. "You miss me?"

Joshua and I leaned against my car in the cool air, side by side, my arm around him. I thought about shoving him into my back seat, throwing the car into reverse, heading back to Lexington, taking leave from my new job, finding another life in another place. Because my baby was my life, wasn't he? I was better off without

Collis. Maybe Joshua was too. Then Joshua shouted, "Daddy!" and ran toward the truck.

This was how those news stories happened, the ones where the estranged parent runs off to Mexico with the child, never to be heard from again. Adrenaline rushed through me at the prospect of that kind of freedom. I figured we could make the border in twenty hours or so. I could explain it all to Joshua in that time. Maybe it would be long enough for him to understand. Maybe he'd learn to forget. We'd be safe.

Collis turned off the truck and opened his door in one big movement. Before I could stop them, Joshua dove into him and let Collis lift him off the ground so his legs flew out and his little red high tops hovered above the pavement. I crossed my arms to hold myself together. How could either one of them breathe? I couldn't. I wasn't sure if I should even look at Collis and Joshua, caught up like they were, saving each other from drowning. My fantasy of running withered. There was no way I would ever keep them from each other. I looked at the pavement until they came back to me and remembered why we were all here. Collis put Joshua down but kept his arm around him. They could not let go of each other.

I put my hands on my hips, "You know what he did, don't you?"

"All boys fight, Ava. You want him to get run over? He's got to stand up for himself. I got suspend…"

"This isn't about you, Collis. I want my son to act better. I want people to know he's been raised right." Joshua slid a little behind his Daddy, aware what I said might cause trouble. Collis just laughed and shook his head.

"You're about the closest thing to perfect ever was, Ava." He thought his smirk covered his pain, but I could see it. He'd lost a few pounds that he didn't need to lose. He had always been wiry like the rest of the Maynards, but I could tell he'd been struggling.

"Let's don't start, Collis. I'll meet you right here, Sunday at five. Take good care of him. Don't be late."

He almost spat his words at me, "Take good care of him? What kind of father do you think I am? I'll get him here, safe and sound. And on time."

"I love you, Mama," Joshua said. I walked over and Collis moved out of the way.

"Love you, too, "I pulled Joshua close, kissed his smooth hair. "Be good." His body was still tiny, his pants were cinched on the inside with as-you-grow elastic, his blue and red underwear covered in superheroes. Sometimes I forgot how small eight was. It hadn't been long ago that he depended on my body for survival. It hadn't been long ago that we all depended on each other.

Collis ruffled Joshua's hair, looked up at me. The smirk had disappeared. "You could come with us, you know. You could put things back like they were." I shook my head. "What I figured." He put his arm around Joshua. "Come on, Buddy. Let's go home." I turned and walked back to my car, but I could hear them talking about the fight, Collis clapping Joshua on the back. They threw mock punches to show how it should have gone, happy to hear each other's voices. "You should've seen his lip!" was the last thing I heard before they slammed the truck doors shut and disappeared from me, down the narrowing road, toward the tree-carpeted mountains. I watched them until the road curved and I could no longer make out the diminishing black dot of the truck.

I don't know if it was some magnet in the earth's core, or just the part of me still connected to Joshua, to Collis, even to Iona itself that made me want to turn around and follow them. Maybe it was knowing when they first got to town, they would pass the Highway Inn, where the rooms hadn't changed since the '70s, and a sign out front still boasted color TV and air conditioning in every room. They'd slow down as they passed Hubbard's Funeral home and read the name of the person who had died the day before posted on the marquee. It would be somebody's grandmother Collis knew. "I'll have to give them a call," he'd tell Joshua. "She used to teach my Sunday school class, mean old bat." Maybe they would wave to the people gathered on the porch, lighting each cigarette on the end of another cigarette, leaning on the porch railing, talking about anything in order to avoid having to go inside and view the body laid out for display. The children playing on the front lawn would yell out Joshua's name and he'd lean his head out the car window to see who they were. Some grown person would tell the kids to act right and keep quiet out of respect for the dead.

They'd curve around Main Street, by the newly renovated courthouse that put the county deep in debt, and take a left on River Road, twisting with the quick current of the stick-colored river by the high school, where the Iona Indians would be practicing late for Friday night's football game. They'd hear the smack of plastic football helmets pounding into shoulder pads. "Looks like a good team," Collis would say. Joshua would stare at the players in their hulking uniforms and nod. After they turned that corner, the first thing they would see—and Collis would definitely talk about— was the Dairy Cheer sign. It had been broken since before we were married, maybe all of our lives, so when it was glowing in green neon, it read, *airy Che*. "They still have the best strawberry milkshake in the world," Collis would tell Joshua and Joshua would agree. They'd pull into Alice's gravel driveway, where Collis was living now, tires crunching almost into the yard, and smell whatever she was cooking, probably pot roast, seeping out through the cracks around the storm door. If I closed my eyes, I could taste the soft, cooked carrots and onions and the tender meat. Her Pomeranians, Prissy and Beau, would yip at the door, then quiet when Collis snapped, "Hush now, it's just me and Joshua coming home."

I rolled up my windows, which I had kept down to let in the cool air and the warm, bitter smell of burning coal seeping out of chimneys. That smell meant home. My car smelled like the coffee I had spilled on my way to work the day before. I had so much to catch up on, I wouldn't even have time to miss Joshua. I would get the house together, sort through all the files in my bag. Maybe I would plant some pansies or mums. No, mums were ugly. I wouldn't even wear one as a corsage to the homecoming dance senior year. I'd stick with pansies. Maybe I'd go ahead and get a pumpkin, too—give Joshua something to look forward to. I turned the radio to a station that played only jazz, out of Richmond. It was a song I never heard before, and I had no idea how to sing along or follow it. The trumpets screamed, loud and shrill, accusing me of something horrible. The drums whispered behind my back. I turned the music off and drove in quiet. I tried to sing something to myself, but there was no song I knew all the words to, except "Amazing Grace." Not exactly the way to cheer yourself up. I was stuck with a patchwork of refrains, mostly one hit wonders from the eighties, all out of tune. Collis had always been the musician; I was the audience, so I stopped singing.

The hills receded from me, and I was floating along, rather than driving. I'm sure I passed all the landmarks I had seen on the way in, the water towers, the highway markers, but I didn't remember. I just knew I was still driving. The empty, harvested fields stretched out before me and pulled me back to the highway. I followed hundreds of smearing red brake lights, blurry yellow lines, and row after row of some builder's idea of the ideal house reproduced over and over and over again in various shades of beige, until I got to the one I was calling home.

<u>**11**</u>

Waiting

The house echoed. I wished now that I had given in when Joshua begged me to take in the emaciated orange cat we found wandering the neighborhood and name her Iona. In Iona, there was nothing like this. Families added new houses or trailers to their land when grown children wanted their own place. Plots of land owned for decades by the same family along a creek became little communities with deep roots. They sprouted their own churches and schools. Why would anyone dream of leaving a place when the people they loved most were their next-door neighbors?

The brand-new beige carpet in the living room still gave off an odor that I suspected was toxic. Every place I had ever lived before had the smell of years living inside, a smell so comforting and familiar, you'd know it with your eyes closed if you walked into the house twenty years from now. I opened the windows a crack to let in fresh air and let the noxious fumes slip away. I craved the scent of long, slow family meals and years of pine cleaner, the faint must of old rugs, the hint of cedar in the siding.

There was an enormous, empty living room in the front of the house, with little half walls making a show of where the living room ended and the kitchen began. It was meant to let people talk while someone was cooking. It was meant to create togetherness, but it didn't work if you were the only one in the cavernous space. I ached to call Joshua and make sure he was okay. I was scared something might happen to him, that Collis would let Johnny come around, that Collis might do… I didn't even know what. Instead, I unpacked the boxes I had left in the corner of every room, my own obstacle course. Whenever I started to think, I unpacked another box, until there was a mountain of broken-down cardboard boxes on the living room floor. Every box was full of home.

Collis had always come to me in spells. He would sink down from time to time to a place he didn't want to take anybody else. He didn't like to call it depression, just said he didn't always feel like being around people. Then, all of a sudden, he wanted to fill the house with people every day. Sometimes he wanted to be with me every waking minute, didn't want me out of his sight. Other times, he came home just long enough to change his clothes after work and lay out half the night with people I didn't want to know, partying and spending money we didn't have, slipping into bed beside me just before daylight, reeking of smoke and beer. I could feel the electricity coming off of him then, even in his sleep.

There was a part of him that needed me desperately, and a part that tried to prove he didn't need any other person, ever. By the time I left Iona, he had been gone from me a long time. But when you've grown up with a person, learned about the whole world with him, it's impossible to unwind yourself from the tangle of it. I didn't believe in the kind of love people sang about on the radio anymore, but I was certain of another kind, a feeling that as much as air and food and water, you could be essential to someone else's survival. I was for Collis, and maybe he was for me. Or now, maybe Joshua was for both of us.

I turned on the TV to fill the room and began to clean, even though we hadn't been there long enough for the house to really get dirty. I mopped all the floors and scrubbed the new bathtub and sink. I worked until I broke a sweat and felt a little bit tired, but still, I was restless. I made Joshua's bed, smoothed the comforter that showed the entire layout of the solar system when it was spread out. The pillows were dark blue, with Earth on one side, covered all over with stars that glowed in the dark. Cassiopeia stretched across the middle of the bed. Joshua had left his covers in a heap that morning, ignoring all the universe offered.

Out Joshua's window, I could see the neighbor across the street sitting on his porch as darkness fell. His house was a clapboard model, with a brick foundation, a dormer, and a wide porch across the front, a builder's guess at what old houses in town had looked like new. I was sure he'd got it wrong. The driveway was white concrete, but it already had a few oil stains on it, even though they were still advertising for people to build their new dream home here. The sign at the entrance to the neighborhood read, "If you lived here, you'd be home!" The island of dirt around the sign was planted with purple and red pansies. Someone had made an effort to make it look settled in, but that wouldn't last. The pansies were already dried out.

When the alarm went off the next morning, I threw on some clothes and gathered up my papers and coffee. I left mostly dressed, like someone fleeing a fire. At the office, I sat down at my desk, took a deep breath before I read the sign-in sheet. Rosa, my supervisor, sat behind me. She looked settled, like she had been here before anyone lined up, and had had time to read the paper.

"What happened to you?" She was looking me up and down.

"Couldn't sleep." I wiped my fingers under my eyes, in case my dark makeup had smeared.

"You will tonight. Look how many we have on the books, and that ain't even counting all these walk-ins." She waved her arm out, presenting the evidence of the waiting room full of people.

"They need to hire more case workers," I said.

"They just did," she said. "You."

My plans to take myself out to dinner, get a drink with Rosa, even to go to the grocery store evaporated by lunch time. Instead, I went straight home after work and slept for a few hours, read and drank wine in my pajamas as the sun went down, then searched the cabinets for whiskey. I knew I had some when we moved. The phone rang and I grabbed it.

"Hey Mama," Joshua said. "I was just calling to say I miss you. I'm getting ready to go to bed." I found the whiskey in the back of the cabinet and poured a big glass full, then added two ice cubes and took a sip.

"I miss you too, baby. I'll pick you up Sunday evening. We'll straighten everything out at school Monday morning. Don't you worry. I love you."

"Ok, love you too. Hey, Daddy taught me a song on the guitar. You want to hear it?"

"Sure." I could hear Joshua put the phone on the table in front of the guitar and strum out what sounded a little like the beginning of "Magnolia Mountain." Then he came back on the phone.

"You like it?"

"I love it. You could be a rock star. Now get to bed, sweetheart."

"Goodnight, Mama. Here's Daddy." I sat up straight in the kitchen chair, tried to sober myself.

"Hey, Ava," Collis said. "You okay?"

"I'm fine," I said, trying not to slur. "You?"

"Why don't you just come down here for a day or two? Stay here at Mom's. I miss you." His voice was sober, serious. I wanted to say yes. I could picture where he was sitting in his old bedroom. He'd be laid back on the bottom bunk of the bunk beds he got for his twelfth birthday. His head would be resting where he had carved his name in the wood in high school. Through the slats of the bed above him, he'd be able to see the brown covered wagon pattern on the tan box springs. I had studied those before, when we held each other close, crammed into the narrow bottom bunk, rolling across imaginary plains.

"Collis, you know..."

"Work ain't everything. Think about it. Think about what's important. We can still make a life here. We could still be together. Joshua needs to grow up near his Nana."

Maybe he did. I wasn't sure what was right. I could hear Joshua and Alice in the background, shouting answers at some TV game show. Joshua always liked to imagine he would win the vacation for two to Hawaii, and he would take me. We would drink out of coconuts. This seemed more likely somehow than me moving back to Iona.

"I will think, Collis," I said. "I miss you too." I wasn't sure I could live in a place with no old handprints on the wall, no stickers in the closet of the child's room.

By morning though, in the bright sunlight, I remembered that if I went back, we'd be stuck in the spot I had barely gotten out of. I remembered the peaks and valleys of Collis's moods, the drugs, the jobs I didn't want to know about, the darkness pulling him away, toward all sorts of oblivion. Things weren't going to get better there for a long, long time. I couldn't go home to stay.

To kill a little of Sunday morning, I drove the highways that circled the city, identical shopping centers every two or three miles. Brightly colored restaurant signs beckoned on every corner. I could circle forever without finding my way home. I got myself lost and made a game of trying to find my way back to the circle. Was it the green or the red gas station I had stopped at last? Finally, I got on the highway and drove to the Quick Stop in Camden, where I bought a Coke in the store, then sat in the car and read case files with the radio on. It was all I could do not to drive full speed on to Iona.

They came into the parking lot too fast and Joshua had his hand out the open window, catching the air with his palm. He was too young for the front seat. Collis knew better. Joshua waved at me and rolled up the window. This time, Collis had nothing to say. He barely raised his head.

"Nana says hi, Mama," Joshua said. "We went out for pizza and took a hike to the Pinnacle. She said you could see five states from there, but I could only count three. You should go with us next time. Daddy said it'd be fun if you went."

"Maybe I will," I said. "Thanks, Collis." He nodded, handed me Joshua's bags and a walking stick Joshua had found on the trail and carved his initials in.

"Let him keep that," Collis said.

"Sure," I said, holding it like a staff. "Did you talk to him about school?"

"Some. He knows what to do. Don't you, Bud?" He patted Joshua's shoulder. Joshua nodded.

"Collis, you were supposed to…"

"I was supposed to do a lot of things. So were you. Shit falls through the cracks."

"Only if you let it," I said. "And that's not the way you should talk in front of your son."

Collis's face began to burn. His eyes were wet, but he held back. "Why are you doing this?" his voice was almost a screech. He leaned toward me as he spoke.

"We both chose this," I said.

"I don't know about that," he said.

A woman parked next to me walked past us, carrying a twelve pack of beer on her hip and two plastic bags full of snacks in her other hand. She was short and wide, and struggled to keep her balance. Another time, Collis would have offered to help her, given her his lightning wink. This time, he kept staring straight at me. The woman looked away from us as she loaded the back of her rusted green station wagon, then slipped inside it and rattled away.

"Do you really want to talk about this, cause we can," I said. I was ready, making lists in my head of what to say.

"Stop it!" Joshua yelled. "Just stop!" He was leaning against my car, covering his ears. We stopped. Cold filled my chest. It would not get any easier. The cracks would widen and so much would fall into them that could never be recovered.

"It's okay, Baby," I said. He still held his hands over his ears. I put my arm around him and pulled him tight to my body. Like me, his face showed everything he felt. His small body shook.

"I love you two," Collis said. He looked me in the eye, but the anger was gone, replaced with sadness. "We won't have problems no more, Ava. Joshua won't have to hear this again." I nodded.

"I love you, Daddy," Joshua said, hugging Collis, picking up his bag and pillow he brought for the trip. He brushed past me, eyes fixed on the car. Collis walked silently to his truck, looking down at his work boots.

"Drive safe," my voice seemed to echo. "Come on," I said, gently pushing Joshua toward the back seat. "We better get home." He climbed in and buckled himself, waving me away when I tried to help him.

"You have to make sure it clicks," I said. "I need to get that seatbelt fixed."

"I know that," he said. "I always do it by myself." His scowl was inherited from his daddy. He shut and locked his door, and I settled into the front seat.

"Ready?" We could have been going to Disney World and the gloom in the car would not have budged. Joshua said nothing, just twisted around in his seat to keep Collis in sight as long as possible.

We both watched Collis walk into the store, like he knew what he had come there to buy, like he had a purpose. I waited for a minute to see what he would come out with, but he didn't come out. He was making sure I was the one to leave first, so he could say how hard he had tried. He was chatting up the salesclerk, who looked about fifteen, with thick orangeish makeup covering her cobbled skin, her green eyes rimmed in circles of dark blue eyeliner. I didn't care what Collis did, but Joshua stayed glued to him and the salesclerk through the thick plate glass.

In the back seat, Joshua stared out the window. I drove on and chattered at him about his school, my work, the weather, barely taking breaths, so he wouldn't have a chance to tell me what he was thinking. His eyes were Collis's. The thin mouth belonged to me. His words sounded like me, too, when I finally left a small space in the air for him to fill. "Daddy drives too fast," he said. "He's flying."

———

I remember Collis flying when we were first in love, like some kind of red-tailed hawk, off the houseboat on Norris Lake. I've heard hawks are messengers, but I was too stunned to figure out what it all meant. We were all there, everybody who worked at The Depot, which was not a depot to anywhere at all, but a restaurant that served anything fried you could want, including pickles with ranch dressing on the side. Somebody's grandmother owned the boat, but she was in assisted living now, so we took it over on Mondays when the restaurant was closed. The lake belonged to us, except for a stray bass boat wandering by every now and then. The pleasure cruise, we called it. Amy, the manager, was twenty-seven and had a hook-up for coke. I didn't try it, just sat on the deck in my light blue ruffled bikini and sipped fuzzy navels, which kept me hovering in a haze and put a glow around people. Collis was an angel. His skin had burned red and when he raised his arms, the untouched white of his body showed.

"I can do a swan dive," he said.

"Do swans really dive?" I asked. "I mean have you ever seen one fly?"

He grinned and shook his head. "Just watch."

I sat up in my lawn chair on the flat roof of the boat and followed his giant steps, one, two, some kind of hop, then he was airborne, flying, hovering for minutes, suspended from the world. It terrified me. His arms were outstretched, longer than his body, his head reached out, looking at the hills on the other side of the bark-brown water. "Careful," I whispered as I stood up to watch the end. Collis pointed his head down at the last second, folded his wings in and disappeared into the muddied water.

Hoots and cheers went out from both levels of the boat. "Six point 0 from the Russian judges," Amy yelled. "Buy that man a beer!" I watched the water for several minutes, staring at the sinking ripples, but he didn't resurface. I held my breath and counted, sure he was on the bottom of the lake where it would take weeks to find him. Please God don't let him drown, I prayed, already at the darkest conclusion. And then Collis was wrapping me from behind in a breathtaking, slippery hug, electric relief.

Now, I was the one flying away. My tires hissed on the highway. The shadows were deepening until the sky was nothing but black, and headlights on the road ahead began to pop on like lightning bugs in summer. The yellow centerline glowed and I followed it. I couldn't see any stars, or even the tops of the hills. I turned on my lights and concentrated on the road in silence. When I looked in the rearview, Joshua was slumped against the window, asleep or pretending to be, worn down from trying to hold our whole world together.

———

"Did you practice your subtraction?" I asked from my end of the living room couch. Joshua looked up from the TV show he was watching.

"Yeah."

"More than once?" Joshua didn't answer; he was like me, a bad liar, everything in his heart rose to his face.

"Okay, okay, I'll do it again," he said, stomping off toward the kitchen where his homework was spread across the table. "Daddy says homework's just busy work. He says I'm smarter than anybody in my school."

I added that to the mental list of all the things that Daddy didn't make him do, which I'd heard about several times in the few days since we got home. It was clear that Collis had convinced Joshua that I was the problem, and if I'd just move us back, everything would be like it used to be. Maybe some of that was true. I was trying to decide what to say to Joshua, if I should say anything, when the phone rang. I grabbed the phone in the kitchen by the refrigerator and forced a cheerful hello. I half hoped it was Collis. I both missed him and wanted to cuss him out, but it was his mother.

"Has Collis come up there?" Alice asked.

"You mean to our house?" I guess I shouldn't have called it "our house," but that's what it was.

"Yes, your place, or anywhere in Lexington. I haven't seen him in three days."

"What do you mean, Alice?" I took the phone into the hallway, away from Joshua.

"Is that Nana? I want to talk to her. Hi, Nana!" Joshua shouted toward me. I held my finger to my lips and scowled at him.

"Collis said he was taking a little trip but wouldn't say where." She sounded despondent. "I figured he was going to see y'all."

"He's not here," I said. "Three days?" I tried to breathe, but panic filled me. That had been since we left him. I had kept making excuses for him to Joshua. We both knew he should have called. Daddy just needs a little time alone, I told him. Or he's out looking for a job. Or he must be planning to come up here and surprise you. Kids know lies though. "Nobody's seen him?" I asked.

"I was really thinking he was there," Alice said. "I thought you all needed some time together... to work things out."

"Did you check at the lake? Sometimes he likes to stay in Evan Hughes's cabin there." I thought he just didn't want to call. He ought to be angry after the way I talked to him. "Or did you try John Bentley's? He might be holed up out there." My voice sped up as I thought of any place he might be.

"John's the one told me we ought to call you," Alice said. "I didn't find him at the lake, neither. I drove around up there." I was quiet long enough for her to say, "Ava? Can you hear me?" It took me a minute to find enough breath to speak.

"I'm coming. Right now," I said. I had already grabbed my keys off the kitchen counter.

"No," she said. "He'll be around soon. A mother just worries."

A dark feeling filled me, pulling down. He could be drunk, high, or in some cheap hotel room sleeping it off. He always said he was built like the mountains, up and down. He'd never be able to live flat. It could be that he wasn't alone. Or maybe someone had taken him down an awful road. I'd never be able to forgive myself if anything had happened to him. I'd left in such a cloud of meanness.

"We'll be there in a few hours," I said. "But don't wait up. I still have the key."

"Now, there's no need for that," Alice said. "We're probably worrying for nothing. I wouldn't want Joshua to miss any more school." I looked at my son, working on his math at the kitchen table, pressing the pencil hard into the paper when he was sure he was right. He counted the problems out with his fingers. He stopped, studied my face, trying to figure out Alice's side of the conversation.

"Is sixteen minus seven nine?" Joshua asked, holding up nine fingers. I nodded yes, waved him off to quiet him, and walked deeper into the hallway.

"We're leaving right now."

"Drive safe," she said. I could hear her exhale cigarette smoke before I hung up. She had quit last year after the doctor got on her, but that didn't matter now.

"What, Mama?" Joshua said, "What?" He was staring at me wide-eyed. I must have looked like something ghostly.

"Daddy," was all I could say.

We drove the whole way in silence, not even stopping once. If Joshua had to use the bathroom, he didn't say. I didn't ask. Sound would make this real, especially if we both heard it, then it couldn't be some secret, unlikely dread, something conjured in separate nightmares. I didn't want to know what I knew, deep inside. The hash marks in the middle of the road reflected my brights and flashed the road ahead in even intervals. No one passed us, or I didn't see them if they did. We were alone, tunneling through thick dark air to the sound of the tires turning over and over on the pavement.

There's a crystalline moment after you hear somebody's gone missing that you know what happened, even if you don't recognize the truth of it. Maybe not the first day, that's the day of hope and denial. Everything inside you resists knowing; everything will be okay. Everyone is overreacting. Or the second, that's the day you're angry. I'll kill him when he gets home, you say. At least I did. I cursed Collis. He was a shit of a father to worry his son. I said this in front of Joshua, to Joshua even, and this is one of the things I regret now, but it's part of a long list.

Collis wasn't my husband anymore, at least not completely, but still I told Micah when she came over to Alice's house to sit with us that he was a sorry excuse for a man, probably holed up with some teenaged whore, popping pills. I told her he was worthless as a husband and a father. He was trash.

"You don't mean that," Micah said. "Come on."

"Maybe I do mean it." It was much better than imagining my only love dead.

People came over, people who used to be our friends, who were still his friends. But what I told no one was that I felt what really happened to Collis as soon as Joshua and I were in the car, once we hit the highway, on the long twisting road to Iona. It took a few days for me to let it be the truth. I didn't tell anybody that either.

I cleaned Alice's spotless kitchen over and over, wiping down counters for the familiar motion of it. "Come on Mama, let's get out of here and look for Daddy," Joshua said. It was the longest week of our lives, waiting in Iona, hoping being there would somehow bring everything back to normal, bring Collis back to us. Joshua turned off Alice's TV for the first time all morning. We were told to stay home in case Collis showed up. We were told to leave it to the police and mine rescue, to leave it to the experts.

"Where should we go?" I really couldn't think of where else to look, even though I had retraced so many steps in my head, like you do when you lose a wallet or a watch. Where was I when I first lost Collis? It was hard to say. Maybe I had been losing him since the first day we met.

"Look, Mama. Nana and I made signs on her computer. We can put them up in town." Joshua held up a flyer with a black and white photo of Collis, smiling, sitting on his mother's porch, his arm stretched out on the top of the porch swing around Joshua. Joshua had been cropped out in the photo on the sign, only his small shoulder in the corner of the frame, so it was clear to strangers who to look for. I remembered taking that picture just before we moved. Underneath the photo, in bold letters, it said, "MISSING."

"Okay. Let's go, Baby. You lead the way." I grabbed my coat and handed Joshua his. Maybe someone did know something. Maybe once they saw our signs, they would tell us Collis's secrets.

"He always takes me to the hardware store and then to Cullen's for lunch," Joshua said. "Maybe he'll show up there." Joshua had decided to take charge of the situation. He figured out that Alice and I were powerless to fix it. I was willing to believe he could.

"Maybe so," I said. "Maybe so." I patted his back, but he was too anxious to be touched. He wiggled out of my reach and headed for the door.

We walked. The heart of town was three blocks down and two blocks over, on Cumberland Avenue. Iona had wide avenues, as if the planners had expected more glamour, since they were from Philadelphia and New York, coal company owners turning farmers into miners, bringing in workers from all over the world, more people, more business, more life, maybe even a parade! Wide floats had gone through with miniature coal tipples and beautiful girls on top, with "Power! Beauty! Progress!" plastered to the sides. Alice said the streets had once been full and wild. She said there had been people brought here from everywhere, all over the world, come to work in the mines. But not in my lifetime, and only the beginning of hers. There was always a boom and bust, and since the late '50s bust, people had followed other jobs North to Ohio, Indiana, Detroit.

The sidewalks had not been repaired since I was a baby, in the late '70s boom. We walked over ridges where tree roots had forced the concrete to crack open, wide as an evil mouth. The old oaks that had been planted to line the streets were broad and tall, though some of them were strangely bobbed, with thick, armless stumps where they had to accommodate electrical wires, or where branches were amputated to stop blight. The shops had not fared as well as the trees. The Snooty Fox Hair Den was boarded up. The Stone Healthcare Center had moved downtown. That happened just before we left. It took up the space that used to hold the Tog Shop and Office Supply. Most of the plate glass windows of the shops along Cumberland Avenue were covered inside with butcher paper. Signs in faded marker thanked passersby for all the years of good business. Some directed them to the mall on the bypass, where a pizza place, a few big box stores, and a Chinese restaurant had gone in. The three of us used to go there, to Hunan's, to celebrate Joshua's birthday.

From here, this wide vein, we were surrounded by the muted peaks of mountains worn down over millions of years. They were taller than the Rockies once, but with the coal companies blasting off the mountaintops to get the thinner, deeper seams of coal, to squeeze out anything else they could sell and burn, the wasting away was accelerated. Maybe what was supposed to take a million years took twenty. When the land flattened, the people flattened too. I grabbed Joshua's hand, still small enough to be hidden in my own. When we got closer to the living part of the street, he sped up, almost to a run.

"We should check there," Joshua said, "In Noble's!"

Noble's Hardware sat right where it always had, across the street from Cullen's Drugs. Joshua still held tight to my hand, something he had refused to do on the way into his school, or anywhere public in Lexington. "He took me here to get tulip bulbs for Nana. We planted them in her front yard. Maybe he's planning to surprise her with more," he said. Anna Noble waved to us through the window, blew us a kiss, and shook her head. This answered our question and led Joshua's gaze to the other side of the street. "Or maybe he's gone into Cullen's to get a cheeseburger. He loves their cheeseburgers. We could try there first."

"Maybe." My heart sunk down into my stomach, and a low watt fear radiated from my skin. I was sure Joshua could feel it too. We crossed the street to Cullen's. Deana Cullen was at the lunch counter, slicing lemons. She had gone to high school with my parents. I'd known her my whole life.

"What can I get you?" she asked. Years of grease from the thousands of hamburgers made there had soaked into the walls. Old cigarette smoke was in there somewhere too, a faint memory, even though Deana kept the place spotless.

"How about a milkshake, Baby?"

"I'm not hungry," Joshua said.

"We'll have two Cokes." Deana got to work on that. She was thin, with deep crevices radiating around her lips from years of smoking. Her hands were smooth and soft from a lifetime of slicing lemons. I had never seen her hair any other way than the way it was now, bangs sprayed up high in the front, a thin blonde ponytail sticking out the back. Her white apron said "Cullen's Drugs" across the front and "Deana" in a beautiful embroidered red script across her right breast, as if anyone around here would have to ask her name. We sat at the old round stools in front of the counter. Joshua twisted his around, pushed off the counter, and made a full, squeaky circle. When he came to a stop, he sipped his soda through the extra-long bendy straw Deana gave him special.

"Have you heard from him?" Deana asked. "He ought to have told somebody where he was by now." Word had spread about Collis. Everybody was looking for him. Any news would have raced back to us like fire, would have burned just as much.

"Don't he like to go down to the lake? I guess you never know around water." Deana shook her head. Joshua stared at the ice floating in his Coke.

"I want to go home," he said. "Maybe he's home now." I pulled out a five-dollar bill to pay.

"No charge for the Cokes," Deana said.

"Thanks." We didn't speak on the way back, but Joshua gripped my hand so tight it went numb, and he pulled me toward Alice's house.

"He won't acting right," Evan Hughes said. He stood behind a ladder-back chair at Alice's kitchen table, held onto the top rung of it. I sat in the chair across from him, elbows on the table, resting my chin in my hands. I wasn't sure if I could hold my own head up. Joshua stayed in his room, playing with the old Star Wars action figures Collis had saved for him. Alice turned on the TV in the living room to give us some privacy, though I know she was straining to hear what we said in the kitchen.

Evan had gone to school with us. He had been all-state in basketball, but now, fifteen years later, his belly hung over his belt and he owned a string of convenience stores throughout the mountains. Alice told me that since I'd been gone, he and Collis had been hanging out, playing poker and watching ball games. Neither of Evan's two marriages had taken, so he had time on his hands. "He gave me all his chips the other night, told me to keep them," he said. "Asked me did I want his guitar, or even his truck. I thought he was joking, you know, maybe he'd had a little too much to drink. I really did. Told him he couldn't pay me to take that old truck." Evan sat in the chair, reached his hands across the table toward me, but I got up and crossed the room. I wouldn't be a part of their sick plan. I could just imagine how they cooked this up over beers, thinking how he could get me to come down here and stay. Evan was clever; he'd always had good ideas for getting into trouble. I glared at him.

"That's not the way to joke," I said, "He's probably keeping an eye on us and laughing. He probably thinks it's hilarious I'd come all the way down here to look for him."

"Wait a minute," Evan said. "I don't know who you're talking about, Ava, but it ain't Collis. He would never hurt you and Joshua. No matter what you did." He loathed me. I could tell by the pinch of his mouth when he looked at me.

"You don't know him like I do," I said.

"I guess Collis was right about you," Evan said. He shook his head, walked into the living room to say his goodbyes to Joshua and Alice and left. He didn't look at me again.

I couldn't help it. I said the worst things I could think of. I was scared to death he was dead, so I had to try to hate him alive. How could you hate somebody who was dead, especially someone you once loved? Still loved. The good memories rose to the top like cream, but I pushed them down. Alice came into the kitchen, filled the red teakettle and set it on the flame. "Want some chamomile?" she asked. "It might help calm your nerves."

"You know where he is!" I shouted. "Don't lie to me, Alice." I pointed my finger at her. My hand was shaking. My whole body was shaking. She drew back a little, but her eyes stayed fixed on mine. Her body stayed steady.

"You don't mean that, Ava." She stepped toward me, put her hand on my shoulder, but I moved away from her.

"You don't know what I mean," I said. After I called her a liar though, and she knew for sure that I wasn't covering for Collis, letting him sleep off some drug-hazed depression, she said nothing. "Alice?"

"I'm still here," she said quietly. "I've had a bad feeling since the first day he went missing." She put her hand over her mouth. I could feel my face heat up with fear, or shame, or both.

When Alice did decide to make a noise, the next morning, she alternated between bawling and nervously listing the people we should call. She had been the one to alert the police, to actually file the report. She was the next of kin, not me. I didn't know what I was to Collis now.

Collis usually ate supper with Alice or called if he got some fast food to take home, or if he didn't feel like eating at all. He wasn't a cook, and he was the only child Alice had. She left a place at the table set for him at each meal, just in case. I held on for a while longer. Collis would come back and shock us all, I thought. Jesus made it back in three days, didn't he? But Collis had already been gone a week. I tried to push that truth to the back of my mind and keep on looking for the impossible, the beautiful unharmed man of my imagination.

The next morning, Joshua was parked in front of Alice's TV, eating handfuls of sugar cereal right out of the box, listening to pre-recorded laughter. I didn't comment on the sugar or the TV, just sat close enough on the couch to touch him as he watched his show. Children know that in a crisis, rules change. Alice came in the back door with a bag of groceries. She walked right in front of us and turned off the television.

"Hey! I was watching that," Joshua said.

"Don't talk to your Nana like that," I said.

"I heard something down at the Save A Lot," she said. "There's signs somebody camped out for a few days on the side of Oak Mountain. Old bean cans and charred wood. Lots of footprints, looked like they came from work boots."

My heart beat faster. I needed more air. "Let's make a plan," I said. I hid my hands in the pockets of my jeans. Joshua dug his arm into the cereal box all the way to the elbow, but he was considering Alice's words. He withdrew his hand from the box and studied the last dry pieces as if they were runes that could tell the future and the past at the same time.

"That's got to be him," Joshua said. "I told you he liked the woods!"

"I'm going up there to see for myself," I said.

"I want to go too. I can find him. He'll come out when he hears my voice," he said. "He misses me. You'll just run him off again."

Alice carried the groceries into the kitchen. She couldn't stand Joshua's hope.

"No, Baby. You need to stay here with Nana. She needs some company. I'll call you when I find out more," I said. "You be good." I kissed his cheek, hugged him tight.

"Stop it, Mama," he pushed out of my arms, stood up. "I want to go. I'm big enough. I can help."

"You stay here in case he calls. You're the one he'll want to talk to." Joshua understood this. He went into the kitchen after Alice and sat dutifully by the phone.

Evan and some of the other men Collis worked with at the Lynchco mine just after college had gathered in a cluster of trucks on the side of the steep mountain road near the mouth of the mine. Evan's beat up truck bed was the conference room. Two men sat on the tailgate, and the other four leaned against the sides of the truck, drinking coffee, quiet, ball caps pulled low over their eyes. Even Johnny Roberts had joined the search. He nodded at me and kept staring as I got out of my car.

Evan walked out to meet me. "We looked all up around here," he said. "Been up here a couple hours already. We ain't going to find him here. We're going down to Hard Rock Falls. He likes it up there. You can just go on home, Ava. In case he calls. We got the search under control. You don't need to be up here alone anyhow." The anger he'd had toward me at Alice's was gone; pity had taken its place. He didn't expect to find Collis alive. Evan put his arm around me, walked me back toward my car like some lost child.

"Okay," I said and slid into the driver's seat. "Okay." Evan shut me in and leaned down to my window so he could face me. He reached in and touched my cheek.

"We'll call you right away if we find a thing," he said. "You'll be the first to know." I nodded. I sat there for a while, drinking the coffee Alice forced on me as I left the house. The only warmth in the car was the steam from my travel mug. I waited as they drove off one by one, a battalion of searchers. I waved at each truck as it passed. Then I moved.

The cold morning air burned my face. I wrapped my red scarf tighter and walked faster. The sun was coming up over the mountain, so I wouldn't need the flashlight I brought in my pocket. There was mist rising from the ground, as if the mountain itself was on fire, except it was cool. I could feel the chill the air held on to.

In high school, Collis and I used to ride up Potter's Fork to the Lynchco mine and park. Everybody did. On autumn nights, kids would burn old tires for bonfires and hang out getting drunk. You could see the whole town from here. Miles of pine tree covered ridges rolled like green ocean waves. Little pockets of lights showed where the other towns were and when we saw them, we didn't feel so far away from what was happening in the world. After all, Hubbard was just over the ridge. I could point to it.

This was the place I always came when I needed to be alone. It made sense that Collis would choose it too. He needed to be alone more often than I did. He held grudges longer. A single fight would linger with him for days, either the anger or the guilt, then he'd finally shake it off and want to celebrate. Up on the ridge alone, I'd hike around, throw rocks off the side of the mountain and watch them fall. I never went inside the mine, but I knew Collis would. He often talked about the way little private caves branched off from the main shaft, how there were places where the men had mined all they could, then moved on to another shiny black seam of coal, places people forgot about.

"It's like a cavity that's been dug out and never filled," he told me. "It's so empty, but comforting and warm. Sometimes I go there on a break. It's a good place to think. You know these are some of the oldest mountains in the world, Ava? All kinds of spirits in there." Maybe he was thinking about those spirits now, camped inside the belly of the earth. I had to check. I walked slowly into the mineshaft. It was warmer in the mine and the path descended gradually. It was rocky and rough, it had been years since anyone worked here. The company had gone under not long after we graduated. Collis worked here for only three months, the summer after my freshman year, but he always said there was something special about it, that the men here were old school and understood each other.

I stepped over the tracks where the mine cars had taken men to the depths, turned my flashlight on and panned the mine walls with its weak beam. Men had always told me that a woman in the mines was bad luck. I thought this wasn't true, but I shook off a shudder, just the same. Maybe Evan was right. He said they had looked up here, but they didn't know how Collis talked to me about this place, how perfect it was for being alone. They might find him at the falls and I would miss it. Still, I had come this far, and I had to look.

The mine took a hard right turn, about twenty feet down. I followed that. My eyes were becoming accustomed to the dark as it came and I could make out the rocky surfaces of the walls. Water dripped a steady beat behind me and I could see its sheen on the rock wall when the flashlight bumped with my gait. I thought I saw something. When I shined my light on it, though, it was just more rock. Small creatures meant to live without light skittered ahead of me. I went deeper into the mine. I could still see the daylight of the opening behind me. As long as that dot of light remained, I would be all right. There was a small opening to the right, and though I would have to crouch down to get inside it, I had to try.

It was even darker in here, if you believed in degrees of pitch black. Rock crunched under me. Once I got through the opening, I could stand up. When I raised my arm up, I touched the ceiling. It was rough and dry, but solid enough that I wouldn't be trapped in a rock fall. This place was a rocky womb, warm and protected. Somehow, there had to be air coming in, going out, but I couldn't tell from where. If I stayed too long here, I would lose my orientation. I took a deep breath to calm myself and smelled something I couldn't place. It was a sweet and raw smell. I flashed my light on the wall and saw nothing. Then I turned to the other wall and saw something dark and wet. At first, I thought it was water, or some kind of strange algae that only grew underground. My mind made up anything else it could be, but my body didn't stop moving. I didn't make a sound. I stepped forward, and even though I wasn't close enough to touch the wall, it became unmistakably thick and red, the closer I brought the light.

I followed the blood down the wall with my flashlight, unable to make a sound. My breath was short and shallow. The light beamed on Collis's mustard colored, steel-toed work boots, the ones I bought him last summer, spattered with what I had first thought was mud. His body was slumped against the wall, but his legs stuck straight out on the ground. I trained the light along his worn-in jeans, ripped at the knee. I could see his dark leg hairs poking through, his skin pale in comparison, the scar he had gotten from a bike wreck when he was twelve slicing under his kneecap. The light moved onto his tan canvas coat and across the once white, now blood-soaked thermal shirt that was torn at the neck from the force of the shot. I couldn't feel my body now and didn't know how the light was moving, or where it came from. I wanted to hold him, change him back to alive, but I had no idea how to move.

What had been Collis's face was splayed open from the mouth, where he had placed the pistol. Blood pooled in his ears and covered everything behind him. A wave of nausea went through me, and I sank down to the floor, vomited. I began to rock and to make a noise that I could not identify as my own.

I touched his work boot, held onto the toe of it, the hard-lugged sole, as if I could hold him down in this world before he floated away. The steel-toed boot was heavy. His left arm hung down by his side, palm out. His hand looked perfect. If I focused on it, it looked like nothing had happened. I studied the fingers, the rough skin of his fingertips, the long lifeline that ran right up to a blue vein. Nothing was flowing there. *No life, no blood, no, no, no*—a word began to take shape over and over, to dislodge from the depths of my throat, so I could hear it and understand it. It was a human sound screamed as if from an animal, *No, no, no, no, no!* I could not stop, couldn't breathe, *No, no, no, no, no—Collis!*

His face had been so beautiful, his smile and perfect white teeth. I wanted to touch him, but not this, that was not him at all. I wasn't sure where I was or how I had gotten here. What was this mess that had once been a person—once been my husband who had loved only me, in spite of me?

He had wanted to talk. I had said no. That was a small word. I would say yes a hundred times now—a thousand, a million—if I could change everything. *I love you. I love you. I love you.* I pulled at my hair to hold onto something. My mind was playing tricks in this dark cavern. The devil could be right around the corner, laughing. *Collis! Collis! Please, no, please, no!* I climbed back through the hole, ran up and up toward the tiny dot of light and the mouth of the mine. I sat down hard on the cold dirt road with my head in my hands, listening to the wails and cries that echoed out of the mine like ghosts.

12

Reclamation

I tried to keep track of what had happened, so I wouldn't lose sight of what was real. I would still be sitting outside the mine if Evan had not accidentally dropped his UK ball cap by the side of the road and remembered it once he got to Hard Rock. When he saw my car, he said, it wasn't hard to figure where I had gone. And once he was near the mouth of the mine, he had heard me, or what he thought was a human sound, gone back to wild.

I refused to go home. Finally, Evan led me to my car and let me rock and moan by myself while the crowds of searchers came back to gather at the mouth of the mine. Collis's friends and co-workers, men he had gone school with who were now EMTs and police in the county, even a few who served in the national guard, began to scrape what was left of him off the inside of the mountain. A fire truck backed up to the mine, its never-ending white hose snaking deep inside the opening. An ambulance was parked next to it, but only for the men who couldn't take what they saw and needed to be revived. Blue and red police lights swirled around us where they'd blocked off the road to the mine. Evan drove me back to Alice's once I was too tired to protest.

After the wailing stopped—or at least calmed to sobs: mine, Alice's, all the people who heard the news—a weighted silence filled us. My heart locked up in the middle of my throat, so I could hardly breathe or swallow. Alice functioned for us, talked to the people who came bearing casseroles and condolences. She made arrangements. It was like she had an autopilot that kept her body going and packed her grief down into a manageable suitcase behind her heart and lungs. My grief ran wild circles around me until I was dizzy and only wanted to lie still, so I wouldn't be sick. I had to be the one to tell Joshua when he came home from putting up "MISSING" posters with the neighbors and came into the bedroom to find me.

"What's wrong Mama?" he asked. He was still wearing his backpack and jacket. I was lying on the bed, under the covers.

My voice was not my own. "He's gone, Baby." I was floating above myself, watching my mouth give this sentence to my son.

Joshua looked confused, then angry. He came closer to make sure I could hear. "You're wrong! You're lying! Daddy's coming back." He tried to punch the bedroom wall over the bedside table, his fist no bigger than a plum. He made a tiny depression that cracked the pale blue paint, like a concave robin's egg, just under a picture of his grandmother, posed in a black velvet drape for her high school portrait. Joshua's fingers began to swell around the knuckles and turned red, but he could still bend his fingers, open and close his palm. Nothing seemed to be broken; nothing was fixed.

The old deep freeze in the garage was full of lasagna, chicken casseroles, each with a name written on masking tape and instructions, "Heat for thirty minutes at 350," or "Thaw First!" The refrigerator was full of deteriorating salads and deli meats, stacked on top of each other, waiting to be offered to anyone who came in to pay their respects. A few dirty cups and plates sat in the sink. We made Joshua eat, but we couldn't find the energy to clean up afterward. Eventually, a neighbor would come by and wash the dishes, sit with a cup of coffee and a piece of the cake she'd brought. She would just want to straighten things up a little, and we would let her. Beautiful hummingbird cakes and pecan pies wilted on Alice's kitchen counter. I stuck my finger deep into the middle of a carrot cake, just to ruin it, then threw the whole thing into the trash can, upside down.

The work at the mine took hours, Evan said. Yellow plastic police tape marked the boundaries of danger and told people not to cross, but they did anyway. I got reports from the men who were there, but nobody could tell me the thing I wanted to know. I got out of bed to hear what they had to say.

"Sorry for your loss, Ava. We're doing the best we can," Joe Maggard said. He stopped by the house after his shift on the recovery team when it was already dark. He stood at ease in his trooper uniform in Alice's kitchen.

"Thanks," I said. "You want some of this pie?" He took a piece to be polite and because when his mouth was full, we didn't have to talk.

"I wish you didn't have to see that, Ava," he said. "I wish it was one of us who found him."

I nodded.

When I came out to sit in the living room, women I knew tried to put their arms around me. Micah sat beside me, silently holding me up. My mother was there too. She and Daddy had driven through the night from Indiana. She held me and said, "You've got to keep going, Baby," but she couldn't tell me why. Nobody could. I heard stories, awful ones of men exploding in mines, roofs caving in and crushing a woman's only son, suicides too. We were just supposed to shake our heads, live the same lives, and hope for better. Most of these women wanted to pray with me, but I couldn't.

Mournful ballads were made up about tragedies like this because the only thing to do was to tell it, over and over, but that changed nothing. No one really listened who could do something about it. The voices of the women in Alice's living room drifted up and dissolved, but I wouldn't sing high and lonesome. I should have kept Collis from that deep dark place.

Joshua liked to sit on the bed Collis had slept in for the last month. None of us could bear to change the sheets. I knew Joshua hoped to find one of Collis's precious hairs or catch the scent of him. Any proof that he recently lived might mean this never happened, that Collis was still here, that I hadn't led him to this.

"I don't ever want to leave here, Mama," Joshua said. "We can't leave him now."

"We'll see, Baby," was all I could say. I knew I would have to get back to the world, to my job, that in spite of death my child would grow, would want and exist, but I surely could not forgive. I guess this made me a sinner in the worst way, cursing God and my husband. A man might be better off left in the depths alone if that's what he really wanted. Collis would have wanted me to honor his desire. He left no note, at least none anybody could find, but words wouldn't explain anything to me anyway. How had I not known that death was what Collis wanted more than life, or our family, or anything? Did I ever know him at all?

Joshua slept with me now in the guest room with the pink floral wallpaper. At least we both lay still and tried, curled into each other like forest animals, blankets twisted around our limbs. I almost wished Joshua hadn't been born, so he wouldn't have to live through this.

A few days later, when I tried to get dressed, I pinched a nerve in my lower back and couldn't move. I was stuck hunched over. Every inch I tried to straighten up sparked jolts of pain. "Mama, what happened?" Joshua asked, sitting up in bed. He looked panicked. Any sign that my body was weak meant that I could go away, that I might leave him behind, too.

I closed my eyes as I took a slow step, bent a little at the waist because it hurt too much to stand upright. "Don't worry. I'll be okay," I said. "Just let me take my time. It'll work itself out." I had only felt this before when I was pregnant with Joshua, going into labor. The weight of his tiny body inside my body, his big Maynard head pushing down inside my narrow pelvis, put pressure on a nerve. Collis had rubbed my back then, over and over through my dress until he rubbed the skin raw. His hands were strong and sure, intent on helping me.

"You sure you want me to keep rubbing?" he had asked. "You're bleeding through the fabric."

"Rub harder," I said. "Don't stop."

"I love you and this baby so much," he said. He did, every touch told me so.

I answered with a rhythmic pattern of short breaths, then a long one. I managed to puff out, "You. Too." before another contraction overtook me.

Even after I walked through the house and sat for a while in the kitchen, the pain still came from the weight inside me, but this time there was no way for Collis to give counter pressure. Alice told me this was my body's way of trying to release the tension, though the way she moved, I could tell her body hurt too.

"You've been tense since you left here the first time," Alice said. "Now you're sleeping and your body's trying to let the pain go. You can't hold it together forever." It used to bug me how certain Alice was when she spoke, all the authority she claimed, but now I was glad to hear that somebody knew what was happening to me. "Everything that's happened is tied up in knots in your muscles. Your body's fighting itself." She was right, I knew, but I also knew that once I let go of that pain, Collis's death would be final.

I called Anita at the clinic. "How can I get rid of this pinched nerve? It's killing me."

"I can call you something in, a muscle relaxer. You can pick it up this afternoon," she said.

"You sure that's okay?" I asked.

"It's no problem," she said. "I'll give you a few extras in case this happens again. It has a pain reliever built in."

"But what if I like them too much?" I said. "What if I get hooked?"

"You're not the type, Ava," she said. "These aren't too strong anyway."

I couldn't help wondering who was the type and who wasn't. I liked the idea of numbing my pain as much as anybody else did. Alice could talk about how I should take care of myself, but she didn't do it herself. Her hair seemed to have grayed more in the two weeks since Collis had died, and she was already losing weight. I could tell by the way her high-waisted jeans hung around her hips. She hadn't eaten much of anything. She nibbled on some cheese and crackers when I was looking, but I knew she'd throw most of them into the trash later. She knew what she was supposed to say to visitors, that it was all God's plan, that Collis was in a better place. She'd said that for the first day or two, but quickly wore through her resolve. I used to be jealous of Alice for the way Collis would open up to her instead of me. Now, I wanted to hear everything he'd ever told her, and she wanted to know about what he shared with me. For the first time, we really needed each other. Alice didn't say a word about me finishing off the whiskey people had left, or taking the pills Anita had prescribed; I didn't say anything about her smoking menthols again. Maybe that was the only way she could make herself take a breath at all.

"Try this cheese," she scooted the plate toward me. I shook my head.

I breathed deep with each movement, didn't bend to get the napkin I dropped.

"You okay?" Joshua asked.

"It's getting better," I lied. It still hurt after two days. "Here, try this cheese and crackers." I pushed the plate toward him. He finished it off. I knew more about my clients now, about all the people who got on these same pills I was taking and never got off. I knew even more about Collis than I ever had. There were ways to escape pain forever, but I had to be here for Joshua.

My brother Travis was traveling for work in northern Indiana, selling restaurant equipment to fast food chains. I told him not to come down since we weren't having a regular funeral. The last two weeks of visitors hadn't helped anything. "You sure, Ava? I could be down there tonight."

"No, Trav. We'll have a memorial service in a few months. There's nothing you can do now. Mother and Dad are still here."

"That's why I thought you'd need me." I came close to smiling at that.

"I can handle them. I've dealt with them longer than you. I'll need you later, Baby."

"Okay," Travis said. "I love you."

My parents got a room up at the Highway Inn but sat with us at Alice's house during the day. My father was the kind of older balding man who didn't believe there was ever much to say, about death, especially. He took refuge in the TV news, politics, and basketball, but still he hugged me tight enough to hold me together. "I'm so sorry, Baby," he said, "So, so sorry." When I didn't say anything back, all he could think to say was, "Maybe it'd do you good to watch a ballgame. How about those Cats? Maybe we could get some tickets and go up to Lexington in a few weeks."

"Daddy, no," I said. He hugged me again until I let go.

My mother always had words. She tried to talk things away. She used a cheerful voice and always focused on the positive, the upside of the situation. "You're so lucky that he didn't do this in your new home," she said.

"There's no good to this. It is nothing close to lucky."

"Now, I didn't mean that, Ava. I just meant…"

"There really is nothing to say. Nothing." For the first time in my memory, my mother was silent for hours. I let her stay around at Alice's, feed me, hold me, then later take Joshua to the hotel, so I could have some time to myself. They were trying, really they were, but this was just another step in them pulling away from Iona, from Joshua and me. The poverty and the pain of Iona embarrassed them. I embarrassed them by staying. They couldn't disown the place if Joshua and I were still in it. And now the shame of this.

"Why don't you come home with us?" my mother said. "You can wait until you're ready to work again. We have wonderful schools. I've planted a garden."

"I have a job in Lexington, Mom. I'll go back to that, eventually. I have a life and Joshua has a school, with friends. We'll be okay there." The part about the friends and being okay, I didn't know about, but the worst thing I could think of doing was becoming a child again, giving up everything that made up the life I knew, the memories of Collis and home, the hopes of the life we'd wanted to make.

"Well, think about it. Think about what's best." Mom held me tight, my face in her blonde hair. I could smell her thick, spicy perfume. It was a new scent for her, so she didn't even smell like my mother. She kissed me on the forehead, leaving a trace of the red lipstick she had reapplied.

The psychologist I saw at the new health clinic across from Cullen's, Dr. Isaac, told me that if a person really wants to kill themselves, there is nothing you can do to stop them—nothing.

When he told me this, I studied the spider plant on his desk and the God's eye wall hanging above it—made of orange, green, and yellow yarn wrapped around sticks—that someone, probably his daughter who was close to my age, had made him at church camp. Dr. Isaac said it took two people to make a relationship, but one to end it.

Dr. Isaac also said no way was it my fault, that it was "a final choice made by the mentally ill person alone." But calling it an illness didn't bring Collis back, or right the wrong he had done to Joshua. The truth still stood. I knew nothing about the man I had loved and married. Dr. Isaac offered me a prescription for Klonopin. "It'll take the edge off," he said. I took it. When I kept feeling the edge a few hours later, I took another.

I didn't offer to view Collis's body or even go near the mine when I drove on that side of town. I couldn't bring myself to leave Iona, even though Micah said it would do me good, that Alice could take care of the arrangements, and maybe I had some loose ends to tie up at work before I came back for Collis's memorial service. Micah also offered to look after Joshua, but I wouldn't let him out of my sight. I don't think he wanted me out of his, either. We sat together, watched the icy glow of the television. Alice had done this before, with her husband, Frank, and other friends and family before him. She was my guide, and I held fast to her. She knew the ritual, how long you could go without showering, when you had to eat, and when you could just sit and stare. Micah called to check on me every day.

A week later, I woke to Joshua gently pulling my hair. He hadn't done that since he was four. "Get up, Mama," he said. "I have an idea."

"It's too early for ideas. Let's go back to sleep. We can have ideas later." I pulled the covers over my head. He pulled my hair again. "Stop it! That hurts!" I sat up in bed.

"Let's plant some flowers for Daddy," he said. He had a shovel in his hand and had dragged in a potted azalea someone had brought by the house. It had been stranded in the small bay windowsill, sequestered with the other struggling condolence plants.

"Okay," I said. "Okay. Can you dig a hole?"

"I already started." Joshua ran out the door with the shovel tilted on his shoulder. I got up out of bed and slipped on the jeans and T-shirt left on the floor the night before. It made sense to want to put something in the earth that would grow, and die, then grow back again.

Joshua dug deep enough to cover the root ball of the plant. He dug until his hair stuck to his forehead, damp and sweaty. "Remember when you and me and Daddy planted the garden in the backyard of the old house?"

I nodded. "I do." We had spent that whole last summer tending to the rows and rows of tomatoes, beans, corn, squash. Collis's garden never had a weed for long. He tended it like some kind of sculptor. It was a beautiful thing to see. So perfectly alive.

"We grew that great big watermelon," Joshua said.

"That was a delicious watermelon. Your Daddy was good at growing a garden. Nana taught him."

"She's the one who told me I should plant this," Joshua said.

"Let me have that shovel," I said. He handed it to me.

"But I get a turn again next."

I dug and dug, pitching the dirt behind me, anywhere it wanted to land. I dug deeper and wider, I couldn't stop. I dug until the hole was big enough that I could curl up in it.

"Mama, we don't need a hole that big," Joshua said. I stopped and wiped the sweat off my forehead with my sleeve. I let the shovel drop and wiped my hands on my jeans. He was staring at me. "You okay?"

"Yeah, I'm fine. You're right. Let's fill some of this back in." We knelt on the ground and pushed the dirt back into the warm hole, until it made a false bottom. It was enough to support the azalea.

"What if it doesn't make it?" he said.

"It will."

After that, watering the azalea was what got Joshua and me out of bed every morning. It was what made me put the pills back, when I wanted just one more. We watched its hot pink petals turn dry and brown, even as we watered it. We were denying the facts of fall and winter, only wanting to see the spring ahead of us.

The preacher from the Methodist church, Billy Brown, came by later that day and wanted to comfort me, but I stuck my hands down into the pockets of my dirty jeans and refused to make eye contact. I was filthy and smelled a little bit like old sweat, but I didn't care. Billy Brown was very clean, so clean the bare parts of his pink scalp shined through thin layers of wiry brown hair. His hands smelled like Ivory soap and the rest of him reeked of herbal cologne that was meant to seem exotic, even if you could buy it at Cullen's. He had bad breath barely covered by the bright green mint gum he chewed, which I could see bouncing around the back of his mouth as he talked. He touched me on the shoulder with his wide, thick palm.

"Let me get you some coffee," I said. I tried to step away, but he gripped my shoulder now.

"Pray with me, Ava," he said. I shook my head, but he took that for a yes somehow and grabbed both my hands in his anyway. His palms were warm and soft and slightly clammy when he gripped my straightened fingers. "Our Father, who art in heaven…" I let go of his hands once his eyes were closed. He opened them again and stared at me. I must have looked a mess with my greasy ponytail, my shallow eyes. I wouldn't be the one to look away though. "Maybe another time," he said. "Looks like you need some rest. Find comfort in your faith, Ava."

He went on to pray with Alice and Joshua on his way out, standing by the front door with one hand on the top of Joshua's head and the other raised to Jesus. I turned on the radio that Alice kept on the kitchen counter so I wouldn't have to listen to him. "Hits from the eighties, nineties, and today!" the announcer cooed.

If you believe in things unseen, you can believe in miracles, salvation, any of it. All of the wonderful things that were supposed to exist high above ground, or once you're deep under it. I struggled with my faith now. I knew the truth of what I had seen, and how the unseen had betrayed me.

13

Remains

I couldn't spend December in the coalfields. Not with the memory of Collis in that mine. The mountains turned bare and brown, crosshatched with trees. The low sky dropped its dark curtain early. Even the news wouldn't leave me alone. Already, six miners had been trapped in West Virginia, like they were nearly every year, and twenty-three were entombed in the underside of Belarus. I couldn't find that on a map, somewhere near Russia, but I knew where those people were now, in the same thick darkness of anyone ever buried alive. Any time a man set foot in the mines, he was courting death. The only difference was, Collis embraced it when it came toward him.

We were watching TV in Alice's den, me stretched out on the brown velour couch, covered in a blanket, Alice in the recliner with her feet up. The overhead lights were dimmed, and all the dinner dishes had been cleaned and put away. It was some kind of documentary about wolves. At the commercial break, a preview for the news came on that mentioned the good weather forecast for the weekend. It would warm up a bit, almost spring-like. "Take off those winter coats!" the announcer said, "But you might not want to store them in the attic just yet."

Alice had been quiet for the past few days. She busied herself with cleaning sticks from the yard since the weather started to turn. She looked at me straight on now, determined. "I'm ready to do it," she said.

"Do what?" I asked, pulling the blanket up to my chin.

"Spread the ashes. We may not get weather like this again for a while. We need to take him up to the ridge. Collis would want to be out when the mountain wakes up this spring. We can't keep him on the mantle forever."

It had been up to me and Alice to decide what to do with Collis's body. I couldn't bear the thought of him ending up underground, turning into earth, then getting dug up again someday by a huge dozer. We decided to cremate him, with no real funeral. Collis hated the funeral home with its chemical smell. I knew he wouldn't want his name on the lit-up board out front. Friends wanted to have a vigil. I kept telling them we would do it eventually.

"Okay," I said to Alice. "Okay." I would never be ready to let Collis go, and I might never have whatever mettle Alice had that got her through. The air was dry and still, the sun would be shining. He would land where he wanted.

It was just the three of us, Joshua, Alice, and me, hiking up the mountain to throw the ashes over the side. Joshua led at first, the way little boys have to race toward everything, but as we got to the ridge, he realized what the finish line was, so he slowed and took my hand. Alice kept up, but I could tell her bad knee was bothering her. Still, she would not be deterred. She had some kind of reserve, like she made a pact of survival with somebody, or for somebody. She had faith too.

She found an open spot on a small rock bald and sat down on it. Joshua and I sat beside her. We could see the side of Black Mountain, where miniature dozers were clawing into the bare rock hillside and backing up. They were twice the height of pickup trucks, with lugged tires as tall as a man. We could hear them faintly. Up close, there would be a din of rumbling and beeping. The rest of the hills were covered in a quilt of tree limbs, with patches of dark green pine. The scent of plants growing and dying mixed together. I put my arm around Joshua. Alice held the oak box that held Collis.

"Are you sure this is Daddy?" Joshua asked.

"I'm sure," I said. Joshua reached for the box, and Alice gave it to him. He opened it, closed his eyes, grabbed a small handful of ash and threw it as hard as he could over the mountain. It landed right in front of us. He brushed his hands together then wiped them on his jeans. He looked at me, "Your turn, Mama." I shook my head. Tears slipped down my face, but I didn't let a sound out. I couldn't toss him away, even to land on the mountain. I couldn't touch him turned to ash.

Alice took the whole wooden urn and hurled the ash out and over, as hard as she could. She was small, but Collis flew beyond where we could see him, down the mountain, into some brush. "I love you, Baby," she said. Like Collis, she had always been better with actions than words. She brushed her hands together to set him free. "It's over," she said.

I never thought about it before, a mother putting the final end to the life she had begun, but it had happened that way. I hoped Joshua would outlive me, so I would never know the pain of that, of finishing what you'd started. The life you help make seems eternal. We hiked back down the mountain, Joshua in the middle, our hands linked to each other in a chain.

"Can we sing him a song?" Joshua asked. "That one they sing in Nana's church?"

"Amazing Grace?"

"Yeah, that one," he began to sing, lining it out like the preacher did. Alice and I responded like we'd been taught: "I once was lost / But now I'm found / Was blind, but now I see."

—

"You'll be okay, then?" I asked, standing in Alice's carport, ready to get on the road back to Lexington. I flushed the ten remaining pills Anita had given me down the toilet that morning. I knew I had to, even though it made me sad to see the last little round blue pill circle down and disappear. I had begun to think of those pills all day, even though I'd said I was done with them. I felt dizzy when I tried to skip a day. I knew what that meant. This had to be a real new beginning, for me and for Joshua. I slung a backpack over my shoulder and carried a bag in each hand. Joshua was already in the car, buckled in, writing his name on the fogged-up window with his finger. Alice tucked her hair behind her ears. She had lost weight, but she was standing straight.

"I've made it this far," she answered. She believed onward was the only way. "You do remember I twirled a fire baton in high school?"

"I've heard that story many times. It just means you don't have much sense. Stay away from anything burning, except maybe the stove." I knew her majorette days were all about performance, keeping a smile on. She was still good at that, at least for Joshua and me.

"What do I need with a stove?" she said. "I've got some Ensure they sent me from the church. I'll get plenty of calories." She grinned. I knew it irked her that the church put her in the category of *elderly*.

"Warm up the damn casseroles," I ordered. That's what we had taken to calling them because they would never go away. Seemed like they bred in the deep freeze. We'd sorted them into colonies.

"Good Lord, I can't eat another lasagna." She laughed. "I'll be fine. Don't worry. I'll come visit soon." Alice was staying put, though I asked her to come with us. She needed to be in her own house, she said. She insisted on it. She wouldn't even step outside the threshold. It was too cold outside. "Feels like it's gonna snow before it warms up for good," she said. "You could wait a day or two. It's supposed to clear up by Monday."

"We'll make it. It's not that far." I had been on leave from work for two months now. My time was running out. I needed to make the break or forget about the life we had in Lexington. Joshua could start fresh in the new semester. He grabbed Alice up in a hug so tight, he almost knocked her over.

"Go easy now, Baby. It's not like you're leaving me forever," she kissed him on the cheek and he released his hold on her. She stayed at the door, watching us drive away. Joshua twisted around in his seat until we rounded the corner to Main Street and he could no longer see her.

On the way to Lexington, toward Neko, the snow began to fall. Flurries thickened to a storm, much heavier than I'd anticipated. The white reflected in my windshield blinded me. My headlights shone back at me like lasers. We pulled over at a gas station diner for burnt coffee and hamburgers wrapped in greasy paper. Johnny Cash sang "Ring of Fire" on the cashier's AM radio. I didn't say anything when Joshua ate two bites of his burger, then began playing with his French fries as if they were soldiers battling each other, lots of ketchup for blood. The glass of the restaurant windows steamed with a white film of heat and breath. We peered through it and waited for things to get better. They didn't. The snow was coming thicker and faster. It wouldn't pass. We were still two hours from Lexington; it was closer to turn around.

"Can I get y'all anything else?" the waitress said, leaving the check.

"No, thanks. We're fine."

"Well, whenever you're ready. Don't look like any of us is going anywhere in a hurry in all this."

"I grew up driving these roads," I said, holding my coffee cup with both hands, for the warmth.

"Me too, but anybody'll slide on ice," she said. "Slick as bat shit out there. Y'all be careful."

I sipped my coffee and watched the snow, trying to tell when it would stop. "Mama, let's go back," Joshua said. "I'm scared." He concentrated on sipping his soda and pushing his fries around his plate. All the soldiers had been in some bloody massacre. I had no other plan to get us home safely. I couldn't subject Joshua to any more fear, so once the storm eased a bit, I headed back slowly to Alice's and the place that claimed us. The snow didn't make as much difference in this direction. I could feel my way home blindfolded. I'd have to work up my resolve to leave again. Alice was at the door in her pink bathrobe when we got there, unlocking the door to let us in, like she knew we wouldn't really leave her or the hills that had swallowed Collis. She didn't say a word, and neither did we. She just opened the door and let us make our way to bed, then turned out the lights.

The first dream I had of Collis came two weeks later. Joshua was back in school in Iona, and after the first week, he slipped right back into his old friendships, his old routine, even the same small desk. I officially quit my job, let the house in Lexington go, had our stuff moved into storage. I wasn't working yet, just thinking about it. I had worried about money, but Alice wouldn't let me pay for anything, said her teacher's retirement was plenty. The fog over my brain wouldn't lift. It was a Saturday that I woke up shaken. At first, I didn't know why, but Collis had been in my dreams, sitting on the kitchen counter, soaking his feet in a sink full of water. I reached for him and he came apart. His flesh dissolved into the water. I lay awake in my bed for the rest of the night and held Joshua tight. In sleep, he still had the smooth, innocent face of a little boy.

I was the first one up in the morning. The day was bright, sun reflecting off a few inches of snow on the ground. I drew the shades in the kitchen and made some coffee. The dream of Collis wouldn't disappear. Maybe if I moved my body, it would shake my brain free. I bundled up in my red scarf and down jacket and headed out through town, up the trail that began at the playground the city finally built. There were a few footprints in the snow, but not many. Some were made by dogs, or other four-legged creatures. I wouldn't have to talk to anyone on my way to the peak of the mountain. With the leaves gone, I could see the curve of the land, covered by a thin layer of crystal tree branches. Through this veil, as I climbed, the town of Jensen came into view. I turned away from it. The rock face of the mountain stared back at me, shelf rocks dripping with icicles. In them, I could see visions. I imagined that Collis had become a part of the rock. Stone to stone and dust to dust. To this you shall return. That was the only truth I was sure of.

"Ava?" the voice came from behind me, a man's voice. At first, I thought it was Collis, that I was imagining it, but it was real.

"Ava, it's me, Jason." I turned to face him. Jason Hayes had grown up with us. His voice was nothing like Collis's, actually. It was deeper, but softer too. I always thought he should be a singer, but he wasn't. Still, he could have been a radio announcer, not the happy-voiced kind, but the kind that seems solid and assured, able to tell even the bad news. Now, he wrote for the *Mountain Lion*, which had a history of telling the truth. That had gotten them burned out twice, and reporters run off the road more times than they could count. People like Jason usually did a year or two in Iona then moved up to the *Courier Journal* or the *Herald Leader*. One or two even made it to the *New York Times*.

Jason wrote mostly about the environment. I liked that he often wrote on the good parts of Iona that were still left, like Hard Rock Falls and the Mountain Laurel Festival, with floats full of beautiful teenage queens who were set on going to college. He balanced that with the depressing articles on disappearing mountaintops and destroyed aquifers. Like me, he was old enough to remember when Iona looked almost as pristine as the mountains in North Carolina. Every now and then, he'd write about going fishing in some old creek he'd haunted as a child. About how that had made him who he is. Those stories were my favorites.

"Hi," I said. "I didn't think anyone would be up here, with the way the weather has been."

"It's beautiful, my favorite place in the world to be right after a snow. If it's thick enough, you can't even see the strip jobs."

"I like that too," I said. I couldn't think of much else to say. My dream-spell was broken, and now I was only hiking.

"I don't mean to bother you, Ava. Just wanted to say I'm sorry for your loss. Really, I'm so sorry. Collis was a good man."

"Thanks," I said. I didn't mind condolences now as long as people didn't say Collis was in a better place, or that he was at peace. I didn't think he would ever find peace here. This was a place where the earth fought back. The dark and bloody ground. That's what my Uncle Gil used to scare me with when I was a kid. But I didn't tell Jason this.

"I was trying to see Alice's house from here," I said. "See, I think that's it over there. The yellow one." I pointed to my right, down the mountain. Jason came up beside me.

"I see it," he said. "Right there by the river. That one next to the railroad trestle, right?" I thought I could see somebody on the bridge, crossing the low icy water of the river, ant-like, walking slowly across the trestle. "Can you see who that is walking across the river?"

"Nobody can see that good, Ava," he patted my shoulder, as if he was worried about my mental state.

"I just thought it might be Joshua." Joshua wanted to cross the trestle and hike the hill on Sanders until he reached the White Oak Mine. It had been closed since before he was born, but he wanted to see inside. I didn't want him anywhere near any mine, ever.

"Well, even if he fell off the bridge, he'd only drop a few feet. The river isn't much more than a trickle," Jason said.

"You don't have kids, do you?"

"No, I guess I don't."

"Sorry," I said.

"I'm hiking to the Pinewood Trail," he said. "It's beautiful in the snow. Where you headed?"

"Just getting out for air, not really headed anywhere. I better get back."

"Well, let me know if you need anything."

"Thanks," I said, watching him walk away, toward Pinewood, leaving new prints in the snow behind. I followed my own footprints back down the mountain.

The trees began to drip as the sun rose higher. I wished the town could always feel as magical as this. The snow covered the scars where the mountains had been stripped and gored. The trash along the creeks and the river had disappeared and the water flowed clearer, a deep brownish green. The cold air sliced my lungs as I worked my way down the mountain. In my head, I heard Collis singing and playing guitar: "I traced her little footprints in the snow / I found her little footprints in the snow. // I bless that happy day when Nellie lost her way / For I found her when the snow was on the ground."

"Where'd you go? Why didn't you take me?" Joshua asked when I came through the side door into the kitchen. His mouth was half stuffed with cereal, and he was pouring another bowl so high, stray flakes washed over the side and landed on the table. He was still in his pajamas.

"You weren't up yet. I'll take you next time. Plus, it's cold. You wouldn't have liked that."

"You never take me!" He crammed another huge spoonful of cereal into his mouth and chewed loudly.

"We'll go. I promise. Soon as it warms up." He focused on his cereal, ignoring me.

Lexington seemed oceans and mountain ranges away. It might not have ever existed. It had pushed us away in the snowstorm. I had to stay here. I needed Alice to mother us both. She looked older now. We both did. New lines spanned my forehead. Her shoulders might never come up again. It was as if she had shrunk a few inches, when she was already petite, pushed down by the weight of everything. Even Joshua seemed older than his almost nine years. His eyes looked dull and tired. I pushed him to go outside to play before his childhood evaporated.

"Y'all need to get busy," Alice said. "Get out of the house. Go to the mall and don't come back until after lunch."

"I've got plenty to do around here," I said. Sometimes I resented that she thought she knew more about survival than anyone. We'd all survived.

"Go!" She wouldn't take no for an answer. Alice was usually right about what would dig us out of our own caves. She had come back from spots like this so many times. She'd reinvented herself as a mother, a teacher, and now, as our guide. I was working on getting through each day. Trying to resist the temptations around me that would make it all go away.

When the mail came, I got a life insurance check from Collis's old job, but I couldn't look at it. I handed the unopened envelope to Sherry Johnson at the bank. We were cheerleaders together in junior high. She used to be able to do a backflip. Sherry opened the envelope carefully, looked at the check, flipped it over and handed it to me.

"I'm sorry, Ava. You have to endorse it."

I signed it and slid it back to her. It was documentation, death money. Sherry deposited it in a savings account for Joshua. "Take care, Ava. You're doing the right thing with this money. That's what it's for."

I needed a place to go, other people with problems to focus on, problems I might actually be able to help fix. I had to get back to work somehow. Staying in the house all day made me anxious. I knew I'd take it all out on Alice eventually if I didn't make myself busy. I called Gabe, my old boss.

You didn't need the sign on the outside of the building to know where Stone Healthcare Resources was. You could just look for the line of people smoking out on the sidewalk, their smoke billowing into the cold air. I breathed in the scent. Addiction transfer, it was called. If someone was lucky enough to kick alcohol, oxy, even meth, they found something to at least patch the void. We didn't even mention smoking cessation programs to them at first. They lived on cigarettes and caffeine. They both sounded good to me right then.

Gabe met me at the door. He must've seen me coming down Main Street. His office faced the street and he kept his blinds open. He liked to keep an eye on things, inside and out. He hugged me before he spoke. "How you holding up?"

"I'm here," I said. "I guess that means I'm flat out crazy."

"Well then, nothing's changed." He hugged me tighter, then let me go. Gabe was about fifteen years older than me, more of an uncle than a father. He had been a football star long ago, recruited to play college ball at Union College, but now he was just broad-chested and bearish. He still had a head full of wild gray hair and a beard that covered his double chin.

"I want to come back," I said.

Gabe looked at me for a minute. "Sit down, Ava." I took a seat on the chair across from his desk. It was meant for clients, so it wasn't very comfortable. Hard plastic chairs kept them from camping out in the bad weather, Gabe said.

"I don't think it's good for you all to stay around here. You need to move on, Ava. This job ain't gonna cheer you up, you know." I smiled. Gabe had a photo on the wall of him and his daughter, Lizzie, holding up a huge bass they had caught at Cherokee Lake in the summer.

"You might," I said. "I can't leave here yet. And I know this place. Hell, I even know most of the clients standing out there on the sidewalk this morning. There's a comfort in that. I mean, not the addiction part, just knowing people."

"Don't they like oxy up in Lexington? They'd probably be able to pay you a living wage, too. Aren't there a couple of meth-heads you could adopt up there? Shake-and-bakers?"

"Sure, just none I've known since kindergarten. None I feel like I could actually save. I need to save somebody, Gabe."

"Tall order," Gabe said. "Take my advice: save yourself."

"Gabe." He looked at me, shook his head. He knew I wouldn't leave him alone until he gave me my job back.

"Okay. You can come back part-time. No more than twenty hours per week. You need to plan for your next move. Plus, that's all I've got funding for."

"It doesn't matter. Get me a desk. I'll be here Monday."

He shook his head, as if there was nothing he could do to get me to act right, but I knew he was as happy as I was.

"Gabe, thanks," I hugged him.

"Don't thank me yet," he said. He walked me out through the cubicles. No one had left. I knew every single face I passed, worker or client. Gabe led Ben Ayres back to his office for an appointment.

"What up, Ava?" Ben shouted toward me as I left. I looked back to see his meth-eaten grin, his caved in face. He had been on the basketball team my freshman year and led the team to the state tournament. Now, he looked gaunt as an old man.

"Hey, Ben," I said. "Same old, same old."

Joshua fell back into his old world. I fell into mine, mostly. Life wanted a rhythm and we gave it one. The same thing I worried about, falling back into a tired pattern, comforted me now. A few weeks after I started back to work, I stopped by the elementary school, the same low brick, flat-roofed building I went to as a kid, to surprise Joshua and pick him up early. I figured we'd go for ice cream or take a hike up the mountain.

He was gluing different-colored construction paper countries onto a map of the world when I came into his class. Mrs. Johnson gave me a smile and called Joshua's name. All twenty-two children looked up at me but didn't say anything. Mrs. Johnson ran a tight ship.

"Ten more minutes," she said. "See how much of the world you can put in the right place." Tall order, I thought. The kids went back to their work. Joshua gathered his small red backpack and metal lunchbox and left the room quietly. Mrs. Johnson waved to us and whispered, "See you tomorrow!"

Joshua didn't speak to me until I got close enough to unlock the doors of the car. "Why did you come?" he asked, on the verge of tears.

"I wanted to do something special, Baby—just you and me." Joshua slunk down in his seat, looked into the rearview mirror.

"I am not a baby! And I don't want to be special. I want to be normal."

I pulled away from the school. "Well, how about some mint chocolate chip anyway? Normal people like that, I hear."

"I guess so," he said. We drove on to the Dairy Cheer, pulled through the drive-through, and sat in the parking lot to eat our cones, just like we used to. Almost.

Compared to the broken people I tried to piece together and quilt into functional human beings at work, I was doing fine. I had lost one man. I had left him too, if I cared to remember. It was worse knowing that we might have never worked it out, and we would have drifted apart to new lives if he had lived. Now, I could only love him and be his widow—and the confusion of having hated him in the end burned. We had lost him, our past, and our imagined future, but so many had lost entire families here. I couldn't wallow in my own troubles. I knew the worst of drug orphans' lives around here, the mamas pimping their pre-teen children for another hit. They needed my help.

The caseload was bigger than I could ever handle. I knew that. Gabe did too. Seemed like the more people we helped, the more came in. When I started this job a few years ago, I felt submerged by it all. I really didn't know how we'd get the drugs out of Iona, unless only the sober survived. Nobody else seemed to know either. If the money dried up from the drug business, maybe it would move on like a bad storm, but there would still be a lot of destruction to clean up. It had settled, low and foreboding, in the mountains.

In the last few years, I went to more funerals of people under forty than I could count, even before Collis. Children were parceled out to nearby kin or foster homes when their mamas and daddies got arrested, grew too strung out to do anything for them, or died in some communal drug shack at the head of a holler. The first home visit where I found a toddler crawling through garbage on the floor, stereo blasting—meth-head Mama passed out cold, face down on the carpet—I held that little girl tight. She couldn't stop crying, as if she didn't know that she was safe once she was in my arms.

14

Flight

I stopped by the Save A Lot after work. It gave me an excuse to stay out a little later, to avoid getting lost in the paperwork that bordered my desk, and to delay going home. Grocery shopping was something I could do for Alice. She didn't like to drive after dusk. It was a Wednesday evening, so no one was there but the cashiers and maybe a few people who had run out of milk for the next morning. Most people were at church suppers—"putting the holy in the whole week," as the sign in front of First Baptist said. The Save A Lot had been updated since I left town the first time. They started working on it last spring, tore it down to the foundation before bringing it back. None of the other buildings in the shopping center had changed, so it stood out like an overdressed girl at a party—hat, gloves, and all. I was almost embarrassed for it.

The ceilings were vaulted now, with a green metal roof. The doors slid open when you stepped on the rubber mat. They didn't stick anymore or need to be propped open when they stopped working altogether. The problem was that I couldn't find anything now. Even the milk wasn't where it was supposed to be. The only thing I recognized in the whole store was the cashier in aisle three, Sheila Hobbs, a girl who was two years behind me in school. She married a boy from the next county over but brought him back to Iona because her Daddy built them a house. She had worked in the various versions of Save A Lot since high school. Her little girl, Sasha, was in Joshua's class.

"Hey, Ava," she said, looking unsure whether she should smile at me. I knew this look by now. It meant, *God, I hope nothing that bad ever happens to me.*

"Hey." I waved and walked toward the vegetable aisle, trying to concentrate on the Muzak. A heavy metal song I recognized from high school had been softened so it was palatable enough for the old women who wandered aimlessly through the aisles. I hated this song, damn it, but it was making me tear up. I looked up at the light and blinked to try to keep it together. The store light was so bright it was almost blue. I looked away from it, and in the peak of the roof, I saw a nest. A small brown bird flew into it. It stopped for a minute to rest, then swooped down toward the frozen foods. Maybe it was a sparrow? I stood still, clenching the plastic handle of my cart. A bird in the house was an omen of death. What could a bird in the store mean? That's the kind of thing Micah would know, from her grandma. I tried to continue shopping but kept watching the bird instead. Two or three other birds swooped and dived and landed on the high exposed beams of the roof. Maybe they flew in when the electronic doors opened. It was clear that this was their home now. They had everything but fresh air and freedom. I kept watching them, but it was hard to move forward and look up at the same time. I almost ran into another cart as I rounded the corner to the bread aisle.

"Whoa!" Jason said. "Careful driving that thing."

"Oh, sorry!" I flushed. "I was looking at the birds." I pointed up and Jason followed my finger to the rafters.

"That doesn't seem sanitary," he said.

"I didn't think about that. I was just wondering if they were a bad omen. You know, birds in the house?"

"You're not superstitious, are you?"

I looked down at my cart, chips, Cheez-Its, chocolate, and peanut butter. Not only was I crazy, I was feeding my kid crap.

"No," I lied. "But haven't you heard that all your life?"

"Oh, my mother would never shop here if she saw those birds, but I don't worry about stuff like that. Those are old wives' tales." Jason's cart was full of good foods: pears, spinach, skinless chicken breasts.

He might call my fears old wives' tales, but we were still from Iona and there was plenty unseen in the world. "There's more to life than facts," I said. "Like, no matter how far they wander, sparrows always return home. So, maybe this is their home, and somebody built over it."

"Ok, sure, I guess there's plenty that can't be explained. Isn't it a little odd they don't shoo the birds out of here? Do they clean up after them?"

"You'd think they'd try," I said. "I wonder what the birds eat when they have their pick of the whole store? What do they make their nests out of?"

"Old boxes? Trash people drop, maybe? I guess they hit the fruit and vegetable aisle pretty hard. Or maybe the bakery."

"I wish they'd shop for me. I'm too tired to think."

"I'll shop with you," Jason said. "I just came in for a few things." He reached for a loaf of wheat bread and put it in his cart next to a carton of low-fat chocolate ice cream. He saw me looking at it. "Don't worry, I'll leave you alone before it melts."

We pushed ahead through the pasta aisle, discussing the merits of penne vs. spaghetti, as the birds circled overhead, waiting for us to let something fall. It felt good to have a guide through the store, even though we talked about nothing, or maybe because we talked about nothing. Maybe the birds weren't a bad omen after all.

Jason left me at the checkout, and I drove home slowly through town. I wondered what kept him here when he could have made it at a big paper in Lexington or Louisville, or even New York. I wanted to stretch the minutes until I had to go back home to Alice's. I knew how the night would go. I'd unpack the groceries and then get into bed, pretending to read a book. I might eat some Cheez-Its, wash them down with a glass of wine. Alice would cook Joshua something. "You okay in there?" she'd ask, talking through the closed door of my room. I knew she'd want me to sit with her on the porch. I was stronger now, and I didn't need her to mother me anymore, but I didn't know how to tell her. Maybe she could volunteer somewhere, so I didn't have to be her project.

"I'm fine," I'd say. "I'll eat later." I'd drift off with the scent of her cigarettes seeping through the house from where she smoked on the front porch.

I drove on. The ridgelines were steeped in orange dusk fading to gray. Lights came on in the houses dotting the hillside, early stars in the night sky. Smoke rose from chimneys, and nothing looked different than it ever had in my whole life, mountains, houses, and trees for as far as I could see. I passed Ward's Branch, the neighborhood where people who wanted to pretend they didn't live in the mountains lived. It could have been picked up and plopped down in suburban Lexington, or Knoxville, and you would never know the difference. Then, I curved around toward the high school. The lights were on at the football field. I could see joggers and walkers, thick and bundled up against the cold, circling the track. Iona was a comfort to me, in spite of everything. It was mine.

As I neared the turn toward Alice's and crossed the bridge, I saw a kid in a green jacket crossing the railroad trestle over the river. I knew that trestle well. It was only about six feet above the river, but most of the timbers were missing or rotten. The railroad gave up on Iona years ago. Now the coal was driven away in overloaded trucks spraying tiny black rocks on everything behind them as they powered up the narrow, curving hills.

I knew that green down jacket, unzipped in the cold. Joshua wasn't supposed to be down at the river in the evening. He acted like all the rules had changed lately, and he was somehow grown. He even tried to tell me to shut up, which would have grounded him for life a couple of months ago. Now, it just sent us both to our rooms yelling, with Alice trying to keep us calm.

Look up, damn it! I thought. The knit hat I sent him to school with was nowhere in sight. I pulled my car to the side of the road, cut the engine, and watched him. He was looking down at the trestle and the water below it. *Please, look up.* I couldn't yell at him. He might fall. The most that could happen if he fell was that he might break an arm, but I was terrified watching him. I felt Joshua's balance shift as he looked up and leapt from the last timber to the gravel road. No cars pulled up behind me. This was Iona, after all. But when I started my engine, Joshua turned and looked up toward my car, then ran up the hill toward Alice's.

I took my time pulling into the driveway and sat in the car for a few minutes, so Joshua could get settled in and pretend like we hadn't seen each other, as if he had been home the whole time. From the moment I'd known he existed, I'd been trying to protect him. No one tells you that job is near impossible, that you can control food, shelter, affection even, but the world or fate or something else can render all of that useless. At some point, you had to trust that something or someone unseen would provide protection. "Okay, Collis," I said aloud. "Help me."

I didn't mention anything to Joshua or Alice when I went inside the house. I unpacked the groceries. Alice was smoking a Pall Mall on the porch, sucking the life out of it. Joshua sat at the kitchen table, focused on his homework, not looking up, daring me to say something about the railroad trestle.

"What do you want for dinner?" I asked. "I just stopped at the store."

"Nothing," he said. "I'm not hungry." His breath was still unsettled from his sprint home. He smoothed his math paper and started figuring. Like me, he whispered to himself when he thought out loud. "I hate word problems," he said. "Who cares which train gets to Wichita first? Where is Wichita anyway?"

"I'll make something," I put a pot of water on to boil and dumped a jar of tomato sauce into another. "It's in Kansas. Out in the Great Plains." Maybe the smell would make us hungry. The sky was darkening fast. Through the kitchen window, I watched the birds dart across the sky in pairs and fly to the safety of their nests.

15

Perennial Stream

Micah and I kept our standing weekly lunch date. This Friday, she was hounding me. I'd given her every excuse I could think of not to go out for anything but work, but she kept on, as soon as we'd put in our orders. "You need to get away. It's been months since you've been out of the house. You didn't even come to my Christmas party!" she said. I didn't tell her that Christmas blew past us, that Alice and I spent a marathon day shopping for Joshua, trying to find the one thing that would make him forget—if only for an hour or two.

"Well, what would you want to do?" I took the rubber band off my wrist and pulled my long hair back into a ponytail. Micah made me aware of how I looked by the way she studied me, trying to make sure I wasn't about to break into pieces. She had always looked freshly scrubbed, the kind of woman who looked better without makeup, who would never seem old because she radiated her own light.

"My friend Gina has a cabin," she said. "Up on the mountain. And before you say no, you know Alice will watch Joshua and Gabe will let you off work."

"Ok," I knew Micah would wear me down. She was stronger than me and way more persistent. She was about to take a bite of her burger, but she put it back on the plate.

"Really? That's all it took? I had a whole other sales pitch prepared."

"Well, I could say no if you want to keep working on me. Does that sales pitch include a trip to Hawaii?"

"No, you already said yes. Pack a bag, we're going this weekend."

"Yes, ma'am," I said, picking at my salad. She finished her burger and began telling me everything she already planned for us.

The cabin was set back from the road, down a quarter mile winding gravel driveway in a patch of pine trees, so you had to be looking to find it. It was built to blend into the land, to tie a person to the mountain for a few days at a time. Micah's friend Gina had made it with her own hands with leftover building materials, over maybe ten years. She took her time, so it all fit together perfectly. Every piece was in the right place.

The cabin was a hideaway, with one small, dark bedroom and a stone fireplace in the middle of the wide-open living room. Micah lit a fire in the fireplace and poured us some wine. She dragged me out onto the deck, which overlooked the good side of the mountain. No mountaintops had been removed; nothing had been cut away. There wasn't a coal seam on this side, so it was deemed worthless enough to build on. The other side of the mountain, toward Harlan, was scarred and cut open. There had been a rich coal seam there, but it was mined out now. The coal company had abandoned its mess, tried to cover it with pitiful brown sod. This side was beautiful still. I could imagine it untouched and ancient. Trees covered the gentle slopes of the mountains, which rolled on for miles in a tide. They were covered in shimmery frost. Night was falling fast.

"I'm freezing my ass off," I said.

Micah went inside and got a few blankets. She threw one at me as she came outside, and I wrapped up in it. "To the future," she said, raising her glass. I couldn't say that, but I clinked my glass with hers anyway, just so I could drink the wine.

"This is what you need—relaxation!" She wrapped up in her own blanket.

"To relaxation!" I downed the glass. I was glad someone knew what I needed, what would bring me back into the living world.

Way down below the cabin, I could see the sparkle of the Kentucky River in the moonlight. The river never looked this beautiful up close, where it was the color of chocolate milk. Big tree limbs fell into it during storms and caught all the trash floating by: milk jugs, diapers, Diet Coke cans. No one ate the fish out of the river unless they were really poor and had to—but plenty had to. The mercury levels were high from mine runoff. Other oils and toxins were mixed into the milk, too. You can't dump the land and water back together every time you tear it apart. Sometimes, it just won't hold. But I still loved that river, the way it wound through town and ran off toward the hills. The way it belonged to us.

The high school always held the senior picnic on the riverbank. I sat next to Collis for ours, his hand on my knee, our feet dangling in the muddy water. He played me plenty of songs there, too, on picnic dates—just the quiet strum of his guitar with me humming along. The Old Regulars still got baptized in the muddy water in their white robes over swimsuits. They sprang straight up after the preacher dunked them back, robes dingy, faces radiant. The modern Baptists used the indoor swimming pool at the YMCA in the next county. They worried about pollutants that God seemed to have no control over.

"Isn't this the most beautiful place in the world?" Micah spread her arms wide across the deck railing, as if she was a game show host showing me all the prizes could be mine.
"The world?" I leaned back in my Adirondack chair. "I wouldn't know. I haven't seen much of it." We were shivering in our jeans and T-shirts, which I suppose was a sign that I really was alive. Knowing Micah, this was her point in sitting outside. She wouldn't accept anything that couldn't be felt. I wrapped my blanket tighter, wishing I'd worn my coat or at least a sweater out here.

"You know what I mean—in our world," Micah said. "It is the most beautiful place that we can actually call ours. Not like Hawaii or Italy. I bet people in those places never think about what we've got. You have to live here to know it. Plus, there's nothing for you to worry about here." I looked straight at her.

"Nothing to worry about in Iona?" I asked. "We must be talking about different places."

"Not as long as I'm here," she said. "You watch. It'll get better. I'm working on it."

She had given me the push to leave when I needed to, but now she was trying to make sure I stayed. We talked long into the night, drinking and eating sandwiches Micah had brought from the Stop Inn Café in town. I knew if anyone could make things right in Iona, it was Micah. She was always trying to get me to come to some meeting, to sign some petition, meet good people. I didn't think it was really possible to fight companies whose pockets were filled deep with money when you had nothing but hope and lint in yours. If they could actually move mountains out of the way, how hard would it be to move a person like Micah or me? I figured I had a better shot saving the people than the land. All most people wanted was a job, a place to call their own. I wondered if Collis would have made it if he'd had that, a steady mining job with benefits and a future, not just a few weeks mining here and there, mixed in with questionable errands for Johnny. I wondered what I didn't know about how we got by, and what he had had to do to make it happen. I wondered how I had been so blind.

"We're having a meeting next week," Micah said. "Against mountaintop removal. You need to come." I shook my head. "Wait, let me try it this way," she said. "Please come, my best friend in the whole world."

"Maybe," I said.

"Maybe means no. You never say yes, Ava. Come on, just this one time! Please. It'll get you out of the house. Say yes." Micah had sat in front of bulldozers to protect the land; she'd marched into the governor's office with a couple of retired miners, a handful of Vista volunteers, and half the Iona United Methodist Church behind her. Once, she filled a bucket full of sludge from Tolliver Creek, which was supposed to have been reclaimed by the mine company, and poured the whole thing across a corporate secretary's desk when she wouldn't let Micah into the board meeting. Of course, Micah had been arrested again. She took pride in her arrests. Her picture made the front page of the paper more than once.

Sometimes, I worried she would go too far, push some fat cat over the edge with her coal company protests, host a sit-in in somebody's secret pot patch up on the mountain. She wouldn't be the first to be hushed up and hurt. We were right next to "Bloody Harlan" after all. In the thirties, my granddaddy Andrew had been shot by what he called company goons, men sent in from Philadelphia and New York to keep the miners in check. People here weren't so easy to quiet though, even now. Micah had a lot to say.

"Okay, okay," I said. "Will you hush up about it if I go?"

"Maybe."

"Maybe means no," I said and swatted at Micah with my blanket.

When we started drifting off and the morning birds began chirping, I nudged Micah and made her go to bed. I slept a little while on the couch, next to the smoldering fire. At nine, I checked on her. She wasn't even close to waking up. She was sleeping untroubled as a child. Her arms and legs were sprawled across the whole double bed. Collis and I called this pose "the surrender" when Joshua was a baby. Even Joshua didn't sleep like that anymore. He curled into himself, wrapped into his own limbs for comfort. I clutched a pillow all night.

I made a pot of coffee and took a cup out to the deck. It was even colder than the night before, despite the sun and clear blue sky. At home, Joshua would be up, watching cartoons. Alice would be cleaning or reading and smoking on the porch. I missed our routine. It was what held our days tenuously together. I heard Micah get up and bang pans around in the kitchen. She slid the glass door open and beckoned me in. "Breakfast!" she said, waving her arm toward the table. She had made scrambled eggs and toast. "Happy New Year!"

It was a few weeks past new years', but maybe it was the start of a new year for me. "Sure," I said, raising my coffee cup. "Happy New Year."

After breakfast, Micah was restless. "Come on," she said. "Let's go for a hike." I couldn't say no to any of her adventures, so got on my boots and coat, and as usual, followed Micah up the mountain.

"Where are you taking me now?"

"Somewhere you'll love. Somewhere I bet you haven't had the guts to go in a long, long time."

"Got the guts to go? I've been everywhere in this county. I'm not afraid of this place. At least not the mountains," I said. "You act like I've never been anywhere."

I followed her ponytail swishing ahead of me, just like high school.

"Pick up the pace, Ava!" she said. It was true, she was the one in better shape now. She was headed toward the falls. I thought I wanted to see the water rushing too. We hiked a single-track trail through towering pines and thick laurel, stepped carefully over slippery patches of snow, and came to a waterfall, half-frozen, half-running.

"Hard Rock Falls," Micah said. "We're going behind the falls, and we're gonna stick our heads in to start the year. That'll wake you up!"

I had been there so many times with Collis. I had even stood naked in the cool waterfall a time or two, the hot sun shining on my back. I'd watched the water stream over him. But that was so long ago it didn't seem like it had really happened. We went a time or two with Joshua in the spring, but eventually, the falls became Collis's alone. This is where he went on his own, to get away from Joshua and me.

"I can't," I said.

"Can't what?" Micah said. She wasn't used to the word *can't*. She never had to think about anyone but herself.

"I can't go closer to the falls. That was Collis's place. I can't go there now."

Micah looked up at me. I was shaking a little, trying not to fall apart.

"Okay," Micah said, "It's okay." She walked toward me, put her arm around me to guide me back.

I felt older now, frailer, more like eighty-three than thirty-three. I examined the wrinkles radiating around my mouth when I looked in the mirror, the ones that reminded me of my Grandmother Cox. Her face ended up carved deep with lines, around her mouth where she'd puckered to savor the deep inhale of her filterless cigarettes, around her eyes from squinting through her thick cat-eyed glasses, and the deep furrowed rows across her forehead, each one a different worry.

"Let's go the other direction," Micah said. "We can hike the Dogwood Trail. It's prettier anyway." I followed her, again, down a never-ending trail of rocks and roots, away from home. My heart was pounding hard, traveling up toward my throat. We didn't speak for a mile or so, and I kept going. "There's supposed to be some Native American pictographs up here," she said.

"Who told you that?" I was grateful for something else to think about.

"It was in the paper. Some hunters found paintings of a couple of deer and a man spearing one. They say they're a thousand or so years old. Painted by different people, some kind of special meeting place."

"In Iona?" I asked. "Wouldn't that have been blown up by now or dug away?" The mountains were full of stories, but most people didn't listen. They were trying to figure out how to make the land pay.

"Scout's honor. It was in the *Mountain Lion*."

"You know where they are?"

"No. I have an idea, though. Right around here. I've heard rumors there's already some graffiti been sprayed near them, stupid-ass teenagers."

"Probably 'Junior was here,' something like that." I said.

"I guess people still want to make a mark. I bet they're near a mine site too. Maybe a hard-to-get-to spot they've only just found a way to dig the coal out of. If they get a place on some historical register though, nobody could mine near it. Wouldn't it be something if the spirits actually did save this mountain?"

"What if it's some kind of ceremonial ground?" These were the oldest mountains in the world.

"It's all a burial ground, Ava. The whole damn place is full of ghosts."

"You don't have to tell me that," I said. My ghosts stayed close.

Micah moved faster down the winding, rooty trail. She pushed past spindly bare hickory limbs and drooping pine branches. She crossed little streams in giant steps. I was having a hard time keeping up with her. The idea of finding the pictographs had lit a fire in her. I didn't need to find anything like that to know this place was sacred and haunted. I had known that all my life. Collis had known that too. He always came up here to figure things out. Said he felt protected here. I wondered what else he'd done up here and who he had protected.

"Look here!" Micah pointed to a rock face that was smudged with what looked like the smoke from a fire. "Shit. Just a leftover campfire." She kicked at the dried-out coals and an empty Beanie Weenie can. "Damn hunters need to clean up their trash."

"You think it's a hoax?" I asked her. "Maybe somebody's just calling it sacred to stop the mining."

"They sent out archaeologists. They're supposed to be little paintings of deer in red paint that somehow hasn't faded."

"Hard to survive," I said.

"Bet they still hold secrets."

"Well, if the companies have anything to say about it, they'll blast anyway, ancient paintings or no."

"If it was a ceremonial site, that's a lot of bad energy. I guess those rocks seemed permanent to people thousands of years ago," she said. "Only money could find a way to level the mountain."

We hiked on, and I looked more closely at the rocks than I ever had before. It was easier to see them with the leaves off the trees. The rock faces were gray, brown, lichen covered, but we never found the red pictographs. I knew Micah would keep looking every chance she could. She needed to know she had armies of spirits behind her. I was with her, even though I had a hard time saying it. Maybe it wasn't too late to save something sacred here. Micah was the one to do it, if anyone could. Maybe these mountains were worth fighting for, and this wave of destruction would pass, like all the rest, leaving our stories intact.

16

Percolation

At school, Joshua ate lunch with the same friend every day, Robbie Jenner. In kindergarten, in tough tussles on the playground, Joshua talked for Robbie who was shy, and Robbie had backed tiny Joshua's words up with his size, which was more like that of a second grader. The boys still stuck together. I knew this from Joshua and from Robbie's mother, Tonya. When I asked Joshua how school was, he only said, "Fine." When I asked him what they did in class, the answer was always "nothing." His face said different lately. He rarely met my eyes.

Tonya called me, "They've been talking about Joshua's daddy."

"Who has?" I picked up a rag to wipe the kitchen counter.

"Some of the boys—the Tack boy mostly, and the Finley twins. Robbie says they pretend to shoot themselves in the head, point their finger at their temple, that kind of thing. I'm sorry to tell you, but I thought you'd like to know. Robbie told them to stop, but they threatened to beat him up. I think it'll make it worse if I call their mamas. None of them are any count."

"Does the teacher know?"

"Well, yeah. But you know she can't do a thing with them. If their mamas don't care, why should they? She didn't want to call and upset you. I told her I'd let you know."

Timmy Tack's mother had been busted a couple of times for possession. Oxy was her favorite, the click, then release, the floating of the body above it all, not only painless, but feeling good. Her boyfriend disappeared one night last winter and never was found. Nobody bothered to look for him anymore. They were afraid of where that trail might lead. When she went on a long binge, or got arrested, Timmy stayed with his grandmother on Owen's Branch. Nothing right happened there. His grandmother had done her own time. Detention wouldn't do that boy any good. Wouldn't faze the Finley twins either. Nobody would stop them; they'd only push them faster down a dark road. Nobody would try to teach these boys compassion when they didn't expect them to live past twenty. Some of the teachers were already afraid of them, as if nine-year-old boys were already clinging to evil.

This was just one way Iona had changed. There were Tack boys when I was growing up; there were wild kids who smoked pot on the bus on the way to elementary school and carried pocket knives that they intended to use in fights, but there was always some adult they would listen to, some teacher or coach or principal who could shame them or comfort them into acting right. Kids like Timmy Tack couldn't be shamed or comforted. They didn't know that adults were supposed to be in charge, not when they had to stay days by themselves, waiting for their mama to come back with some new man she called her boyfriend and a bag of cold burgers and fries. Child services had been called, but they had plenty to keep them busy, and at least Timmy's mom did come home sometimes. The Finley twins had no grown-ups to speak of, unless you counted their eighteen-year-old aunt. They were fighting their own way through the world. I'd be damned if I'd let them hurt Joshua, though.

Joshua came in the back door, dropped his backpack on the kitchen floor, and turned to run back out. "I'm going to Robbie's!" He yelled toward me in the kitchen.

"Don't you think you should ask me instead of telling me?" I yelled back with my hands on my hips, but it didn't seem to give me any more authority. Joshua knew I would cave in to whatever he wanted right now, especially if I didn't have to think about cooking. I had planned to talk to him about school over dinner, but now it seemed better to just let him move forward.

"Well, can I go over to Robbie's?" He looked happy almost. He looked like a regular kid right then.

"Tell me about school first. You can't just run in and out of here. What happened today?"

"Nothing."

"The whole day? Not one thing happened? Who did you play with at recess?"

"Robbie. Now, can I please go? He got a new ball hoop and we're gonna shoot free throws."

"Okay, be home by six," I said. "And don't forget your coat!" It was back to winter, even though the weather was fighting with itself, trying to keep spring from coming too early.

Robbie lived two doors down in a two-story brick house. His dad, Tom, was obsessed with the yard. The grass looked like a golf course, even in winter. Every blade was exactly the same height, unlike Alice's yard, which was brown and ragged, more weeds than grass. A few wild onions had sprung up since we'd had some warm days. Our azalea held on. Its tiny tight buds knew better than to open yet; it knew the few spring-like days now and then were a cruel trick. Joshua checked on it every day, hoping for a bloom.

Alice sat on the couch and grabbed the remote, "well, we might as well see if there's anything good on the TV."

I walked to the kitchen, "Might as well."

Alice was a big fan of reality shows. "Here's that one where they drop them in the jungle or the desert and see who makes it out. They ought to try dropping them in these hills sometime. Then we'd see who really knows how to get by." She narrated the whole show, so it didn't really matter if I was in the room. "I put some chicken on the counter to thaw," she called over the low rumble of the show. If the world blew up in a mushroom cloud, Alice would make sure we still had something to eat.

"I see it." It looked almost gray with yellow globs of fat in the package. A thin white layer of frost lay on top of the plastic. It was nothing I could stomach. I ignored the chicken and Alice, and went back to my room, which is what Collis's room had become. I started going through his things whenever I had a few minutes to myself, and I came upon a shoebox full of old letters and pictures and report cards. I was pictured in some of the photos, though I looked nothing like that now. Joshua was in a few photos, but I had most of his baby pictures packed away. I moved everything from the Lexington house into a storage unit on the highway. It was one of many things I couldn't deal with yet. I didn't have to. It was all climate controlled. I guess Collis had thought enough ahead to make this box. He probably knew I'd find it and hoped I'd give it to Joshua, but I hadn't yet. It held so many images of Collis happy and smiling, so alive.

When Joshua called later and asked to spend the night with Robbie, I said yes. I spent the whole evening in Collis's top bunk trying to fix his image in my head because sometimes it slipped. Not the image I saw in all the old photos, but the living and breathing image of him, the way it felt to be next to him. Sometimes I panicked because I couldn't remember which arm he had a mole on, and which knee had the scar from the bike wreck when he was twelve. I'd run into the living room and ask Alice. Between the two of us, we would remember.

"You know the one about the boy scout camping trip where he almost got frostbite because he refused to take a coat?" she said.

"Oh, yes. He never did think it was cold enough for a real coat. What about that time in college when he danced on the table at Frisch's when UK won the tournament? I've got a picture of that." We laughed at how foolish he could be. It's the quirks you miss, the things you can't see in any other person. Alice and I needed each other to conjure him now, though I suspected she blamed me for his disappearance as much as I wanted to blame her.

I started keeping a notebook with physical facts about Collis. On the front of the green wire-bound notebook, I wrote "Daddy". I figured I'd give it to Joshua someday, along with the box of photos and papers. With all that and all the stories Alice and I told about Collis growing up, he'd be able to make up some memories. I'd keep out the bad ones. I also had a message on my phone, not a nice loving one, but still, his voice. "Ava, it's me," he said. "Answer your damn phone… Ok, I'll get back to you. Tell Joshua I love him." I kept it for the last part, so Joshua would always be able to hear his daddy say he loved him. He would know for sure he was never the cause of all this. Still, I hadn't played it for him yet. He had been so, well, normal lately. I didn't want to jinx that.

I woke up before daylight. Some birds were chirping, but it was still the blue border of night and morning. I got dressed without turning on the lamp. In the kitchen, I turned on the light on the vent above the stove. The coffee pot steamed and sputtered, but I didn't think it would wake Alice. She was taking sleeping pills Dr. Thomas had prescribed. She said she was running low, but Dr. Thomas told her he couldn't legally prescribe any more until next month. I worried she liked them a little too much and took them whenever she wanted to check out for a little while. Collis used to get her a few from his friends when she needed them. She'd offered me some, but I didn't want something to just knock me flat. If I needed to sleep, I usually popped half a Xanax, so I could float for a little while in frothy nothingness before I drifted off.

I slipped out the door, coffee mug in hand. I'd walk until the sun came up, then make breakfast and get Joshua early. Talking was the last thing I wanted, but my tenth-grade teacher, Mrs. Pinsky, was walking her lab, Max, around the corner, making a beeline straight for me.

"Oh, Ava! I've been thinking about you," she said. Max sat dutifully beside her and waited.

"Thanks. That's sweet of you, Mrs. Pinsky."

"How is your little boy doing? I just hate it for him." Max got distracted by a squirrel and stood up. Good dog.

"He's doing well. It's good to have Alice." I loved the dog for pulling on his leash. "Your dog looks like he's ready to go," I said. She started going on about her Max.

The few warm days we'd had showed in the mountains. The air was full of wet earth smell. There was a faint green tinge to some of the mountainside. The trees were still bare, but the ground underneath was coming to life. I could see it from Cumberland Avenue, looking past Mrs. Pinsky, up at the mountains. Still, the mountain behind the airstrip at the end of the wide avenue was nothing at all like I remembered. I hadn't really noticed it until now. I was finally looking at the world again. The hillside was the red-orange color of the clay dirt. It had been stripped of coal, emptied and left exposed, a huge chunk of the mountain carved out. Red mud trickled down the open wound. From here, I could see what looked like tiny dozers moving around. They must have been enormous up close.

"Mrs. Pinsky, when did that happen?" I asked, pointing to the mountain. "It wasn't torn up last summer."

"Oh, honey, I don't know. It's some sort of new process they've got going to squeeze out the last little bits of coal. It's not pretty, but I guess that's what God put the coal in there for, was for us to use it."

"I'm not so sure," I said. "I don't know that he'd appreciate a mess like that. Somebody ought to…"

"Well, Max is getting antsy, I guess we'd better walk," Mrs. Pinsky said. "Come on, Max. Take care, Ava." If I had known how quickly environmental talk would scare her off, I'd have started with that.

I didn't know what one person, especially one person who'd left and come back could do about it, but I knew now that I had to do something to stop the destruction, if only for Joshua. Collis had made Joshua his own myth of family, love, and death here, his own murder ballad. I'd have to counter that somehow, find something to build on. I couldn't let the mountains be torn apart too. Maybe Micah's meetings were a start.

I sipped my coffee, but it had cooled. A runner I didn't recognize came down the street at a fast clip. Two ladies in fleece sweatsuits and brightly colored running shoes walked past, swinging their arms, their lipsticked lips pursed as they exhaled. I waved at them and walked faster back home, away from the gash on the mountain.

I had agreed to go to Micah's meetings many times over the last few years, but I had never followed through, afraid of causing a fight with Collis. He had been gone for almost five months now though, and there was a bigger fight to fight. I was ready for it.

"So you're really coming this time?" Micah asked.

"I promise this time I really, really will come," I said.

"You swear?" She glared at me. We'd agreed in seventh grade that a swear was irrevocably binding. We saved them for extreme situations.

"Micah!"

"Well, do you swear?" I'd broken promises before, it was true. But the gash in the mountain, the Mrs. Pinskys, I couldn't stand by anymore and watch it all disappear.

"Okay, I swear I'll come to your damn meeting."

She winked at me and said, "I knew I'd get to you sooner or later."

The meeting was at the Iona Diner, and it was packed. I was late, of course. I usually was when I was nervous. This meeting and fighting Big Coal seemed almost futile to me, a little sad, but not to everyone else. The two middle-aged men standing closest to the door made a space for me when I walked in. They were clean, with shiny bald patches on the tops of their heads, bellies rounded out, standing like some kind of sentries on either side of the glass door. I thought one of them worked at the barbershop. I didn't know the other one. There wasn't an empty chair to be had. The place smelled of fried food and cigarettes. The heater made an intermittent clang, but it wasn't loud compared to the rumble of voices. With all these bodies, we didn't really need the heat on anyway. All the booths were full. The tables had been moved out of the way and replaced with folding chairs. Micah's voice filled the room. She didn't need a microphone, though she was holding one and gesturing with it. When she raised her voice, the speakers distorted it. "We can't let them take our air, our water, and our mountains!" she said. "We can't let them take away this place. It's who we are! We are the mountains!" The room erupted in cheers and applause.

"Damn straight!" a man in front of me shouted. He was older, maybe in his seventies, and he wore pressed jeans and a light blue collared shirt. His thick white hair was combed and set neatly in place with a little Brylcreem. His face had some color from working outside. "They want to take off the top of the mountain on

Taylor's branch," he said, "up above the home I've lived in my whole life. The home I was born in. Everybody I've lost is buried up there. They gonna just blast them away? My wife's up there. Our son, Chuck, he was a veteran. But we see what Big Coal thinks of our dead. And our living!" A thin froth of white spit collected in the corners of his mouth. His voice shook, but it was more from anger than sadness. If he lost his dead, there would be no proof of his life.

A younger man stood up. He was about my age, but I couldn't place him. He looked uncomfortable. "I'm sorry for Mr. Taylor's loss," he said. "I really am. But we do got to think about jobs. I've got a family to feed. A truck to put gas in. Lights to keep on. Working at the Wal-Mart ain't going to cut it. If I could even get a job there." Some people glared at him, other heads lowered so they wouldn't have to face him. One or two people, probably his co-workers, clapped. A few people hissed, soft and low, coiled snakes ready to strike.

Micah spoke, calm and confident, "You think they'll stay around after everything's mined out, Morgan? They're already stripping and running. All they'll leave is a mess in their wake. Cancer rates are going up. Birth defects, too. We've got to fight for living wages, not dying ones." This sent the crowd into a roar. Morgan looked torn. I felt for him, but Micah was right. There was a kind of syndrome where people fell in love with the coal companies or at least stood with them because they thought they'd survive that way. It was like living with an abusive lover. They still believed that somehow the companies would bring more jobs and money, as long as they didn't question the CEOs or look to anyone else for salvation. They'd get as much as a bullet to the head with their homes destroyed by Big Coal and nothing left worth keeping, not even a job. It was suicide.

Most of the people in the room looked harmless, like you might meet them at a church supper and ask them to pass you the potato salad. But here, they were furious, pushed into a corner and ready to fight their way out. I listened to story after story of people's drinking water getting contaminated with mercury, arsenic, and run-off. There had been a rockslide that piled up flyrock behind one family's house. They couldn't open the windows for fear of being buried, enveloped by the broken mountain. Micah passed the microphone for people to tell their stories, then took it back when it had made its way around the room.

"Who loves these mountains enough to fight for them?" she asked. A cheer rippled through the room, the wildest sound in town on this Thursday night. "Okay. We'll meet here at six o'clock Monday morning to leave for the capitol. That should put us there by nine or so. If you can't sit in at the governor's office, there are lots of other ways you can help. We need food and drivers and places to stay in Frankfort. I'm sending around this sign-up sheet. Put down whatever you can do. Let them know which side you're on!" On cue, the room broke into "Which Side Are You On?"

I joined in on the chorus because it was the only part I knew. Jason was in the front corner of the room, wearing a fitted T-shirt that said, "I Love Mountains!" I looked away. A person who's mourning has no business having feelings for another man, no business with a pulse that quick. I focused on the low rumble that had filled the room as people made plans, or talked about what was happening where they lived, how much of the hillside was missing.

I had known Micah my whole life, and I had known what her job was for years, but to be here, to see the mamas with babies on their hips, the teenagers with gauges in their ears and Goth clothes, the old men in overalls and pristine ball caps, and Micah pulling them all together to fight, this I'd known nothing about. I waited while people lined up to talk to Micah. Brent, a guy she worked with who lived in Lexington and came in for meetings like this, was typing people's information into a laptop. I signed the petition somebody passed to me, asking if I opposed the destruction of the mountains. Of course I did. Finally, Micah saw me.

"You came!" She hugged me, and the people there looked at me like I must be something special because I was close to Micah. "You going to help us? We need more bodies."

"Sure," I said. "As long as you don't put me on the microphone." How could anybody say no to her? To me, she was Micah, my best friend since second grade. To these people, she was some kind of mountain savior. Maybe she was.

17

Strata

I stared into the bright light of the refrigerator, and nothing looked like it could possibly taste good. I closed the door. Alice and I had been getting in each other's way. The house was shrinking. "Let's go out," I said.

Alice thought I was too distracted when I drove, but I wasn't. I'd reach to change the station on the radio and she'd grip the handle above the door that nobody but nervous old ladies uses and gasp, "Watch out! There's a truck coming." I always saw it coming in plenty of time. "I'll drive," Alice said.

"Suit yourself." She was used to being in charge, and I didn't mind somebody else carting me around. I was seeing a side of Alice that wasn't her mother-in-law self. We were closer kin now. We were more honest with each other too, for better or worse. The one thing we had stopped talking about was Collis.

I slid into the passenger seat of her wide brown sedan. Joshua sat in back. He rolled his window up and down, making a rhythm. "Stop it!" I yelled. Alice looked at me and raised her eyebrows. She and Joshua exchanged a look in the rearview mirror. At least I didn't smoke around him like she did. "I can't take you rolling the windows up and down," I told him. "It'll break the switch. We can't afford to get things like that fixed." He put his hands in his lap and looked at them. Alice glanced at me. I looked straight ahead.

"You'll like the Ranch House," she said. "Everybody does."

"When did they put in a steakhouse?" I asked.

"Oh, Honey, I don't know. I don't even know what day it is anymore. I guess right after you all left. It went up quick."

We drove up on the bypass, and Alice wedged the car into the full parking lot.

"Hop out," I said to Joshua. I grabbed his hand and led the way. He didn't resist, but he held onto his silence.

Inside, the buffet line wound around the inner perimeter of the building. We found the end. Some people waved; others looked away. I didn't blame them. About three people ahead of us, I recognized Mrs. Kinder, my second-grade teacher. Her name was different now, of course. I think she married a Cranfield a few years after the mine explosion killed her first husband, but she would always be Mrs. Kinder to me. Her red hair had faded. It was mostly white with a few faint reddish streaks now, swooshed to the top of her head and sprayed still in a peak. She had widened too. The flesh of her upper arms drooped. Still, she was neatly dressed in a navy pantsuit, with a ruffled pink blouse underneath. Not a hair out of place.

"Mrs. Kinder!" I called to her. She turned around. I guess she was used to this, being taken for her old self in her new life.

"Ava, how are you?" She frowned when she said this, touched me on the shoulder. Everybody in town knew about my crazy, dead husband. They talked about it, I knew. That was the shorthand for me in conversations, my legend. You know, Ava, the one whose husband shot hisself? I could tell it hurt Mrs. Kinder to think about me and how we had something horrible in common. I was too tired to lie.

"I'm terrible," I said. She nodded, pulled me into a tight hug, and I was in the second grade again, enveloped in her soft, full body.

"It takes a long time," she said. "A real long time." She patted my back softly, like I was her child.

"Mom?" Joshua said. He was tugging at the bottom of my shirt. "The line's moved up." He was used to this now. As he walked, he ran his hand along the brass railing that divided the buffet line from the dining room. Alice had already stepped ahead with the line. Mrs. Kinder let me go but kept her hand on my back as we moved forward. The line had grown behind us, too.

"Ava," Mrs. Kinder said. "People have no idea how what they're saying sounds." Her eyes were not like I remembered them. They were set deep in her face now.

"I know, Mrs. Kinder."

"I'm a Cranfield now!" she said. She grabbed her husband by the arm, as if to prove he was alive and well. As if to prove I could move on too, maybe marry again. He looked our way, smiled, held out his hand to me, and I shook it.

"Larry Cranfield," he said. His smile was broad and warm; it filled his whole face. I just nodded. I couldn't imagine finding or even looking for my own Larry Cranfield. She was still a Kinder and always would be, as far as I was concerned.

Joshua filled his plate. He was getting ready for a growth spurt. I'd put money on it. He piled the plate high with mashed potatoes, minute steak, green beans, a roll. Alice's plate was a miniature version of his. There were tiny piles of food, neatly spaced around the rim of her plate, like numbers on a clock face. I put some mashed potatoes, a piece of fried chicken, and salad on my plate, knowing I would only eat the potatoes. I might only have a bite of everything else, but I wanted to encourage Joshua. We sat among the after-church crowd, even though we had not been to church. Most of the women wore dresses that covered their knees. Their shoes were sturdy. The men were in shirts and ties, at least. Some wore suits, ironed so many times they shone with spray starch. The older the people, the more formally they were dressed. We wore jeans and t-shirts, heathen, but there were others dressed like us too. We weren't going to church, but it still felt like prayer to eat with other people.

There were a lot of Mrs. Kinders in this town. Some who'd lost people already; some who hadn't yet. I guess we were all trying to understand why we stuck around a place that beat us up so bad, why we loved the way it held us, the way we held each other up.

The high ceilings carried conversations around the dining room. The low chatter burst every now and then with laughter.

We ate and talked quietly about Joshua's school and who was the best player on his basketball team. "You should see Davy Michie!" Joshua said. "He can almost dunk. He's like five feet tall already. I think maybe he was held back a grade or something. Maybe they could hold me back, so I'd be bigger than everybody on the team."

"No way," I said. "You're plenty big." He was four feet eight when I took him for his check up a few months ago, and his face had narrowed a little more. His fat baby cheeks were long gone. Joshua was slipping back into a nine-year-old world, going forward. And I knew now, despite it all, Iona was the place we had to be for that to happen. We had to understand what had happened to us here before we could ever decide to leave. And once we looked closely, we saw ourselves in every part of it. We had to stay. I couldn't fight it anymore.

A waitress came by, some girl I'd never seen before, but she was cheerful. "Can I clear everything away for you?" she said.

"Please," I said. "Take it all."

Joshua had gotten past his trouble with the Tack boy and the Finley twins, though I knew this from his teachers and Anita, not from him. He, Jonah, and Robbie were a trio, and that carried enough weight in the third grade to protect him. He wasn't interested in schoolwork, but he liked being around his friends, like any other kid his age. That was enough for now.

I had started to look forward to work in the same way. I got up and showered, got dressed in the cleanest thing I could find, grabbed a cup of coffee and got out of the house every morning. In the car, I turned the music up as loud as it would go. I needed to feel it. I needed it to stir up my blood. Even though he followed me everywhere, I only let Collis slip into my real world at lunchtime, or maybe when I'd take a coffee break. Then I could savor him smiling, holding me close, and ignore our troubles. Usually, I'd eat at my desk, looking at my reflection in the computer screen as I chewed, trying to picture his face next to mine. I could almost imagine it.

"You know, that's bad for the digestion," Gabe said. "You shouldn't eat while you're looking at a computer." He stuck his head in my half-open door. He had a bag of fast food in his hand, and he was headed for the break room.

"What you've got is a bag of indigestion, no matter where you eat it," I said, nodding toward the bag. "You know that'll kill you dead."

"A man's got to eat. A woman too. How 'bout just a fry or two?" He waved a fry in front of me, as if it would tempt me, then popped it into his mouth. "Delicious!"

"Disgusting!" I said and shooed him off. I'd lost interest in my peanut butter and jelly sandwich by now, so I put it back in the bag and tossed it into the trash. Collis had slipped away into the air.

The electronic chime on the front door dinged. Kayla wasn't at the front desk. She had gone to lunch. Wayne, who was homeless, was asleep in a chair in the corner, a fixture. We didn't have a shelter in town. The closest one was thirty miles away in Hubbard, and he wouldn't take his meds if we left him outside, so we didn't kick him out unless he got wild. He'd been sleeping most of the morning. The only disturbance from him was a low snore. I went to see who it was. I was supposed to be covering the phones too. I took in my reflection in the glass door.

Why did I wear these old corduroy pants? This shirt looks like I slept in it. I didn't believe in laundry anymore unless there was visible dirt. My clients didn't seem to mind.

"Just who I was looking for!" Jason said as I opened the door. I tucked my hair behind my ears.

"What can I do for you? Things slow over there at the paper?"

"No, we're busy. I just had a minute, and I was wondering if you had plans this weekend?" I looked down at the pile of papers on Kayla's desk and straightened them into a neat stack. "It's just, I don't know that many people here to hang out with anymore. As friends, of course."

I looked back at him, trying to decide how to say no. His face was boyish. He wore thick-framed tortoise-shell glasses. I could imagine kissing him, though I pushed the image out of my mind a second after I let it in. I hadn't dated since I was seventeen. He was giving me his most genuine, open smile. He did have nice lips. He held his hands up to indicate there was nothing under the table, nothing to fear, then ran them through his hair.

"Ok, well…" The door dinged again.

"I'm back!" Kayla said. She was breathing hard, a little flustered. "There was a line around the corner at Cullen's. I didn't mean it to take so long. Thanks for watching the phones." She looked at Jason, then at me, then back at Jason.

"No problem." I turned to Jason, "why don't we talk at my desk?" He nodded and followed me down the hall to my cubicle. "Make yourself at home." I pointed toward the worn blue plastic chair across from my desk. He sat. I had hoped he'd read my mind and say he had to go, scoot out gracefully, leaving us both unscathed.

"I'd like to hang out with you," I said. "I really would, but I can't."

"You need to get out sometime, Ava," he said.

"I do get out," I said. "Joshua and Alice and I eat out a lot. We just went to the new steak house on the bypass. It's got good fried chicken and biscuits."

"How about a hike then?"

Can you cheat on the dead? It's till death do us part, but then what? I had every right not to feel this hollow after our three months of separation, and six months since Collis's death. What it would be like to touch someone again, warm skin to warm skin?

"I could maybe take a hike," I said. Jason smiled. "But not too long. I'm out of shape!"

"Not that I can tell," he said. "How about Saturday? I'll pick you up. Is eight too early? I mean, that way we can get back by lunchtime. I'm going to Lexington that evening."

"Eight's halfway through the day for me," I said. I was relieved that he'd set an end time to it. I only had to stay until noon. He'd even leave town after that.

"See you then." He got up to leave and gave me his lopsided smile. Already I felt guilty, as if Collis was watching me, betrayed.

"Just some good clean fun. Healthy living. Fellowship," he said, as he walked out the door.

"I said I'd go, didn't I?"

Gabe passed Jason in the hallway and said hello. I knew he had overheard us, but he kept walking toward his office, pretending the walls weren't paper-thin. Kayla buzzed my phone.

"This is Ava," I said.

"Can you take a walk-in?"

"Sure. Anybody I know?"

"No. A girl. Says she's from Ohio. Just moved here."

"Why would she do that?" Nobody just moved to Iona. You had to know about it, have some kind of tie here, or a reason. It was two hours from the nearest airport. The closest bus station was half an hour away, in Hubbard. Plenty of people had moved from Iona to Ohio, or Michigan, or Indiana. Hordes of people left in the sixties to find work. The only outsiders who moved here were hippies going back to the land, Vista volunteers, or drug runners.

"Should I send her on back?" Kayla asked.

"Sure."

The girl was maybe eighteen, smooth skinned and lanky, but her eyes already looked old. Maybe it was just the makeup. Her hair was long, streaked white blond and chocolate brown. The right side was shaved close to her head, so it all fell to the left. I could make out the faint memory of freckles through her foundation. I stood up and offered my hand.

"Ava Maynard," I said. "What's your name?"

"Brianna. Brianna Roberts." She slid into the seat in front of my desk.

"What can I do for you?"

"Well, I need food stamps," she said. "And Section 8. I need a place to live. You know, the basics."

I nodded. "There's a wait list for all that, but you can get food from the food pantry at the First Baptist Church every Wednesday morning at 7:30. I'd recommend you get there early. There's always a line. Do you have kids?"

"One," she said. "But he's in Ohio with his dad's family. It's just me here."

I looked at her. "Is your family here?"

She looked toward the window, as if to make sure nobody in the family was passing by and might hear her. "Not any of the good ones. They're in Ohio too. I came down to take care of my granny before she died, which she did last month. I been living in her place, but my uncle wants it. He had the lights and the water cut off to try to force me out. I have to wait for the probate. She said it'd be mine. She wasn't even speaking to him. Hadn't talked to him for two years. She said it was my place. I know a little bit about the law, Miss Maynard. I've been researching. He can't take the house just because he paid her utilities and groceries every now and then. That ain't ownership."

"Who's your uncle?" I asked. Chances were, I'd gone to high school with him.

"Johnny Roberts. You know him?" She didn't give me time to answer. "Of course you do. Everybody around here does. He thinks he's notorious or something, but he's just a pill head like the rest of them. He's been in prison, but not for everything they ought to have got him for. I'm not telling you anything everybody in town don't know. He wouldn't care to burn me out of the house. He's like that." She fidgeted in her chair, couldn't seem to get comfortable, boney as she was. "He done worse before," she said.

There he was again, when I thought I had gotten rid of him for good, Johnny Roberts. For all I knew, she had never met him, wasn't related to him, just saw a chance to squat in a house. I'd never heard anything about him having a niece. Maybe he sent this girl to keep some kind of eye on me.

"And you, are you on anything? Selling?" I asked this as I read her papers, then looked up, to see if she was telling the truth. I would look up her records as soon as she walked out the door.

"I'm clean. It's hard to stay that way in this fucking place, but I am clean. I'm going to get my son back and live in my Granny's house. That's the plan. Can you help me, Miss Maynard?"

"I can try. It depends on what you're willing to do for yourself and your son."

This girl didn't look clean to me. It was in the eyes. They looked too alert, ready to jump. She had drawn thick lines of lavender eyeshadow on the top lids, but there was way too much grey in the skin around them for anybody under sixty. This girl had felt each day she'd lived, and it didn't look like there'd been many good ones. She had chewed her fingernails to the quick. I could see where they had bled some, around the edges of her chipped green polish. She started chewing them a little then, pulling at a tiny hangnail with her teeth. I looked at the insides of her arms, her wrists. She was wearing a short-sleeved shirt, no track marks, no cutting that I could see. She had four or five tattoos, professionally done, all in dark blue ink, but spaced-out kind of strange and jagged. Maybe she was planning to fill the gaps with color but ran out of money. There were a couple of fairies, a Chinese-looking symbol, and on her thin right bicep a name, Tyler Devon. Maybe she was telling the truth, at least about some of it.

"Oh, sorry," she said. She caught me staring at her chewing her fingernails. It had to hurt. I could see the raw pink where the skin had been peeled back.

"Bad habit. Sometimes I don't even know I'm doing it." She put her hands in her lap, overlapped, like a church lady.

"It's okay. There are worse habits."

"Don't I know it," she said.

"Okay, Brianna. Fill out this form and we'll start working on food stamps. As for your uncle, do you think you need a restraining order? Do you want to find another place to stay for now?"

"No. I'll be okay. I've got a few friends here. I'm safe." There were so many ways friends around here could get you into trouble, but I didn't say that to Brianna. There was so much everyone wanted in return; it was hard to believe she was safe. I'd heard all my life that mountain people were survivors, but we were really just the same people you find all around the world who learn to expect things to go the wrong way and don't seem too surprised when they do. I still believed in the inherent good in people, but

I knew the destruction drugs could do, too. They erased families, left no trace of the people you had known, the way things used to be. I'd seen it in my own home.

"There's an NA meeting Tuesday nights at the New Believers Church on Perry Street. 7pm. Can you make that?"

"Sure. It's not like I've got a job or nothing." I always try to keep my face neutral. The people who came for pity wanted too much; people like Brianna were offended by it. Still, eighteen was young as I was when I started dating Collis. I wanted her to tell the truth. "I really am clean, Miss Maynard," Brianna said. I nodded.

"Well, once you get settled, come back. We have a job-training program. I can place you somewhere in a paid internship."

"Doing what?"

"There are lots of choices, healthcare, retail, dental hygiene. Whichever one you'd want to do. We can find you something."

"I don't know what I'd want to do," she said. "I never really got far enough to think of something like that."

"Did you have a job in Ohio?"

"Fast food," she said. "It was a shit job, but at least I paid for diapers. My mom paid for the rest. She thinks I can't handle my son, but I can. I just need to get settled. I need a new start." I doubted Brianna would find that here, but I handed her flyers on Job Corps, the community college, and childcare vouchers.

"Thanks, Miss Maynard."

"Call me Ava, please."

"Thanks, Ava," Brianna smiled and moved out of my office like I had done something to help her. I waited until the electric bell dinged on the door and she was gone before I shook my head. I couldn't care about Brianna, or any of the other people who came in after she left, wanting food stamps, section eight, childcare vouchers, all kinds of help. I was still trying to get a new start for myself. Maybe a hike was a step in the right direction.

Kayla buzzed me again, "It's Micah."

"Uh-oh," I said before Kayla put her through. I tried to preempt her attack, "If you're calling to get me to go out somewhere, I can't do it."

"Well hello to you too!" she said. "I was calling to check in on a friend in need, but I can't go anywhere with you, no matter how you beg. I happen to have a date tonight with James, you know, that new doctor who works at the clinic? You'll probably be watching movies from the eighties with your old mother-in-law. Just saying."

"You don't know what I'm doing. Maybe I have a date soon too."

"You do not! The earth will shake before you let that happen." I actually managed to surprise her. I could count on one hand the number of times I'd done that.

"I told Jason I'd go on a hike with him. As friends, but that counts."

"Well, well. I guess it does count. Look at you! Wonders never cease."

"Stop. You'll make me want to cancel."

I drove home, even though it was close enough to walk, because I picked Joshua up after school every day. He was too young to be a walker, even if Alice thought it would do him some good, give him some independence. There were a few kids on our street who walked to school together, and Joshua would probably be fine, but I couldn't know for certain. If I drove him home, I had a guarantee he would get there as long as I did.

In the car, I put Brianna Roberts out of my mind, let Jason slip in for a while. He might keep me distracted for a month or two. Maybe longer. I didn't really care about anything more than getting away from who I was and maybe touching somebody who was warm and alive. I didn't want to be mired down or tied to anybody I might care about losing. But I did want to feel something good. I turned on the radio, music, never the news. How could I care that ten people died in a highway crash or another mine shut down? How could I worry about the state of the economy, or Congress passing some bill that kept people struggling? The news just showed how hard the world was to live in, which made me almost understand why Collis left it. Maybe Jason would show me the good still in the world, at least in Hensley County.

I pulled up in the car rider line and Joshua slid into the back seat. His math teacher, Mrs. Anderson, opened the door for him. She was maybe twenty-four, freshly graduated from the University of Tennessee, moved back home and married. She wore sweaters that had teacher icons on them, blackboards, ABC's, an apple. I had no idea what a girl her age was doing dressing like an old woman, even if she was a little thick. She had a pretty, round China doll face and long brown hair to her waist. I guess it was some kind of status symbol. She made herself a teacher, and she wanted to show it everywhere she went. She was good to me and to Joshua.

"How you doing?" she said.

"I'm doing."

"Let's go, Mom!" Joshua said.

"You buckled?" I looked back to confirm he wasn't buckled. The radio station was the same one I'd always listened to, 80.8 FM. It was locally run, so you never knew what you'd hear. Today it was the rock and roll show. The DJ was a guy who graduated a few years before me, Chris Evarts. He had always been a hair band metal head.

"I'm buckled now," Joshua said, clicking his seatbelt. "Turn it up, Mama."

I did and the drums shook the car. He felt it too, and we were both shaking our heads to the beat, trying to get something to come out of our insides. For the first time since we'd been back, a smile stretched across my face before I noticed it. For that moment, we were ourselves again, until the final note, the drums crashing in a fury, and the DJ coming on to announce that we should stay tuned, the weather would be up next.

18

Run

My body was beginning to look middle aged. I wasn't fighting it, even though thirty-four seemed young for that. I had always had a belly, but it was softer now and more present. At first, after I found Collis, I couldn't eat a thing, now I wanted all I could fill myself with. I was taking most of my pleasure in food. I truly believed in the medicinal qualities of chocolate. And wine.

I was thickening in the middle, like my mother, getting a little sturdy in the thighs, a little broader in the ass, but nobody would say anything, not after the last five months I'd lived through. Around here, I was still on the small side. But when I looked in the mirror, I was shocked. If mountains wear down and lose their shape over time, what chance did I have?

"Come with me to yoga class," Micah said, "It's in the basement of the Baptist church and it's only five dollars. You need it." She always told me the truth, whether I wanted to hear it or not.

"Thanks. I need a lot of things."

"I know, Smartass, but this will change your life. You ought to try breathing every once in a while. It's what living people do."

"Is it?" Who knew it was that simple, breathing? Thoughts of Jason reminded me that I had a body, that it could be more than a carrying case for my grief, that there was pleasure in moving, in touch, but I didn't want to move and breathe around a bunch of women in a church basement.

Instead, I waited for a cool morning, when I was up before Joshua and Alice. I made coffee then tied up my running shoes, walked out to Cumberland Avenue and began to pick up my pace. I had run cross-country in high school. 7:45 was my best mile, now I'd be lucky to run a 10:45. Didn't matter. I just wanted to move forward. A huge old blue and rust Ford truck swooshed past me and honked. I waved, even though I didn't see who it was. I probably knew them. More than one person slowed their car enough to ask did I need a ride. I practiced my "no thanks" wave. People ran here, but usually they were teenagers, getting in shape for basketball. Women my age walked or ran when there was something wrong. Maybe that's what I was doing now.

I ran to the playground at the end of Main Street. From there, I followed the trail parallel to the railroad tracks. I could hear my blood pumping in my ears, and I began to warm up. My muscles felt longer, my breathing thickened. Sweat trickled down my forehead. I wanted more of it. I wanted to be drenched. The trail went as far as the tracks did, to the town of Hubbard at least, which was thirty miles away. I only planned on running three or four miles, just to get back into it. Just to be alone.

I got out of town in a quarter mile or so, and I was running between the woods and the old train tracks on a narrow strip of pea gravel. The city had worked for years to make this a fitness trail. I imagined it would lead me where I wanted to go, even though I wasn't sure where that was. I settled on one thing, I didn't want to be here, in this place, in this body. I ran. The sky was so blue I had to squint, but I didn't have to look at anybody here. Nobody was looking at me. That was a relief. I listened to the crunch of my shoes on the gravel. I had to think about breathing, and every now and then I let out something between a gasp and a moan. It was as if grief was leaking out of my body with my breath. I would run as far as I could. Each footfall made a beat through my body. My thoughts swirled, and then I could feel something, or someone beside me, Collis. I don't know how to explain it, but I knew it was him. Not the mess I'd seen in the mine, but the real whole him, the Collis I knew when we first fell in love. That's the one I always pictured. He didn't say anything, but he was there, keeping my pace, which surprised me. We had never run together before.

"If you watch runners, they always look like they're in pain," he always said, "I don't know why anyone in their right mind would torture theirself that way." But I could tell he wanted to be with me now, to feel my heartbeat and make sure I was still breathing. I kept running.

My grandmother wasn't running with me, but she showed up in my head all the sudden too. Keep going, she said. Don't stop now. Collis just smiled, kept my pace. All my ghosts were surrounding me, holding me up as I pounded my way forward. I wasn't surprised then to feel my cousin, William, who died in a motorcycle accident when he was seventeen, show up. Out of the whole family, he and I had seen ourselves most in each other. William took his time catching up to me, but I knew he would. He was always cool like that. He seemed amused at me, smiling and laughing, and he hadn't aged a bit. Still that golden hair and green eyes. I had forgotten how I missed him.

Collis stayed the closest. He ran just behind me and to the right. I didn't turn and look at him or stop because I sensed that might scare him off. I could almost hear his breathing, but maybe that was mine? I hadn't run this far in a long time. Was I hallucinating? The gravel looked the same. I wasn't dizzy.

My watch said I'd been going for a good forty minutes. Collis pushed me ahead. I was a little light-headed, but I didn't want to stop. I didn't want all my people to fade away. I ran and ran, parallel to the tracks, until my watch beeped the hour. A coal train blew past, whistled twice, and with the blast of air that rushed over me, all my people fled. They had felt so real, like I could reach out and touch them. For a minute, they were mine again. Now it was just my own gasping I heard. I ran back to the house alone, sweat cooling my skin. Joshua looked up from the cartoon he was watching when I walked in, his sandy hair still messy from sleep. His pajamas were too short again. No matter what happened, he kept growing, long and lanky now, tall for a third grader, a full-on kid.

"You okay, Mama?" he asked. "Your face is so red." He was right. In the bathroom mirror, I saw what scared him. My face was almost scarlet and dripping with sweat. My eyes were red too. I guess I had let some tears go. I wiped my face off with a dish towel and took a drink of water.

"I'm fine, Baby. I'm good," I said.

19

Last Cut Lake

I agreed to meet Jason at eight, which meant I got up at six to get ready. I was trying to look put together, without looking like I'd spent a lot of time planning. No matter how much under-eye cream I used though, dark bags still puffed out. I tried to smile for the mirror to see what I looked like, and fine lines spread out from the corners of my eyes. I put on eyeliner then wiped it off. It made me look like I had a little bit of a shiner, so I washed the whole mess off. He'd have to look at the real me.

I wanted to slip out of the house before I had to say much to Alice. I'd asked her to watch Joshua, told her I was hiking, but didn't mention Jason. This was not a date, but still. I was going somewhere with a man, and maybe I should still be only thinking of Collis, even though we were almost divorced when he died. It was hard to reconcile the Collis of our early marriage, and the Collis I left. The one who loved me and the one who turned away. It confused me. Time wasn't linear. The past and the present folded over each other in sedimentary layers.

I was putting on my shoes in my bedroom. Out the window, I saw Jason drive up in his bright blue pickup up and heard him honk. It felt all the sudden like high school. Maybe I should just call it off. He'd probably understand. Joshua walked into my room in his fire truck pajamas, wide awake.

"Where are you going?" he asked. I pulled my down jacket out of the closet, then worried that might be too warm. I wore it anyway. Better too warm than too cold.

"I'm going on a hike. I'll be back by noon. I got you some donuts. They're in the kitchen."

"Donuts? Thanks, Mama."

I pulled him close and kissed him, "I love you, Baby. Nana will be up soon."

I tried to take my time walking to the truck, like I really didn't care about going, one way or the other. "Morning," Jason said as I slid into the passenger seat. "Looks like a good day for a hike." He was dressed for it, jeans, a thermal shirt, a flannel shirt over that and hiking boots. I second guessed the dangly earrings I had chosen to wear at the last minute. At least I had on worn jeans and a plain purple T-shirt, so he wouldn't think I was trying too hard.

"Morning," I said, immediately regretting the whole thing.

A wide smile filled his face. "I thought we could go up by Pearl Lake," he said, pulling the truck onto the road, his left arm out the driver's side window.

"Okay, as long as we can be back by noon. Joshua will be waiting on me." I had my arms wrapped around myself.

"Is this too cold for you?" he asked, moving his arm in and rolling up the window.

"No, I'm fine," I said, loosening my arms, trying to relax. I watched the trees roll by as we drove higher and higher up the mountain. We parked in the small lot at the edge of the lake, which was maybe a quarter of a mile across at this point. We got out of the truck to look at the lake and stood side by side, but not close enough to touch. The air smelled of moss and engine oil. A man had backed his truck up until his back tires were partially submerged in the dark green water. He waded in and slid his Jon boat off the trailer into the lake. It barely made a splash. He parked the truck, jumped into the boat, cranked the engine, looked up and nodded at us as we passed. A thin fog was lifting. The man motored away until it was hard to make out the lines of the boat; just a silver smudge.

We took the trail that led around the perimeter of the lake, then climbed up into the hills. I decided not to talk, just listen to whatever Jason had to allow. He led the way. The trail inclined gradually. It was well worn, a single dirt track, covered in orange-brown leaf mulch. We had to step over rocks and gnarled roots every now and then, push wayward branches out of our way. The pines cast green-blue shadows on the trail. Sunlight filled the gaps.

"I haven't been up here in years," Jason said. He walked ahead of me on the trail, pointing things out as we ascended. I kept quiet behind him, watching the way he moved, confident and steady. I liked the way his flannel shirt pulled across his shoulders, the way his jeans fit. My breath got a little deeper, and I could feel a film of sweat forming on my brow. I slowed my pace to put a little more space between us.

"There's a great view at the top. We'll be able to see the whole town of Iona. Neko too," he said. "It's the most beautiful view in the county."

I knew I should speak, but I was confused. I was still in love with a dead man, and as we hiked, I could almost feel Collis beside me. Jason held back a branch, so I could get past it without scratching myself. I ducked under it and stepped past him, so he could let it go.

"You okay?" he asked. "You want to take a break?"

"I'm fine."

"Okay, onward!" he said. "I've been coming up here since I was a kid. My mom and dad were always dragging me on some trail, taking me and my sister camping. Now, I don't feel right unless I get out into the mountains every weekend."

"That sounds like a great way to grow up," I said.

"As long as you like granola and tofu," he said. "They got in with the hippies. I've been to more bluegrass shows than I can count."

"You know any Ralph Stanley?"

"Dr. Ralph's my dad's favorite." He began singing "Rank Stranger" and belted out the chorus. "Everybody I met / Seemed to be a rank stranger! / No Mother, no Dad / Not a friend did I see!" His joy in it made me smile. I hummed along quietly.

As we got closer to the ridgeline, the trees started to thin. I stopped to get my water bottle out of my backpack and took a sip, then handed the bottle to Jason. "Thanks," he said. I took my fleece jacket off and tied it around my waist by the sleeves. The sun had risen high above us, warming the ground. The dirt smelled fresh with spring, even though most of the tree limbs were still bare. There was the faintest tint of pink on the limbs across the mountain. Everything was about to come alive.

"I think the best view is over here to the right," Jason said, leading me toward the edge of the trail. I followed through a winding path covered in pine straw and tree roots. I hadn't been up here in at least five years. He stopped abruptly.

I came up beside him and saw the whole top of the mountain across from us was gone, as if God had taken a huge knife and lopped it off, without even trying to smooth the edges. "Wow," I said. The side of the mountain had been gnawed at by dozers, and a few sat perched on the top, triumphant. Trees were felled and left to dangle on the hillside. The rust-orange dirt had washed down the mountain in rivulets. Below, a cluster of neat white clapboard houses huddled together on a wide patch of brown grass. I felt like I'd been punched. I tried to keep tears from spilling in front of Jason. What I loved kept disappearing. "Is that Hawkins Creek?" I asked.

"What's left of it," Jason said. "I'd heard they were doing a mountaintop removal, but they were supposed to reclaim it. Said it would be cow pasture. They talked about Iona beef." There were no cattle in sight, no grazing grass, nothing that could really sustain life, except the families stuck there at the bottom of the mountain, along the creek, banded together against the flow of the land.

"I guess that's the valley fill over there to the left," I said, pointing. The V where two slopes came together was filled in with a huge mound of gray rock and orange dirt. It had leveled the land temporarily, but it would never be completely solid. Any big rain would send all that rock and dirt and sludgy goo, what they called overburden, down to the houses and the creek below. I guess they thought of us as overburden too.

"This place breaks my heart." I turned to go back down the trail toward the lake. I couldn't look at what was left of the mountain. Micah said the whole area was dissolving underground; miners were ripping it to dust above ground. Pretty soon there wouldn't be a solid square of land to stand on. No wonder my office was flooded; if we couldn't hold the land together, what chance did the people have?

"Ava, wait," Jason said. "It's still beautiful here." He grabbed my hand. I let him hold it as we walked back toward the lake. The gentleness of that, the warmth of my hand in his, that was a tenderness Collis and I had lost years ago. I held onto it now. We hiked down the curve of the trail and let our hands slip apart as we crossed a small stream across the trail. I went first this time, gingerly stepping on stones strewn in the water.

"Well done," Jason said, stepping boldly to the rock in the middle of the stream, then jumping across right in front of me. I didn't step back and he caught his balance by holding on to my shoulder. He looked at me, questioning, but I couldn't answer, just looked straight back at him. He leaned in and kissed me. My body felt something, but my heart was still. I kissed Jason back, the way I had wanted to kiss Collis. I couldn't admit this was happening, even though I didn't want to stop it. I let him hug me close. Then I pulled away and started back down the trail. He followed, took hold of my hand again, but this time neither of us said a word. The world was too fragile around us.

Was this the way my life could be? Had I ever felt this way with Collis, this safe, this cared for? Maybe I was making too much of it. Maybe it was too much of a risk to hope. Maybe it was too soon. By the time we reached the parking lot, the man in the Jon boat was anchored way across the lake, his engine now quiet. He was sitting with a long fishing rod in the water, still as a statue. On this level, the mountains looked like they were still standing just fine, the destruction hidden from view. The boat was floating in the deep green water at the bottom of a tree-covered bowl. It was beautiful.

"I guess you should take me home," I said.

"Okay," Jason said. We got into his truck. He pulled out onto the hardtop, and we wound our way back to town. He kept looking at me, stealing glances as he drove, trying to read me, but I looked ahead. I didn't want him to know what I was thinking. He stopped in front of Alice's, and I slipped out of the truck with a small wave, but no words. I didn't even watch him drive away.

"You're back already?" Joshua said when I walked in the door. It was eleven and he was still in his pajamas, reading one of Collis's old comic books, his fingers sticky with powdered sugar, two donuts left in the box beside him on the couch.

"Yeah. I saw all I wanted to." I sat beside him and stuffed one of the donuts into my mouth.

20

Backfill

I pulled up to the high school gym and inched my way toward the entrance in a long line of cars. Joshua was restless in the back seat, anxious to go to the high school basketball game with Jonah. Basketball was the highlight of their nine-year old lives. We stopped a few cars away from the double doors of the gym, which were propped open. Ticket takers had set up a folding table in front of them.

"Right here is good," Joshua said. "I see Jonah!" I stopped the car, and he hopped out. "Thanks, Mama."

"Have a good time!" I yelled as Joshua shut the car door and ran to meet Jonah at the ticket table. Jonah's mom, Anita, had taken Joshua on as a project, including him every time she took Jonah somewhere. I loved her for it. So did Joshua, I think. I waved as he slipped farther and farther from view. Then I drove home, went inside, and sat down at the kitchen table. I didn't have a high school basketball game in me yet, too many people to say hello to, try to smile for.

Anita wanted me to sign Joshua up for the peewee team Jonah was on and I was thinking about it. I took Joshua to watch those games some Saturday mornings and cheered for Jonah, but the Knights' games were a real social scene. They were the big event in an Iona weekend, if you could call anything in Iona a big event. Who knows who I'd run into there? I was coming back into the world, where anything could happen.

In the same parking lot, at a game a few weeks before, when I went to pick up Joshua, I'd seen a girl I didn't know at all, but whose face had been burned in my mind, the wide set, huge brown eyes, the long silky dark hair, the full, dark red-lipped mouth, all this set in mocha cream skin, the total opposite of my freckled skin, seawater eyes. She was slim, but strong too. I don't think I could have taken her in a fight, though I would have given it my all. She was a more serious challenge than the girl at the Quick Mart, the one I'd seen Collis flirt with on our last meet up in Camden. This girl was real. I could even guess what she smelled like, a vanilla scent that was so sweet and thick, it gagged me. I'd smelled it on Collis's coat before.

I don't know what they did, Collis and that dark-haired girl, if they actually slept together or just wanted to. She showed up in our lives every now and then and he'd slip away for hours at a time. Now I wish I knew her name. I'd looked through cell phone records, so I know it was a Knoxville number that he called each night for three or four months at a time. That's the only proof I had. It went in spells. They'd start up then stop abruptly. Then he'd start looking me in the eyes again and touching me first. That's all I know. I thought about calling that old number, but it might not even be hers. She would want to know he was dead, wouldn't she? Maybe she already knew. I wanted her to know. It might have been her who broke his heart instead of me. It might be more her fault than mine that he was gone now. That would change everything. She haunted me.

21

Nobles' Hardware

"Don't slam the back door!" I yelled when Joshua came in the next morning. He tiptoed back and pulled it gently to.

"Hey, Mama," he said. "I think it's broken. I didn't try to slam it." He looked scared of what would come out of my mouth next. I tried to take the edge out of my voice.

"I know, Baby. It's okay. How was the game?"

"Awesome," he said. "We beat the stew out of them. Joey Thomas dominated on the boards."

"Where'd you learn that?"

"Jonah. His mom's boyfriend knows a lot about basketball."

Joshua plopped down in front of the TV and ignored me. I didn't like Anita's new boyfriend. I'd known her for years, and she'd never had good taste in men. This one seemed like a pothead to me. I knew she wouldn't let him smoke around the boys, but still, I wished she would break up with him.

I needed to go to Noble's to get a new latch for the back door, rather than fuss at Joshua every time he came in. Maybe fixing the little things around the house would fix me. It was the kind of thing Alice or I would have asked Collis to do. He never did understand why everybody didn't know the way the physical world worked, or how to fix things that broke. I didn't even know what size Tupperware to put leftovers in, let alone how to fix a drain. Now that Collis was gone, everything seemed to break. The toilet in the hallway bathroom ran until you jiggled the handle, the window in Alice's bedroom had cracked when a bird flew into it beak first, the back door would not stay closed, no matter how many times I slammed it, or how hard I pulled. Alice and I let all the little chores around the house pile up and just complained about it every time the storm door flung open in the wind and smacked against the side of the house.

"Whose dishes are these?" Alice asked, as if she didn't know what I'd eaten for breakfast, or what color imprint my lipstick made on my coffee cup. She liked to keep things straight, as if keeping the house in order would bleed structure into our lives, as if we would ever have control over anything, or either of us could really let go. Still, Alice tried. Years of teaching third grade had instilled a great respect for rules in her. I was just about ready to throw the rules out, but I was still living with her, and she was still my mother-in-law.

"I said I'd get them." I wasn't in any hurry to take care of anything that was out of order. I didn't want her to touch it either. It was as if we were waiting on Collis to get home. We were getting mad at him for taking his time, and we started taking that out on each other in snaps about little things.

Sunday afternoon, I sat at the kitchen table with Joshua, working on his English homework. They were learning about how and when to use verbs, both action and linking. It was raining, a cold, windy rain that was doing its best to remind us it wasn't yet truly spring; it was too soon to relax. The door smacked against the house, loud as a gunshot, and we both jumped. "Damn it!" I said. "That's it. I'm going to fix the goddamned door myself."

"I'll help," Joshua got up. "I used to help Daddy all the time."

How hard could it be? I still had all of Collis's tools in the shed behind the house. I couldn't spend my whole life waiting for someone who would never come home.

"I'm going to Noble's right now," I told him. "You stay with Nana and work on your sentences. You can help me when I get back."

"Okay. I think I've got it now anyway. Action verbs are what you do. Linking verbs just tell what you're equal to." He focused again on the paper, his pencil firmly grasped in his left hand, like Collis used to do.

"Yes," I ruffled his hair. He shook his head to stop me. "I'll be back in a few minutes." I grabbed my purse and my raincoat and drove the half mile to Noble's as fast as I could in the downpour. I was ready to fix something right now, to make something right, and I didn't want to lose my momentum.

The store was empty, except for Anna Noble. She was a little hunched now. She had to be close to eighty, but her smooth white bob and her dark horned-rim glasses gave her a sophisticated look. Anna had a basketball game on the radio, sounded like a girls' high school game. The announcer called out, striiing music! and Anna clapped her hands together. "Go, Lady Knights!" she said. She was sitting at the counter, filling out order forms as she listened.

"How much are they winning by?" I asked.

"52-47 now. It's the third quarter. It's been a real barn burner."

"They'll do it," I said. "Those girls are tough as nails." She nodded. Anna had black and white photos on the walls of herself in a 1950s basketball uniform. She had been a guard.

"How can I help you, Sweetheart?" she said.

Anna and my mother had been friends, even though Anna was about fifteen years older than Mother. When I was young, she'd come over to the house, and they'd read cards for each other. My mother wasn't very good at telling fortunes, but Anna was. She took her time with it, just said what she saw and didn't elaborate. Anna told me I'd have one baby boy, and she told me I'd settle in Iona, even though I knew that. She never told me anything about Collis dying so young. Would she have told me what she'd seen? My mother no longer believed in fortune telling. I believed Anna could see things other people would never know.

"I just need one of these," I said, holding my hand out and showing the broken aluminum latch to Anna. She took it gently from my palm, held it up, and inspected it. "A 5765," she said. "We've got plenty of those."

"You'll want one of these and one of these too," Anna said, reaching her long thin arm above her to a bin full of latches and handing the pieces down to me. There were about fifty milky plastic bins of screws, bolts, nails, and latches on the wall behind her. The sticker labels on the bins were worn and hard to read, but she knew without having to think about it what was in each one.

"Oh, and take a few of these special anchor screws," she said. "They don't come out easy, so you won't have to do this again any time soon. You sink them deep into the studs." Her hand was soft and wrinkled. The nails were unpolished but filed into perfect new moons around the tips of her fingers. I took the screws from her. I didn't know how to ask her for what I really wanted.

"Okay," I said. "Can I do all this with a regular screwdriver?"

"Phillips head," Anna said. "That'll be $5.37, Ava. It shouldn't be too hard to fix."

"Thanks," I handed her the money. She handed me some change and a receipt. I took a little breath. I figured it was at least worth asking. If nothing else, my life in the last year had taught me not to put things off. "Anna, do you still read cards?"

"Lord, Honey. I haven't done that in years." She waved her hand past her face to sweep away the idea.

"Do you think you still could?" She looked at me above her glasses, which had slid a little down her nose. I'd take any kind of sign or wonder.

"Well. You got a few minutes? I don't reckon I'll be getting much business in this kind of rain." The rain was coming down in a dark gray curtain, blackening the afternoon sky.

"Doesn't look like it'll stop for a while," I said.

"I'll see what I remember. Come on in the back room. Let me find where I put those old cards." She locked the bolt on the front door and turned the sign on the glass front door from Come on in, We're Open! to Check Back Later, We're Closed. I followed her to the storeroom where there were shelves and shelves of tools, a desk with a computer, a lamp, a coffee maker, and a mug that said, World's Best Grandma. Anna pulled up two chairs.

"Sit down," she said. I did. All the sudden, my heart was beating fast; my hands were a little shaky. I held on to the duct taped armrests of the beat-up office chair she offered me. What if I found out something I didn't want to know? No. I wanted to know everything now.

"Now, give me your hands." She cupped my hands in her palms and closed her eyes for a minute. Then she let them go. "I always ask a little blessing first," she said. "Just to cover my bases."

"Can I ask a question? I mean to somebody who's not here?"

"Sure," she said. "But I can't promise anybody'll answer. I don't know who will even show up. It depends on the cards you choose. I just read what they spell out."

I looked at Anna, "ask him why."

Anna looked up at me with something almost like pity, but she didn't say whatever she was thinking. She focused on the cards, shuffled them and started to lay them out in a Celtic cross pattern, three cards down, three cards across, and four down the right side in another line. "This card represents you," she said, laying the Queen of Hearts in the middle of the counter.

"I don't know about her," I said. I hardly felt like the queen of anything. "Maybe I'm a Jack of something? She seems so sophisticated."

Anna looked above her glasses at me. "I picked her because of your age and your coloring," she said. "Nobody your age gets a Jack."

"Oh," I said. She gave me a look that told me to keep my mouth shut, so I did.

"Now shuffle the rest of the cards and cut them into three piles," she said. "About equal." The cards were a worn classic Bicycle deck, with a red pattern on the back. They had been shuffled so much they didn't give much resistance when I bent them. Anna gathered the three piles I made and laid a layer over the cross pattern and the vertical line. There were ten cards showing in all. She studied the matches she'd made and looked up at me. "There's no answer to your question, Ava," she said. "I don't see any signs of Collis. But who's this other man?"

"Must be Joshua," I said.

She shook her head and laid another layer of cards on top of the cross. "No, not a boy. It's a man. Blond-headed, light eyes. The Jack of Diamonds, right next to the King of Spades means he's coming back into your life. Watch out for him," she said. "He thinks he can control you." It could be Jason, but he wasn't blond. I wasn't sure what he wanted from me. Could be she just saw me working at the clinic.

"What about a move? Do you see if me and Joshua are leaving? Do you see us far away?" I was leaning closer. She leaned back and took a sip of water from the grandma mug.

"I don't see you leaving out of Iona any time soon," she said. "Not now. Looks like you have to do something here before you get to make a decision. There's a journey too, and a woman leaving your life."

"A death?" My throat tightened. I half expected more deaths. Things came in threes, and I had only had one so far. I almost wanted to hear of two deaths, so I could breathe a little easier.

"No. Nobody's gonna die. It's just somebody moving on. Or you moving on. Don't nothing stay the same, Ava. But you know that."

"What about Joshua? Do you see anything about him?"

She looked at me then laid another layer of cards, "Joshua's best when he's alone. He's not mad anymore. At least not at you."

"What else do you see?"

She laid out the rest of the cards and studied them for a while. "Not much. Except for that man. Sorry I didn't see any more for you, Honey."

"Thanks, Anna."

"I wouldn't do it for just anybody," she said. "Don't put too much faith in it." She swept the cards into a pile and tapped the edges of the pack against the table until they were even and would fit back into the box. She was done with it, even though I had a million more questions. She got up to walk to the front of the store. I followed.

"You hear about what happened up at Case's Creek?" she asked.

I shook my head. I was still thinking about the cards, the King of Spades, the seven of clubs, it all had to mean something important. I was mad that Collis still wouldn't speak to me, even now. He owed me that, at least.

"They had a rockslide, you know, up where they've done that reclamation work. Cover up, I call it. Like a cat covering its shit in a litter box. The dirt and rocks didn't hold, just slipped down into the road and the creek, even into people's yards. They left a big mess up there like always. Piles of dirt, slag, even old equipment, some people say. Benny Jenner came into the store not too long ago and said it was a whole lot of sludge about to break through and flood the whole community. All it'd take, he said, was a real good rain." She nodded toward the window where the rain was still pouring down.

"That's a crime," I said. "Somebody ought to call the EPA on them. They get scared when all the water quality people come in. At least they try to pretend for a few months after. I don't guess anybody wants to stick their neck out like that though."

"Somebody might have already," Anna winked at me. "It's an old neck." I wanted to be that brave. To stand up for this place before it all slid away, like Anna. I wanted clean water, strong mountains, a future I could see without reading the cards. "Don't forget your door latch. Ain't that what you come for?"

I took the small paper bag from her. She followed me out and locked the door behind me. It wasn't five o'clock yet, but she was done fooling with people for the day. Anna lived her life the way she wanted. Each minute.

22

Pine Mountain Thrust Fault

It was almost April. Micah and I had lunch every Friday at Cullen's since the beginning of the year. I knew it was her way of keeping an eye on me and making me go out in the world. I was more comfortable eating at my desk, surrounded by stacks of papers, lit up by the glow of my computer screen. Sometimes I'd get to the end of the day and not remember if I'd eaten the peanut butter and jelly I packed until I saw the plastic baggie in the trash can. Sometimes I forgot to eat at all. I'd found more than a couple of squashed sandwiches with the dark jelly bled through the bread when I cleaned out my bag at the end of the day.

"You eat like some kind of animal hiding in its nest, protecting its food from scavengers," Micah said. "That's how a lot of mental disorders begin. Lack of interaction." Like she knew anything about sanity.

"I was thinking interaction was the cause of most of my problems," I said. "That, and the friends I run with." But I agreed to eat like a human, with her, at least once a week.

Cullen's filled up by 11:30 on weekdays, especially on Fridays. We sit down around 12:00 after waiting in line, at our dark green vinyl booth by the window, and Deana brings us our unsweet teas before we even ask. Some days I order a grilled cheese and soup; other days, I have a chef salad. Micah gets a cheeseburger every time.

"Highlight of my week," she said.

"Me or the burger?"

"Both."

"Pretty boring," I said.

"Me or the burger?"

"Both." She set up jokes for me to make sure I could still smile. I always took the bait.

Lately, she'd been obsessed with geology. She wanted to know more about what was underneath these hills than the mining engineers did. "You've got to beat them at their own game," she said. She knew a lot more than I did, that's for sure. "You know how much limestone we're sitting on, Ava?"

"Tons of it?" I guessed, picking the triangular pieces of cheddar cheese out of my chef's salad and eating them first.

"Yes," Micah said, "but the rivers and rains keep wearing it down. And now, with all the blasting, this whole place could dissolve underneath us, and we'd sink right into the ground. It would just open and swallow us up." It was just like her to make it dramatic.

"Micah, these mountains have been standing for millions of years. We're okay for a day or two. Maybe a million years from now, it'll all slip away, but there are plenty of real things happening right now to worry about."

"But this was the ocean floor! The goddamned ocean, Ava! And you should see the brown water that comes out of my faucet right now because of what they're doing! Undrinkable! She smacked her palm on the table for emphasis. A few people in nearby booths looked our way. I raised my eyebrows to quiet her, but she kept on. "You think I care who's watching? Half this town keeps an eye on my every move. Did I tell you somebody followed me home last night? Some 'coal keeps the lights on' nut."

"Did you call the police? Some of those fools are dangerous, Micah." If anything happened to Micah, that would be it. That would be all I could possibly take in this life.

"You think Talbert and his boys at the sheriff's office are really going to protect me? Who do you think lines their pockets? I've got people looking out for me. Dwight drives by my house on the way home every night to check on me. I won't be afraid. It's what they want."

"Is this place really worth risking your life to save?" I asked her.

"I can't stop now," Micah said. "It's all I've got. And so much history is in these mountains! Imagine what got trapped in the rock, all those weird prehistoric fish, seashells. I've found a fossil of a shell before up on Pine Mountain, haven't you?"

"You're changing the subject. You've got to look out for yourself, mountains or no."

"Okay, I'll be careful. But haven't you found something from the sea on the mountain?"

"So?"

"So, it all broke apart and slammed back together. One side usually gives up and slides under, but not here. The land was too stubborn to move. That explains a lot about this place, don't it?"

"And you think I need to get out more?"

Deana came by and filled our glasses with more tea. "Your burger will be right out, Micah. You need more dressing, Ava? Some crackers to go with that?"

"No thanks, Deana, I'm good."

"Okay, Sweetheart, I'll be right back," Deana said. She was always gentle with me now, almost maternal. She seemed to feel somehow responsible for me finding Collis, even though it had nothing to do with her. I was meant to be the one to find him.

Micah took a sip of her tea, then started back in on me, "Speaking of going out more, I'm going out with James again. You'll be hanging out with old Alice."

"You don't know what I'm doing."

"Is that a fact? Do tell."

"I don't know yet, but it will be more exciting than talking about rocks with your doctor," I took a bite of my salad, so I wouldn't say anymore.

Deana came over with the hamburger to save me. "Hot plate," she said. "Be careful. Anything else I can get for you ladies?" Micah took a big guiltless bite of the burger.

"No thanks," I said. The room was full now, and the chatter and clanging of forks against plates made it hard to keep our conversation quiet. I didn't want anyone else to know about Jason and me. I wasn't sure about much, but I did know I was lonely, and a little bored, which was a big improvement from being exhausted just by getting out of bed and going to work.

"You were saying?" Micah said.

"I'd rather talk about rocks," I said.

"Suit yourself," she said, finishing another bite of her burger. "This place will be pock-marked with dug out mines and sinkholes soon, just like the moon."

"It's already the moon. Have you seen the strip job up at Carver's Fork?" The world was crumbling around us. I was beginning to see things the way Micah did. Maybe I looked like the moon inside too. I could see the door from my side of the booth. It opened and Brianna Roberts came in. "There's one of my new clients," I whispered to Micah.

"Where?" Micah said. She turned around in the booth and stared at the door.

"Don't be so obvious!"

Micah slowly turned her head to the right. She was still too obvious. "The skinny one with the crazy hair? Looks like an addict to me. Pretty rough looking to be so young."

"I know, but she says she's clean now."

"Don't they all say that?" Micah dipped a fry in ketchup and stuck it into her mouth.

"Most of them, yes. But I want to believe her. It's something in her eyes. And she's real motivated. She's got a little boy."

"Well, that doesn't make her new and different around here, does it? Even kids have kids."

"I know. But still, there's something that makes me think she's telling the truth. Maybe I could at least get one of these kids back on track." Micah shook her head. I watched Brianna slide onto a stool at the counter and order a Coke. Deana handed it to her, then gave her a clipboard with a sheet of paper and a pen attached. "See," I said. "She's filling out a job application."

"That don't mean a thing," Micah said. "Deana will make her do something about that hair. Can't do much about the tattoos. Why does everybody need to have tattoos these days? Lord, I don't know which one of us has the more depressing job, me trying to keep the mountains from being ripped apart, or you trying to hold the addicts together."

"I hold families together. Sometimes, anyway. They'll tear up the land to get to the coal, till the last speck is gone. Then they'll get the gas. We can't stop them, Micah. They'll roll right over us."

"Watch me do it," Micah said. "And I better get back at it. Tell Alice and Joshua I said hey." She pushed her plate toward the center of the table and drank the last of her tea. I had eaten all I could.

"Be careful," I said. "I'm serious. I don't look good in black." I left some money on the table for Deana and walked over to the counter.

"Mrs. Maynard, um Ava, hi," Brianna said. "I was meaning to call you today. Can I put you down for a reference?" She pointed to the paper with her pen. "I'm applying for a job here. They said they might need somebody weeknights."

"Sure," I said. "Hey, Deana!"

"Yes, Doll?" Deana moved over to the counter.

"This is Brianna."

Deana looked at me then took the clipboard from Brianna, "She one of yours?"

I nodded. "A hard worker. Give her a chance."

"I'll get back to you," she told Brianna and turned to fill another drink.

"Thanks, Ava!" Brianna looked giddy as any teenage girl.

23

By and By

The sun pushed the first faint streams of light into the dark sky as Joshua, Jonah, and I walked through the parking lot of the Neko Freewill Baptist Church. We joined the twenty or so people from Micah's group who were congregating near a white Ford Econoline van with Neko Free Will painted on the side in blue letters. I promised Micah I'd meet here at five thirty to help arrange rides to the state capitol, but now I wasn't sure why I said yes. I wasn't much help, just company. I had never done anything like this, but Micah said she needed me, and she'd been there for me more than ever now.

Joshua begged me to take him along. "We've been studying the mountains in school," he said. "Micah came to Mrs. Anderson's class and told us all about it. They blow the mountains apart and take what's inside and there's nothing left, Mama, just a big mess. We need to tell the governor about it." I tried to look firm, but he gave me his saddest look, big eyes like Collis.

"Oh, all right. You can come, but only if you stick right beside me." Collis was probably rolling over in his grave knowing I'd take Joshua to protest against the coal companies, but he wasn't here to say anything, was he?

"I will. I promise!" Joshua said. "Can we bring Jonah too?"

"If it's okay with his mom." Anita said yes too.

"Dwight, are you driving your truck or the church van?" Micah asked. She held a clipboard and started checking off something with a pen. She'd been up for hours and looked fully alert. The rest of us were groggy and slow, many sipping steaming coffee from thermoses, murmuring hellos and good mornings.

Dwight was a big man, maybe two hundred seventy-five pounds, with a full dark beard. His clothes were ironed with perfect creases, even his jeans. He smelled like a mixture of soap and musky aftershave. I, on the other hand, had thrown on jeans I wore the day before and a blue T-shirt that said Kentucky across the front in a curly script, my hair pulled into a ponytail. Next to Dwight, I felt like a mess, but it was the best I could do this early in the morning.

"I got the van," Dwight said. "I can fit twelve, I think. Long as they're not too big." He winked at me. Four or five people were already inside the van, waiting to go.

"Good," Micah said. "Ava, you, Jonah, and Joshua can ride with Dwight." Dwight's brother was doing time for cooking meth in his basement. His sister-in-law had been shot in the head in a raid and was in the nursing home in Hubbard, trying to re-learn how to swallow. Dwight ended up with their seven-year-old daughter to raise, even though he was only twenty-three. His size somehow made him seem older, more mature. He had found Jesus and joined this church about the same time he got in with Micah's group. He said it gave him something good to focus on.

I wondered how so many people did it. The funeral marquee and the county jail were always full. I wondered if I was dooming my own son by keeping him here. I wondered what we'd have left if I made him leave.

"Let's get moving!" Dwight said. "I sure hope the governor's ready for us!" A few people cheered. Joshua gave the two-fingered whistle he'd been trying to master.

I sipped more coffee to clear my head. It was still dark out, even though we were calling it morning. We had to tell the governor to stop the destruction of the mountains, but I doubted he would listen. It had been a long time since I was as hopeful as Joshua and Micah. I had almost gotten to the point where I planned to move on when everything had been blasted down, to get away. But I said I would be here, so I was.

Micah finished sorting everybody into cars and gave each driver a sheet of paper with directions to the capitol and everybody's phone number, in case we got split up. Some cars took off in search of more coffee and biscuits before they hit the highway.

"Let's load up, Ava," Dwight said. Jonah and Joshua hopped into the middle seat next to a thin woman who wore a T-shirt that said, "I Love Mountains!" and pristine white Keds. She grinned at the boys.

I sat in the front passenger seat. It was way too early for conversation. All I could muster was, "buckle up, boys." They obeyed then leaned toward each other to share Jonah's video game. It beeped and popped, even with the volume down, but it kept them happily occupied. I was glad Joshua had a friend here. Lord knows Anita had taken Joshua enough for me.

"Give 'em hell, Ava," Anita said when I picked Jonah up the night before. "I wish I didn't have to work." She'd come to Iona as a Vista volunteer and still leaned all the way left. She wanted to make sure Jonah got a good dose of protesting in. "And Ava, let me know if you need anything to help you sleep."

"Thanks. I'm okay." I was trying to keep as far away from any kind of pills as possible, the longer I worked at the clinic, the more I saw. Anyone could become an addict. Even me. I'd learned to make peace with waking up at 3:30 every morning, trying to do breathing exercises, staring at the ceiling for an hour or so, then slipping off back to sleep for an hour around six. This morning, I just gave up at four and got dressed.

Dwight turned on some gospel music and eased out onto the highway. His little niece hummed along as Dwight sang: "We are tossed and driven on the restless sea of time / Somber skies and howling tempests oft succeed a bright sunshine." We followed the taillights of Micah's sedan. It only seemed right that she should lead the charge. A whole convoy fell in behind us and looking back at the lit-up string of cars, I thought maybe something good could come out of this. Maybe we could save this place after all. Dwight sang on. "We will understand it better, by and by."

We watched the sun come up just as we got out of the hills, near Camden. I couldn't help but notice the Quick Stop as we drove past. My mind went to Collis's face, handing off Joshua, the pock-marked teenage check-out girl Collis flirted with. That could have been today or a million years ago.

The other passengers were chattering away. Joshua and Jonah were making up stories behind me. Dwight and I had run out of conversation, or at least I couldn't keep my end of it up. As we drove through Lexington, I wanted to veer off toward the house we'd lived in so briefly. It held something we could never recover, and I knew we'd never go back there, even if I could get us out of Iona. Finally, we arrived in Frankfort. We pulled up to the capitol building just before nine, poured out of our cars and joined a group of about fifty people.

"Okay, everybody," Micah said. The whole group hushed to listen to her. "If you don't want to be arrested, remember to stay in the lobby. Those of us who go into the governor's office have to be ready to be cuffed. Remember the principles of nonviolent protest. I, for one, will sit there until they cart me off, or until the governor talks to us, whichever comes first."

I grabbed Joshua and Jonah by the shoulders. "Stick with me, boys. Jonah, your mama would kill me if anything happened to you. We're just going to stand out in the rotunda and sing, okay?"

"We know, Mom. You told us before."

"Yes, ma'am, Mrs. Maynard," Jonah said.

The rotunda was a round white marble hall, with a domed roof. Voices echoed in it. Micah led the march with a big banner that said "I Love Mountains" in red letters. Dwight was beside her, with a bullhorn, leading the chants. "Save the Mountains! Save the People!" he yelled. Everybody yelled back in a call and response. Once we got inside and the sitters planted themselves, we broke into "We Shall Not Be Moved." Micah was glowing.

The governor's people had expected a protest, but not all this. They'd expected a bunch of hippies, not kids, church folks, and old people. The politicians were falling all over themselves trying to say the right thing, that they needed to look into it more, that they would comment later, none of it was genuine. The TV cameras were rolling. The governor would speak with us when his schedule allowed, they assured us. Dwight started up with "Go, Tell It on the Mountain," and it seemed to reverberate off the capitol dome.

Three policemen came toward our group. "We are asking you to leave. If you don't vacate the premises immediately, you will be arrested," the tallest one said. I grabbed the boys' hands and pulled them back out of the building. Dwight took a head count once we got out of the heavy double doors.

All but six of us got out then and gathered on the wide marble steps outside, but we couldn't keep track of what was happening inside. We leaned in the double doors to see, but the cops blocked the opening. "If you enter the building, you will be arrested!" one near me shouted. It seemed they were trying to silence us, trying to keep the truth from getting out. Micah was right, we had to speak out for the mountains and the people in them, or we would all be forgotten, even if that meant the coal companies pulling up stakes. I was scared, but I felt energized too. I was speaking out, and it felt good.

Micah and five others stayed to get arrested and get some publicity for the cause. I could hear them chanting, "Save the mountains! Save the people!" through the thick glass doors the cops were guarding. I saw the cops lead Micah and the others toward the doors, hands bound behind their backs with giant twist ties. We chanted and cheered them as loud as we could as they were pushed past into the back of a police van, then we followed them to the police station and waited.

By the time we got Micah, the other two women, and three men who'd been arrested for unlawful assembly out of jail, it was suppertime. Save the Mountains paid the bail, but our lawyer had to do some talking to get things moving. Everybody was lit up with excitement; the boys couldn't sit still; the rest of the group couldn't stop talking. Micah was as happy as I'd ever seen her when we filed into the first diner we could find off the highway.

The governor had agreed to sit down with Micah and some other board members at a later date. She thought he'd have to keep his word, since it had all been televised and shared on social media. He would invite the mining company executives too, but something was going to happen. We might make something change. I was beginning to believe in the power of Micah's protests, like I had always believed in her. We were worth saving.

In the diner, Dwight gave the blessing before the dozen or so of us tucked into our sandwiches and fries. "Dear Heavenly Father, thank you for keeping our brothers and sisters safe. Thank you for giving us strong voices and giving us the strength to use them to save your people and your creation." We all said Amen. I hugged the boys, high fived Dwight, and for the first time in a long time, I felt like I belonged to something that would last.

24

Ephemeral Stream

We worked our way back into our various routines a week after the sit in. It turned out the governor was booked, or so he said, for a month. That would give him time to build a protective shell of lobbyists and excuses. Micah was pushing for a meeting sooner. She was back and forth between Frankfort and Iona every couple of days. I heard clips of her speaking on the evening news, but she never had time to talk on the phone.

I was with another client, a retired miner named Jimmy who had been clean for two months. I had just sent Jimmy toddling toward the door with his oxygen tank when Kayla buzzed me at my desk. "There's a Mr. Johnny Roberts on the line for you, Ava," she said. I took a deep breath to calm myself, but my heart kept racing, and my thoughts kept pace. I'd been doing my homework on Johnny. He'd done two years for possession of narcotics, but he'd never been held accountable for the other awful things people speculated he had done, extortion, distribution, burning people out, armed robbery. Some people said he'd moved on to meth production, that he'd hooked up with some cooks in prison, but nobody had any real proof. I still couldn't find out for sure what he'd asked Collis to do, buy, sell, shop or worse.

Pain pills were easy to come by here if you were good at shopping for doctors. There was plenty of pain in mining work, so it started out legitimate, then grew into addiction. Doctors were corrupt, or scared, stuck in the mountains paying off school loans. Some of them caved and doled out the "hillbilly heroin." I'd heard some of the production had moved to Mexico, since the feds were getting serious about it, but that still didn't seem to make it harder to get. People like Johnny Roberts kept their customers well supplied. Pills and meth were easier to come by than alcohol in this dry county. I didn't know one family in Iona that hadn't been touched. All the results of this ended up on my desk, and Johnny Roberts, the king of it, wanted to talk to me.

"Ava Maynard. May I help you?" I said, in my most professional voice, even though my heart was pounding so hard I was sure he could hear it.

"Yes, Mrs. Maynard. I don't believe I've had the pleasure of your fine company in some time. But I'm gonna see you soon, I'm sure. You see, I got a niece, Brianna, says she told you a bunch of stories on me. And it seems you helped her put in some restraining order, says I can't come on my own property, my own fucking mother's house? I'm wanting to know is she telling me the truth, or is this little whore lying like she does about everything else?"

I had been trained to deal with this kind of anger and irrationality, but that didn't make it any easier. I took a breath to steady my voice. "I did advise Miss Roberts on several matters," I said curtly, "but all my clients' information is confidential, Mr. Roberts. I'm sure the Hensley County police will notify you if there's a restraining order against you."

"I'm sure they will, but I wanted to settle this up with Brianna before it got to that. Don't you worry, though, I'll keep in touch. You never know how we might help each other. By the way, Mrs. Maynard, I'm real, real sorry about your loss. Some people, like Collis, just can't take the pressure. Looks like that'd be a big ass mess to clean up, what with a pistol in the mouth and all. I doubt if that rock wall will ever come clean. If Collis had been thinking, he could have faced the other direction, to save on clean up. Don't you think? But he wasn't much of a thinker, now was he?"

"Don't ever call me again!" I yelled. He hung up, but I couldn't let go of the phone. My whole body was shaking. This town was so small, so rotten with corruption, Johnny could know the details of how Collis was found. He was on the search team, but as far as I knew, he didn't go in with the recovery crew. It was a crime scene. Had he been there? Had Collis been pushed? Had someone else killed him?

I couldn't let Johnny get to me. I knew that was how people like him worked. What I had to do now was find Brianna and find a way to keep her safe. Keep myself and Joshua safe too. I searched my computer for Brianna's number, but it wasn't in the system, so I buzzed the front desk. "Hi, Kayla. Can you find me a number for Brianna Roberts?" She was in a few weeks ago, a new client? Thanks."

The phone rang and rang. Finally, I got a message, "You've reached Brianna. I can't come to the phone right now, but I'll get right back at you!" I hung up and tried again, in case she was screening calls, but I got her message again.

"Brianna, it's Ava Maynard," I said. "Call me as soon as you can, okay?"

Deana had given Brianna a few hours a week bussing tables and doing dishes down at Cullen's. Maybe she would know more about where Brianna was and what was going on. This time of day, after breakfast but too early for the lunch rush, Cullen's was empty, except for three old men in trucker's caps and flannel shirts, sitting in a booth, nursing their coffee mugs and telling stories in a low hum. One of them smiled at me. I nodded at him and smiled. He had been the butcher at the Save A Lot when I was a kid. Deana was alone at the counter, sorting silverware.

"Hey, Deana," I said. "Brianna around?"

"I ain't seen that girl all week. Should have known better. She turned out to be no count, Ava." Deana started making a new pot of coffee. "You want a cup?" she asked.

"No thanks. I'm sorry, Deana. I thought she might work out. You know her uncle is Johnny Roberts?"

"Good Lord. Them Roberts is sorry. Poor Catherine died without a soul around her. Every one of her children's into dealing drugs. Now all them kids want to do is to take her house."

"Brianna was with her grandmother when she died. She moved down here from Cincinnati to take care of Catherine." Only now could I see how what I had wanted to be the truth might not be the truth at all.

"That's not the way I heard it. Sarah Bamburg told me Catherine was found after lying in the floor for two days, face down on the living room carpet. Wasn't nobody around until the UPS man tried to make a delivery and seen her. Said the blood had already pooled bad around her neck. They had to bury her in a scarf to cover it. I'd say you're lucky to get shed of that girl. She's probably in with her uncle. That house sets way back from the road. They could do a lot of bad out there and get away with it. It's a lot of money to be made."

"A lot of trouble that comes with it too. Still, I'm not sure she's as bad as you think."

"Hard to tell these days," Deana said. "Ava, you sure you're safe?"

"Safe as any of us. I think I will take a cup of coffee to go if you don't mind, black."

I walked back up Main Street to the office, past the line at the Baptist Church for the food pantry ministry. I thought I might see Brianna there, but I didn't. I saw plenty of regulars, though, and I waved as I passed. A few waved back.

When I walked into the office, Brianna was waiting for me in the reception area, reading *Parenting* magazine. "You here to see me?" I asked. I almost expected this, like I could somehow conjure her, or she had maybe been watching me too. Either way, she'd have to keep up her act, tell me what I wanted to hear and make me believe it was somehow close to true.

"Yeah. I got your message. Everything's blown up this week. I need to talk to you," Brianna said.

"Come on back," I said, leading her down the hallway. "It can't be any worse than I imagine." She followed me quietly back to my office and shut the door behind her.

"I heard my uncle called you." Her hair had grown out a little in the month since she had been here. Her roots were brown, and the streaked part was pulled back into a low ponytail. Her eyes still looked sunken in, and she was a little thinner, if that was possible. Her wrist bones bulged out like big marbles.

"Yes, he did call me, asking about you." I was cautious with her now.

"I'm going back to Ohio," she said. "He's crazy. I know he would do something to me and my baby if he got the chance. He promised he would."

"What about the restraining order?"

"Turns out, everybody needs a favor around here. Johnny's always willing to help them, for a price."

"You're not clean, are you?" I raised my voice more than I meant to.

"I am, Ava, I swear I am. I just needed some cash. Washing dishes didn't get me enough money for food. I did a little deal for Johnny, just to get him off my back. He gets to everybody eventually. He just needs to see a little tiny bit of weakness, a little desperation. He checks to see who's been laid off, then goes to help them like he's some kind of friend, loans them money, everything. He bought me diapers and formula when I was broke. It makes you feel like you owe him something. You ought to know that."

"He hasn't got to me."

"No, I guess not. But maybe your husband? That's what I heard anyway." She leaned back in her chair, stuck her hands in her pockets.

"What did you hear?"

"He was real good on the guitar, wasn't he? Johnny liked that about him, liked having him around for company. Coal mining brothers and all that. I get sick of hearing all that."

"What do you know, Brianna?"

"I just heard Collis was a delivery man. Low level. Sometimes, he'd shop doctors. You know. Everybody does that, making appointments, trying to get prescriptions to sell. It's not like he did anything violent. At least not that I know about."

"I think you need to go," I said. I could feel the blood drain from my face, the ice pick in my gut. Brianna watched me for a minute. She shook her head.

"I'm sorry, Ava. He can get to anybody. Good people too."

"I don't need this," I said. "Come back when you're really clean." I practically pushed her out the door. I had accepted what happened to Collis. It was depression, the lowest of his many slips into the depths. I could understand that. He wasn't able to live with us split apart. At least he wasn't able to live without Joshua. Had I really not known him? Had he been a criminal? Had he been murdered?

A heavyset woman was just leaving Gabe's office. "I'll see you next month," he said. I nodded at her as she passed me.

"Gabe," I said. It wasn't as loud as I hoped, or as steady. It came out in a raw whisper. "Gabe!" I stood in the threshold of his office.

"What's wrong?" My whole body ached. Gabe could see that.

"Collis—what did you know? Why didn't you tell me?"

"Come in and sit down, Ava." He closed the door and sat across from me at his desk. I was the client now.

"Brianna Roberts told me her Uncle Johnny got to Collis," I said. "He smoked pot, Gabe, but he was not a pill head or a junkie. I know he wasn't. Was he? Please tell me he wasn't selling for Johnny. Or doctor shopping. Or roughing people up. He wouldn't do that, would he, Gabe?"

Gabe came around the desk and sat in the chair beside me. He took my hand and held it, as if to still it. He was calm and cool when he spoke, but I was on fire. "Ava, what difference does it make now? Collis is gone. Let the dead rest, Honey. Give yourself a little peace. You and Joshua are settling back into a good life. You can't believe every addict, recovery or no, who walks through that door. They don't even mean to lie. It's just what they do." He squeezed my hand, but I pulled away from him.

"I need to know what was going on." The room felt unbalanced, and I wished for something, anything to steady me, to steady the world. I needed to know if maybe somebody like Johnny pushed Collis toward that mine and that end.

Gabe leaned forward in his chair, "Ava, listen to me now, Collis killed himself. The way he was sitting, there's no way anybody else did it. I talked to the cops at the mine. There weren't any other footprints there but yours and his. No signs of any other person. I thought about it too, but it looks like this was Collis's own plan. You said yourself he was depressed. It wasn't the first time he'd thought about it. Maybe not the first time he'd tried."

"Maybe so, but I wonder what made him feel that was the only way out right then. I thought it was me, the move, Macy leaving, but now..."

"All I've heard is he was considering doctor shopping for Johnny. Here and in a couple other counties. That's all I've heard. Just considering it. It didn't seem worth telling you once he was gone. You've had enough to deal with. We can't none of us claim to be perfect, can we, Ava? Let it go." I got up, feeling like I was going to throw up. Even Gabe forgave these people and this crazy place. "Let it go, Ava!" Gabe called after me, but he didn't follow me. I couldn't stop thinking of Collis and how little I had known. How had I not known?

When I got to Alice's, she wasn't home. Maybe she had known the whole time. Maybe she had allowed Collis to go toward trouble without trying to stop him. Maybe she condoned it, and anything he wanted would be fine with her. I was in the kitchen when she came in with bags of groceries in each hand.

"Can you help me get these in?" she asked.

"Sure," I said. I followed her out to her car and grabbed four plastic bags. She carried the gallon of milk in one hand and a bag in the other.

"Alice, did you know Collis was shopping?" I said, trying to make it sound like a casual question, shifting the bags as I opened the back door and let her walk through ahead of me.

"Shopping for what?" She sat the gallon of milk and the bag on the counter and crossed her arms across her chest, like she had caught a chill.

"Doctor shopping, for Johnny Roberts. Did you know he was trying to get doctors in three or four counties to write him a prescription for pain pills, for oxy?"

Alice didn't answer at first and in that slim pause, I realized she would never tell me the whole truth. She didn't want to admit that Collis had fallen, and that she had done nothing to try to stop it. She would do anything to protect Collis's memory, the one of the son she loved, not the one who had drifted away from us.

"What in the world are you talking about, Ava? Collis would never do something like that." Her eyes said different.

"How can you be sure, Alice? He was desperate to stay here."

"My son would never do such a thing."

"Can you say that, Alice? He had changed. You know that."

"Maybe he wasn't the only one who changed, Ava." Just like Collis, Alice knew the quickest way to get to me. "The only thing he was desperate for was to get you and Joshua back." She glared at me and I realized she blamed me for pushing him to leave, that somehow, she saw his death as my fault and not his. I blamed her just as much.

Alice pulled her cigarettes out of her purse and lit one right there in the kitchen, daring me to say something about that too. I started unloading the groceries quick as I could. It was all I could do about anything.

"Even you, Alice? Why can't anybody around here tell me the truth? I'm going to find Joshua and me a safe place to stay," I said, "until I can get us out of here all together."

"Don't be foolish, Ava. Stay here. There's all kinds of talk goes around Iona. You just can't believe everything you hear."

"I don't know what I believe, Alice. Or who," I said. "You knew there was a reason, but you let me think it was my fault. I think you wanted me to think that."

Now she looked afraid, eyes wide, like Joshua and I were just a part of Collis and she couldn't bear for that part to go away too. "I want you all to stay here, Ava. Please," she said. "Don't take that baby away from me." She took a deep breath and stubbed out her cigarette in the stainless steel sink, rinsed the ashes down the drain and threw the butt in the trash.

For a minute, I couldn't get enough breath to say anything. I hadn't thought there was anything worse than what I had already seen. I had thought that our little family was somehow immune, protected. Alice had known better. She let me believe we were better, stronger, than most people around us. The whole town seemed to be falling in on us, rotting from the inside.

Alice couldn't stand my silence, so she filled it, "If Collis did anything like that, and maybe he did, he didn't do it to hurt anybody, that I know for sure. Collis would never hurt anybody. You have to forgive him, Ava."

"I don't have to forgive anybody, Alice. Least of all Collis. Not you either," I put the milk in the refrigerator and slammed the door shut.

The only place I had left to go was to Micah's. If I asked, she would let us stay with her until I could figure something else out. Micah lived on the edge of the county on a little rocky farm her grandparents left her. It was near Cattle Island, where there was a surface coal seam and a gas pocket underground, so she spent a lot of time out there, fighting to keep the gas and oil companies off her and her neighbors' land. It was beautiful countryside, like something from a turn of the century photo, the old white clapboard farmhouse, the chickens in the yard, even the mountain behind the house was still standing as it always had, thanks to Micah.

I picked up Joshua from school and started driving toward Micah's place. I had already packed our bags. I wasn't going to say anything to Joshua about Collis yet. What could I say? Everybody was right about death not being the end. It was only the beginning of suffering for the ones left behind. Joshua was finally living a pretty happy life in his young world here, in spite of everything. I didn't want to mess that up.

"Where are we going, Mama?" Joshua said.

"Micah invited us to come out for a few days," I said. "She wants you to help her gather eggs." Joshua thought of Cattle Island like some pastoral Disney World, with chickens and cows and a mule. Micah was gone so much, or so busy sitting in front of bulldozers, she had to pay a neighbor to take care of the place. There was always a battle to fight somewhere. But she was home now, when we needed her to be.

"Hey!" she said, as we pulled up. "I was just about to check in on you."

Joshua jumped out of the car and ran to the barn. "I'm gonna feed the chickens!" We watched him run. It amazed me how he kept growing like any other kid.

"You okay, Ava?" she said. I got out of the car and slammed the door.

"No. I'm not okay at all. Can we stay here for a few days?"

"Of course. Something wrong with Alice?"

"I don't know what happened to her," I said. "I mean, she's fine, but she never was fine."

"Come on in," she pulled me gently by the arm toward the door. "I was just about to make some tea. You have bags to bring in?" I nodded. Micah went back to the car, grabbed my bag, and slung Joshua's bright red school backpack over her shoulder, while I watched her come back and forth.

"Here, I should help," I said, but I didn't move.

"You go on inside. I've got this," she said. Micah was the one person who had never let me down.

We sat with our tea at the table I'd eaten a thousand dinners at, in the kitchen that had not been changed since Micah's grandmother remodeled it in harvest gold and avocado green when we were in elementary school. I told Micah what I'd found out. Alice had known how deep Collis was in with Johnny Roberts. She knew he was shopping doctors, intimidating people, maybe worse, and she didn't tell me or try to stop it.

"What did you know, Micah?" I asked. "Did you know and not tell me too, like everybody else in this God forsaken place? Alice thought there was no way around it, that it wasn't Collis's fault. And I sent Joshua here to stay with him. I had to, I didn't have anybody else, but who knows what all went on around my baby?"

"Ava," Micah said, "you knew I thought maybe Collis had a habit. It crossed your mind too. I never thought it was serious, though. And he was good with Joshua. He was a good dad. I'd have known if he was dealing. I hear a lot of the gossip. He wasn't dealing."

"What was he doing then, exactly, Micah? Was he hurting people that Johnny didn't like? Was he making deliveries? Looks like I didn't know a thing about my husband at all. How can I know for sure he wasn't dealing and hurting people?"

"I guess you can't know for sure," Micah said. This took my breath away. She was right. I would have to live with doubt forever.

"Johnny Roberts made it sound like he had control over Collis," I said.

"And you trust Johnny Roberts over everybody else who actually loves you?" Micah leaned toward the table and looked straight at me.

"Collis smoked a lot of pot. Sometimes he sold it to friends," I said.

"Hell, that's been going on since high school," Micah said. "I heard a rumor or two he'd bought oxy, but there are rumors about me that would curl your hair. Some about you too, if you didn't know."

"But I know the truth about you and me, so the rumors don't matter. I thought I knew the truth about Collis. I loved him, Micah. Still do." I was pacing the room now, my voice rising. "What if he was selling, too? What if he killed himself because he couldn't find a way out of all the trouble he was in? Or someone killed him? What if I let that happen?" I finally said it out loud.

Micah didn't say anything. Joshua came running into the kitchen with three eggs in each hand. "Look how many they laid!" He grinned, and for a moment, I could see nothing but Collis in him, the way his whole face lit up with that smile.

"You could make a good farmer," I said. "Now go put those in the carton in the refrigerator."

Joshua carefully put the eggs in the carton. "Why don't you see if you can find something to watch on TV," Micah said.

"Ok," he said and walked to the living room. We listened for the TV to come on.

"I never felt like such a fool," I said to Micah.

She shook her head, "You're not a fool. You just love him." I couldn't respond. I just nodded. "I'll fix up the back room for you all. You put a pot of water on. I've got some pasta we can throw on and a jar of pesto I saved from last summer."

"Thanks," I said.

I woke before daylight with Joshua cuddled next to me in the bed, sleeping deep despite my restlessness. I tried to get back to sleep, but my mind wouldn't slow down. The circle of questions wouldn't stop. Did he love me? Did I really love him? Why did he have to die? How would we live? The rooster insisted on crowing at five. I figured if he was up, I might as well get out of bed too. I went into the kitchen and found Micah up, already working on her laptop at the kitchen table.

"Good Lord, don't you ever rest?"

"Not much." She got up and poured a cup of coffee, handed it to me, then refilled her own mug. "I have to stay one or two steps ahead of them. And don't forget, I have a meeting with the governor soon."

"How do you stand it here, Micah? All the death and destruction? Don't those pushers try to get to you?"

She didn't answer right away. She sipped her coffee and weighed what she was about to tell me. She didn't get caught up in her emotions like I did and fly off the handle. She always kept an inch or two above everything, so she could see the lay of the land. "I know everybody in town, and then some, Ava. I know where plenty of the bodies are buried. I stay out of the way of the users and dealers. They'll ruin themselves and I can't stop them. I try to fight for the land. The people left standing will have something to call home if I do my job."

"But sometimes the whole place feels ruined beyond repair. Maybe you're wasting your life."

"I have to fight for the part I love," Micah said. "This place is my home in a way most people in the world will never have."

"I'd like to have a home," I said. "A real one. I need to rent my own place. Then maybe I can work my way back out of here."

"You sure you don't need Alice? I'm pretty sure she needs you two." Micah sipped her coffee.

"Joshua and I need to have our own place. I don't trust Alice. Who knows what else she covered up for him?"

Micah stared at me for a minute, "You wouldn't do the same for Joshua?"

I hesitated a minute. I would do anything for Joshua, but this? "I couldn't let him get away with something like that, knowing it could kill him. Collis had choices, Micah. He made the wrong ones. Lots of the wrong ones."

"You can't forgive him, can you? Or maybe it's yourself you can't forgive."

I opened my mouth to tell her she was wrong in so many ways, but we heard Joshua pad down the hallway into the bathroom, heard the flush. "Go back to bed," I said, as he came into the kitchen." It's too early," I smoothed his hair down where it was sticking up at the crown.

"Can't sleep," he said, though he looked halfway there.

"Go back and try," I turned his narrow shoulders back toward the hallway, pointing him in the direction of the bedroom. "Read a book if you can't. I brought the one you took out from the school library, *The Book of Reptiles and Amphibians*, It's in your bag."

"I'll try," he said.

I had lost the energy to fight Micah, or to keep her from mothering me. We both knew she was right about one thing, I couldn't forgive anyone, least of all myself.

What I loved about this place seemed all gone, my family, the way people watched out for one another, even the physical rise and fall of the mountains, and the rise and fall of Collis's chest in the bed next to me, sleeping. I missed the way everybody was woven together and belonged to each other in endless patterns, holding each other up. I missed the way I came from a place with its own way of life. But what was once a comfort was now a trap. Was it worth lying to ourselves to be with people we loved, in a place we loved, with no rational explanations, except we were born to it?

25

North Branch

The house I rented was owned by Marvin Daly. He was four or five years ahead of me in school, but he'd married a girl in my grade, Tiffany Smith. She hadn't set foot in Iona since high school graduation. Marvin worked for a bank in Louisville now, and his mother had passed away two years ago, but he still couldn't bring himself to get rid of the house. I understood that, even if Tiffany didn't. He'd have a hard time selling it anyway. There were a lot of old houses for sale, and people who needed a place to live, but not many in Iona with enough money to buy them. People would come back to check on their houses, or to check on the old relatives still living there a few times a year. Then they'd drive out, fast as they could, back to the cities where they'd built a new life. It was hard to see a place struggling to survive, a place so much more beautiful in their imaginations. The North Branch neighborhood was right off Main Street, by the North Fork of the Kentucky River. We studied the river in junior high, and I remembered this, the headwaters, where the river first flowed from deep in the rock, begins on the western side of the mountain. The river flows northwest, through the Cumberland Plateau. It takes on Rockhouse Creek, the Carr Fork, and Troublesome Creek. Then it joins the South Fork and the Middle Fork to form the Kentucky. Eventually, it feeds the Ohio and flows out of the mountains all together. Somehow, one day, it gets to the ocean. So, the North Fork is powerful. The purest water used to be here, at the top of the mountain. There were still places to find a pure spring, but now most of it had been polluted by runoff.

This was the most modern neighborhood in Iona, built during the '70s, when everybody was wildcatting deep mines, when strip mining got big. Everybody had money for a new truck; some even had money for a new ranch style house. It had been a mark of social status to live in North Branch. I'd been to plenty of slumber parties there in junior high, plenty of cookouts in high school, but now it was almost a retirement village, or a ghost town. The twenty or so houses were evenly spaced on a small grid of streets named after flowering trees. We rented on Redbud lane. Every other street in Iona, with the exception of Main Street, wound along a creek, or snaked up a holler. This was not a place of straight lines, of point A to point B. It was a place of gaps and hollows, spaces between ridges. This was a place where stories and lives and streets meandered through the mountains, until they finally came to rest in one spot, sacred to that family, or the ones who recalled what the family had been, remembered that they existed at all.

The Daly's house was a wide low slung brick ranch with a deep front porch and black shutters. It had two bedrooms and a nice big kitchen with pine cabinets and an oval dining table with six chairs. Marvin hadn't gotten rid of the furniture or cleaned out any of his mother's lifetime of possessions, which was fine with me. My stuff was in storage in Lexington. In my mind, our stay here would end with the school year. I could take Joshua anywhere I wanted in June, pack a few boxes and hit the road.

It was odd though, to find Mrs. Daly's thick-lensed eyeglasses on the bedside table, as if she planned to read her Bible that evening, and her half-filled bottle of herbal shampoo still on the side of the bathtub. Maybe Marvin believed she'd be resurrected in the rapture and would need those glasses and shampoo. I sat on the porch after Martin gave us the tour and the keys and drove away. I asked her for permission. I promise we won't change anything, Mrs. Daly. We just need a place for a little while. We'll be out of your hair soon. It was important to keep on good terms with ghosts. You never knew how they could mess up the lives of the living. I believed in such things. Nothing fell from a shelf, no lights flickered, so I took it to mean Mrs. Daly wanted our company. I threw away the shampoo and an old toothbrush, but I kept the glasses in a drawer in the nightstand, just in case.

A few days later, I began unpacking the last of the boxes I left stacked in a corner of the living room. They were marked "odds and ends," so it took longer to figure out where everything went.

"Why do we have to have our own stupid place?" Joshua said. "Can't we just go back to Nana's?" He dragged his fingers along the living room wall as he came toward me, as if to mark them with his scent. I picked up another box and sat it on the coffee table.

"Joshua. Everybody needs their own space every now and then," I said. "We need some room and Nana needs to get back to her old routine. Now, stop running your hands on the wall. You're just gonna make it dirty."

"I thought it was ours," he said. "I want it to be dirty."

"Joshua Maynard," I warned. He put his hands in his pockets.

I didn't take Alice's calls until we'd been in Mrs. Daly's house a week. It was only when Joshua ran to the phone in the kitchen and answered it before I could stop him that I even said hello. "Hi, Nana. Yes, she's right here," he gave me the phone, despite the fact that I was shaking my head and whispering no!

"Hi, Ava. I'm just checking to see if you need anything."

"We're okay," I said. Joshua was shaking his head, as if to say no, we were not okay. I sat at the table and tried to ignore him.

"Well, you left Joshua's basketball shoes," Alice said. "I could bring them over on my way to the store?" There wasn't any getting around this. Sooner or later, I'd have to let her back in, at least let her see Joshua. He needed her.

"Okay," I said. "He's been looking for those."

"I'll bet he has!" she said. And with that, we made a silent contract to bury our betrayals, at least for a while, for Joshua's sake. Alice knew how she'd hurt me, but I didn't have the energy to argue anymore. Instead, we talked about the shoes and what she could bring us from the store. When I hung up, Joshua was still watching me.

"She's on her way," I said. He ran to the front porch to wait for her.

Joshua began to go to Alice's after school most days. He rode his bike to school from our place in the morning—it was just a few blocks—and after school, he rode down Main Street, took a right onto Cumberland Avenue and straight to Alice's driveway. We were only maybe half a mile from Alice's, but I needed that half-mile.

While Joshua did his homework and ate snacks at Alice's, I got to work on making the house ours. I gathered up all of the rest of Mrs. Daly's things and put them in boxes in the basement. I scrubbed out the musty smell of disuse in the bedrooms and sprayed Lysol everywhere. Even though the early spring air was still chilly, I opened all the windows. It was a sunny day, so it made the whole place feel warm and cheerful. Finally, I made a pot of soup beans and a pan of cornbread. That would fill the air.

When Joshua walked in the door early that evening, he said, "See, I made it just fine. It only took me six minutes. It'd probably only be three if I pedaled harder."

"You're fast, Baby. Just watch for cars."

He looked older than nine some days. His face was losing some of its soft roundness; his limbs were on their way to lanky. It looked like he'd take after Collis's lean, muscular build.

"I know how to cross the street, Mama."

"Okay," I said. "You hungry?"

"Yeah. It smells good."

"Go wash up and we'll eat."

One of my clients had come close to overdosing over Easter weekend. She was lucky, the guy she was with was greedy. He wouldn't give her as much as he took. That's what saved her. She spent the weekend high on something called "bath salts," a kind of cheaper version of meth, with the grand finale in the ED. This was the hot new drug. ODs happened a lot. Now, she was sitting in my office as I tried to negotiate with CPS to keep her kid with her, but it wasn't looking good. Foster care was hard to come by. Who the adult was and who the child was had little to do with age, and way more to do with who could make it through the day intact.

"I told you I'm clean as a whistle now, Ava. I'll stay that way. You watch," she said.

She was scrubbed clean with no makeup and faint purple circles under her eyes. Her t-shirt advertised Camel cigarettes, and like her jeans, it was freshly pressed.

"I hope you're right."

She was fidgeting, looking around my office as I waited on hold. "Mind if I step outside for a smoke?" She asked.

"Sure," I said. "Go on home. I'll call you Monday, after I hear more."

Kayla poked her head in my office door and handed me a stack of papers.

"What's all this?" I asked, sifting through them.

"This and that," she said. "Mostly WIC and Section 8 forms for you to sign. There is this one thing from Ohio, though. A custody paper. And don't forget, Gabe's taking us to the Mexican place over the mountain for my birthday lunch."

"Oh, that's right! Happy Birthday!"

"You're a sight," Kayla said, shaking her head. "I don't know how you get out of the house in the morning."

"Joshua's good at getting me together."

The papers from Ohio were for Brianna. She had found a job and a place to live in Cincinnati, had been clean for two drug tests, according to their records. They wanted to grant her partial custody of her son, and they wanted a letter from me, vouching for her character. The lines of good and bad were wavy. On a good day, a straight day, Brianna would make a great mother. I believed that. She was mature. She could handle pressure. She loved that baby the best she knew how. But on a bad day? Not for one minute did I believe she'd take her problems out on the kid. She might be selling though. She might use. What kept any of us on the side of good and clean? What pushed Collis over that edge? Maybe I could keep Brianna on the right side. I wrote the letter, signed it, and dropped it in the mail on the way to lunch.

We drove over the mountain, into Tennessee, to go to the Mexican place. We passed the old fireworks place, now shut down with a sign that said, Thanks for all the good years. "Seems so long since they closed down," I said. I wished I could go back to that night of fireworks on the mountain, before I left, before everything.

Gabe drove on, Kayla told about her birthday plans, and I held my arm out the window, with my palm spread open, to feel the warming air. This was my favorite time in the mountains. Tiny leaves had sprayed the trees with a fine green mist. Here and there, a redbud dared to announce its bold pink self to the world.

When I was Joshua's age, we lived near town, on Sanders Creek, and I'd run up the mountain every day after school. I had a perch on top of a rock shelf, and if I didn't want to be found, I could hide underneath it in the damp, metallic dirt. The mountain made a perfect spot for me, and in springtime, mom couldn't see me up there from the back yard. The trees hid me. She had Daddy mow a huge oval around our house and put a fence around it, as if she could keep our place separate from the mountain, but I knew we were part of it, and it was part of us. She might as well try to take the wet off water. Most days lately, I understood her urge to be separate from a place so full of heartache, but now, with my arm out the window, driving toward never-ending baskets of chips and maybe a mid-day margarita, I felt again the curve that had been carved in the mountain for me.

Soon enough, we'd be thick in deep summer green and staking up plants heavy with tomatoes, squash, and beans. It was considered almost criminal around here not to put something in the ground and tend to it until it gave you something back.

"You putting in a garden?" Gabe read my mind.

"Maybe just some tomatoes and basil, a couple of cucumber and pepper plants," I said.

"Well, I guess that means you're back home for good then?" said Kayla. "If you want to see those tomatoes grown, you'll be here through the summer at least. Then there's a fall garden, lettuce and greens. You'll want that. You can't leave once you start something growing. You might be here clear until December."

The waitress sat us at our usual table and started us off with waters and two baskets of chips, which we immediately dug into.

I was still thinking of leaving, starting new in a month or two, but I didn't want everybody knowing my plans. What difference did it make if I made plans anyway? I'd tried that before. I took a handful of chips and took my time chewing. "I can't seem to get out of here anyway," I said, finally.

"She can't leave us," Gabe said, "It's in her blood."

"Death, destruction, and poverty, you mean? That's in my blood? Great." I took a sip of my margarita.

"Not that part," Gabe said. "Or maybe just a little of it. I'm talking about the other part. You know, 'Being of these hills / I cannot pass beyond.' That's James Still."

"Well, James Still is wrong," I said. "I can go anywhere I want." All the way home though, those lines rang in my head.

26

Headwaters

It had been three weeks since our hike, and I hadn't talked to Jason since. He was on assignment in West Virginia. Each time he called, I ignored the ring and told Joshua not to answer, so the machine would pick up. He left messages saying he'd only been home once or twice to check his mail and get his laundry, but that he'd like to see me the next time he was home. Each time I picked up the phone to call him back, my memory of Collis grew as big as a real man in the room, and I put the phone back down. It's hard to un-marry yourself from someone in your mind, even if he's dead. Hearts stay locked in quiet ways. It still felt like cheating to think of being with Jason, like Collis might show up and find us out.

Jason was working on a story about a West Virginia mine disaster that ran way up the chain of command of the company. I was glad he'd been out of Iona for a few weeks, relieved not to have to make any decisions about him. It was Micah who pushed us toward each other again.

"Don't you think we should find something a little more exciting to do in this town than sit on your porch drinking beer, or sit on my porch throwing feed at my chickens? I mean, I've got my friend Alex in Knoxville, so I guess what I really mean is, don't you have anything more exciting to do?"

"Are you suggesting that I'm boring or you are?"

"I think you can figure that out," she leaned forward in her chair, staring directly at me. "I've got a date to see a band with a hottie in Knoxville. There will be wild sex. There will be food and wine. There will be absolutely no commitment. It'll be perfect."

I shook my head and took a sip of beer, "Hussy."

"And damn proud of it," Micah said. "Whatever happened to Jason Hayes?"

"Nothing."

"Really? Nothing? See what I mean? Boring."

"What am I supposed to do, follow him to Charleston? It hasn't been that long. Collis has just been gone since November."

"You don't have to be lonely forever just to show you loved him, you know."

"Since when are you an expert, Micah?" I wanted to reel the words back into my mouth before I finished speaking, but they streamed away like a prize bass on a line. Silence sat between us after the last word fell. I knew all about Micah's loss.

"Right. Only my sister," Micah said. "What the hell do I know about loss?"

Micah had lost her sister Jody when she was twelve and Jody was sixteen. Jody was driving down the mountain after a bonfire party at an abandoned strip job and got slammed into on the driver's side by a coal truck. Micah's parents still lived on Trace's Rock, but after Jody's death they seemed to age fifty years. Micah saw them once a week, brought them groceries, but they were more focused on Jody's death than Micah's life, as if they still could not believe it had really happened. So, Micah learned a little more about loss every day.

I still had my little brother and my parents in Indiana, even if they all thought I was crazy. It's important to have someone existing in the world alongside you, to know somebody who knew who you had been all your life. In death, all chance of reconciliation is gone, all you were with that person is buried. I knew the difference now.

"I'm sorry," I said.

"Yes, you are," she said. "Sometimes you are a sorry individual. You're not the only one to hurt, Ava. Not by far. You've still got a family."

I didn't talk to my brother often. Sometimes blood separated you as much as it drew you together. Even his accent was different from mine, flatter, like the land he was in. Now he was too busy with work to talk.

I called my parents on Sundays, just to check in. "How's everything at the end of the world?" my dad always said.

"Things are great here on the good end. How're things on your end?" I'd say.

My mom kept asking when I was "moving out of this mess." I'd just tell her it wasn't a mess, it was home, and then I'd put her on the phone with Joshua, to make her feel guilty for saying it. I still had the three of them though, which meant I still wasn't completely alone in the world, and my loss wasn't any worse than Micah's. She was my guide to surviving the world after death, the only person who could teach me how to breathe.

"You've got to come back into the world, not just for yourself. For Joshua, too," Micah said. We drank our beers and changed the subject to her next trip to Frankfort. We couldn't afford to lose each other.

⸻

Jason seemed surprised when I called him, but I had thought about what Micah said. "Is this a bad time?"

"Oh, no. I just, I've been waiting on some calls for work. I thought you'd be someone from Mine Safety."

"Well, I can let you go." I wondered if he had really been expecting some other woman, from here or in West Virginia. I didn't like the thought.

"No, don't. I'm glad it's you. I've been thinking about calling you too, Ava. I just didn't know if that's what you wanted."

"It is," I said. "I'd like to see you again."

"I'd like that too. I'll be back in town Friday."

"I'll be around then," I got the words out best I could, even though I felt nauseous.

"How about dinner at the Diner?"

"Sounds good," I said. "Seven?" After I hung up the phone, it took me a full minute to steady my breath.

Micah came over to watch Joshua. I didn't think it'd be right to ask Alice to babysit while I went on a date. Joshua would be spending Sunday with her anyway. I waited in the kitchen, where I could look through the window and watch every car that passed, and I swept the floor again for something to do. I was ready by 6:30. By 7:00, I was convinced Jason had changed his mind.

"Would you stop it?" Micah said, "He'll be here any minute." Joshua didn't seem bothered by the whole thing. If he was, he hid it well. Micah had promised him a game of Monopoly once I was gone.

He was ready to push me out the door when the truck finally pulled up. "Bye Mama. Come on, Micah," he dragged her off by the hand to the living room. "I want to be the wheelbarrow." I heard him tell her as I closed the door.

"Okay, I'm the shoe," she said.

I got into the truck, and I could smell Jason's soap. His hair was still a little wet, and he had shaved. He had a pressed shirt and jeans on, dressed up for Hensley County. I rolled down the window, since it was still a little warm at sunset, and spring filled the space. We rode in silence at first, then Jason turned on the radio, something from the seventies came on, familiar, good background noise.

"You look nice," he said. I had tried, at least. Micah did my hair and made me put on a little makeup. She'd picked out my outfit, too, even though I thought the jeans were too tight, the black shirt a little low cut. I had to trust her, though. I had already thought through as much of the date as I could bear. I told myself I wouldn't talk about Collis, or death. That sounded like a good start.

The Iona Diner was the only halfway nice restaurant in the county. That meant they put candles on the tables at night and used tablecloths. They still served canned vegetables and fried jalapeno poppers. If I had ever thought I could have a private life in this town, I was crazy. I knew all but four people in the restaurant, and now they all knew I was on a date.

I heard through the grapevine that Jason had been out with Amanda Vinessett a couple of times since we had been together. I wondered if he'd brought her here. I didn't know where else they would have gone. I shouldn't let it bother me, but it did a little. Maybe this was his way of letting me down easy. We ordered as soon as Myra Standfill came to the table to tell us the specials, then we sipped our waters.

"How's your work going?" I asked.

"Good, but I think I'm finding out more than I bargained for. This Macy thing goes all the way to the top." He seemed a little unsure of how much to say.

"They knew about the safety violations and didn't shut it down?"

He took another sip of his drink, as if to give himself more time to decide whether or not to trust me. "Looks like they've known for a while, and they shut down whistleblowers instead."

"Are you safe there?" People had been killed for knowing less. And for writing about it? That was asking for trouble.

"I think so. As safe as I am here." It was so much easier to talk about work, Iona, corruption, anything but ourselves.

"Do you know a lot about what's going on here? I mean, with the dealers?" I couldn't help myself.

"I know who to stay away from. I know who some of the major players are. It goes pretty deep around here. You'd be surprised at who all is involved. I'll write about it soon, when I get enough evidence."

"Don't you get tired of writing about all the ways this place is rotten? I miss your fishing and hiking articles."

Jason smiled. "Those were just getting me to this, Ava. Somebody's got to say something. I want to tell the world about what's happening to this place. I want to tell how it is now, the good and the bad, not how we wish it was, or how it used to be."

"You need to stay safe. Those people, like Johnny Roberts, they've made their own rules. They can turn anybody, looks like."

"I'm tough," Jason said. "They haven't gotten to me yet."

I wondered how long it would take for somebody to get to Jason. Did everybody really have a price? Did I? I took a bite of bread, a sip of tea then broke my own rule and asked what I'd really been wanting to ask all night. "Did you ever hear anything about Collis? If he was involved?"

Jason looked down at his plate and began to work on his salad. I had let the words get out before I could stop them. Talking about your dead husband was a sure way to kill any spark.

"I don't know. I hear a lot of things. I figured you'd know more about that than I would. I mean, Collis worked with Johnny in the mines, didn't he?

"Yeah," I said. "I just didn't know what all went with that."

"Roberts uses anything he's got. And men who've worked underground, it's a brotherhood, like the military. He abuses that."

"You think Collis was dealing for him?"

"I'm not saying that. There's nothing I could ever confirm. Johnny keeps his hands clean. He protects people who are loyal to him."

"I don't guess you can protect a man from himself, can you?" For a minute, we didn't say anything, just ate our salads. I wished I had kept my mouth shut. I wished I could separate the present and the past. Myra came over with our entrees, and we were saved. I began talking about how delicious everything was. I even made Jason try a bite of my lemon chicken. Then I turned the conversation back to Jason's job. I knew how to hurt Collis back, or to at least turn myself away from his memory.

"I never have seen your place, you know," I said.

Jason looked at me, slowly finished chewing his steak. "Well you know, I'm right above Noble's Hardware. The Nobles used to live there in the twenties, when they first opened the store. Then they moved onto Trace's Rock. It's a perfect little place for someone who's coming and going. You've probably seen the metal steps that go up the side of the building? The fire escape? I built that little deck up there, so I could sit out when the weather gets good. Mrs. Noble takes any improvements I make to the property off my rent. I've been working on it for a while."

"I'd love to see what you've done," I said.

"Want to come over for a drink? I'll give you the nickel tour."

We climbed the rickety metal steps of the fire escape and sat on the small wooden deck for a while, looking at the whole town of Iona and the mountains beyond. "What a view!" I said.

"It's a great place to watch the sunset." Over a few glasses of cabernet, we watched the sun slip between the mountains, and I liked this new view of Iona. "I did promise you the tour," he said, as the sky turned a deep navy.

"You did," I said. He led me through the small apartment, newly painted a light gray, with recently refinished heart pine floors.

"You've done a great job," I said. It was nice to be in a space that was different from all the houses I'd lived in here. It had possibilities for something new.

"I want to do more, but I've been gone too much. I'm gonna work on the kitchen next winter."

"I was hoping you'd be around for awhile," I said.

In the kitchen, with its worn linoleum and mismatched appliances, Jason took my hand and kissed it. "I'm so glad you came over," he said.

"Me too," I put my arms around his neck, pulled him close.

I hadn't been with anyone but Collis since I was seventeen. I hadn't even been with Collis much in the last two years. It's hard to love a man who's depressed, and then it's hard to believe you'll ever love another man. Jason knew that. I was the one pushing him forward. I leaned in and kissed him.

I wanted to hurt Collis, even if he was dead. I didn't care about Amanda Vinessett or anybody else Jason might be seeing. He didn't seem to be thinking about anybody else now. We kissed tentatively at first, then soft, but certain, until we pulled to each other. I led Jason through the living room, to the couch, to me, discarding each layer until we were touching skin to skin. I could tell he didn't trust that I knew what I wanted. Above his couch was a little skylight, and as we rocked back and forth, constant as a river wave, I clung to him for dear life and caught a glimpse of a slender fingernail of moon in the dark sky.

When I got home, Micah was asleep on the couch, with the TV still on, turned down low. She stirred and sat up as I shut off the TV. "Well?" She raised her eyebrows.

"Well, what?" I began straightening up the room, so I didn't have to look her in the eye, but she could read my face. I didn't have to say anything, and she knew not to talk too much about it.

"Good," she said. "Good for you. If you weren't going to make a move, I would have!"

"Micah! You'll wake up Joshua."

"Okay," she whispered, "but I still say good for you. Both of you."

"It's not like that," I said.

"What's it like then? Do tell." I threw a pillow at her. "Okay," she said. "Okay!"

I went into Joshua's room, sat on the end of his bed, and watched him sleep in the light coming in from the hallway. He looked so much longer, stretched out on his bed, and his batman pajama top pulled up a little, revealing his belly button. He looked younger too, more innocent with his hair swept off to one side, his eyes closed with that dark fringe of lashes, his mouth open a little, revealing his big new front teeth.

"Good night," I whispered in his ear. Then I kissed the top of his head.

"Good night, Mama," he said as I left the room.

27

Gravitational Pull

I was cooking dinner, tacos as authentic as I could make them from Save A Lot. They had gotten in a shipment of decent avocados and slightly wilted cilantro, which only happened about once a month, but made my world feel a little bigger. Joshua was working on his science homework at the kitchen table, labeling the concentric layers of the Earth and coloring them in. We had fallen into a routine, finally. That was one of the hardest parts of moving forward. Every day brought something brand new, something to be figured out and understood by evening. I craved order and structure. I wanted to get bored, to not be constantly reminded that every moment was so urgent or precious. I wanted to waste time, just because I could.

It almost felt like home here now. There were no traces of Mrs. Daly left in the house. I gradually moved her things to the shed, including her glasses. I had the windows open and smelled the faint scent of flowers, an overeager forsythia that bloomed early, and the new grass my next-door neighbor had begun to cut. I have seen golf courses wilder than his yard. His roses won 4H competitions. I wouldn't have to worry about a man like that dealing oxy or meth. Or, if he did, he'd at least keep it away from my house in some elaborate, orderly system.

There was such a transformation in the hills, and it seemed to spread to the people. They came out and sat on their porches in the evening, as if to see the show. Bulbs started to sprout. Joshua and I even went to Alice's to see if there was anything left of our azalea bush. Little tight buds had formed and were reluctantly beginning to loosen. It was hard to believe that in a few weeks, the buds would be lush clusters of bright pink flowers. It was hard to believe that a year ago, I was looking for jobs in Lexington and Collis was still alive. Our lives were unrecognizable from that now, as if a fault had erupted and built a new landform for us, still hot from the molten core and unsteady.

Alice came over for dinner twice a week. I was beginning to realize she had known down deep she was going to lose Collis, no matter what she did. "He was always running the roads, even in high school," she said. "I couldn't keep him home once he got his own truck. You remember that old Toyota, don't you? The one missing the back bumper? He loved that truck. I'd cook his favorites, pot roast, chicken casserole, so I could see him for a few minutes at night. It worked most of the time, even, well, even until the end."

"Mama, can you help me?" Joshua said, looking up from his work. He erased the line he had just written, then swept the pink bits of eraser from the paper with his hand.

"Sure, Baby, what are you working on?" I sat next to him at the table.

"Gravity. I'm supposed to make a poster on where it comes from and what it's for."

"Well, it draws us to the Earth's core, doesn't it?"

"The book says, 'Gravity's strongest at the Earth's surface. Any two bodies separated by any distance have a tendency to pull each other to themselves. The farther you move away from the center, the more you will experience gravity due to the sphere below you.' Can you help me draw that?"

"I'll try," I couldn't even draw a circle, mine looked more like an egg, but I helped Joshua color a cross-section of the Earth, with a smiling person on the green and blue surface, and a red core of molten iron in the center. Curved arrows went between the two, showing the path of attraction.

"When Daddy was underground, did he feel less gravity?" Joshua asked.

I stopped coloring the sky around the smiling man. "I guess so. I guess he felt less pressure underground. Maybe that's why he liked mining so much." I tried to hug Joshua, but he shook me off and kept coloring.

"There!" he said. "How does it look?"

"It looks great. Is that you on the surface?"

"No. I think it looks more like Jason," he said. "He's always smiling."

Come to think of it, he was.

A week after our date, Jason went back to Charleston to work on the Macy mine disaster story. I worried about him there. I only partly claimed him as a boyfriend, but I still worried about him like one. There was a lot of money at stake, a lot of corruption that went deeper than the mines themselves. If you could send men to work in a hole you knew might blow up at any moment, how hard would it be to run a reporter off the road?

We wrote letters to each other, like we lived in some other time. We were the only inhabitants of this rarefied world. I liked having physical evidence that he was thinking about me. There was innocence to handwritten ink on paper, and somehow, more privacy too. I wrote to him about work, about the newest hard cases I'd seen. He told me about the corruption in the mines, how the company skimped on safety equipment because it slowed down production and cost more. He told me how some men had quit, and others had families and saw no other way but to keep working there. It took a day or two from the minute the stamp was stuck until the letter reached either of us. It seemed a way to slow things down, and to make them more permanent at the same time. Each letter thrilled me and filled me with guilt. The last letter said he was coming back home for a day, then heading to Frankfort to do a story about Micah's meeting with the governor. "Would you meet me and stay the night? I miss you," he wrote. I read it over and over, just to make sure I wasn't reading something into it that wasn't there. It was there, I decided.

If Micah was with the governor, I'd have to ask Alice to watch Joshua. I'd have to tell her why I was going, but I didn't think it was her business. Not yet. There was always Jonah's house. Joshua spent the night there often anyway. Anita divorced Jonah's dad when Jonah was two. The dad had been a legal advocate for coal miners with black lung, but after they broke up, he moved to Louisville and was practicing corporate law. I never did care much for him. Now Anita moved a new man in about every six months. Usually, it was a bearded hippie guy passing through on his way to hike the Appalachian Trail for the spring, or a bluegrass musician with a series of gigs with the old-time greats. Her current man, though, had been there as long as Joshua and I had been back in Iona, seven months. His name was Jake, and he was supposed to be working on water quality issues, but I didn't think he did much more than hike during the day and get high with Anita at night. Anita made a pretty good salary at Stone Healthcare, so she could support him if that's what she wanted. She'd built a modern house up on the hill above North Branch, with a swimming pool and a hot tub. She'd always looked out for me, so I called her.

"Of course he can stay. I'd be happy to keep him," Anita said. "Jake has to go to Tennessee for a conference. The boys can keep me company." Even better, I thought. I could go without worrying. Or try to.

"Thanks." I needed to go, to feel like I was thirty-four instead of ninety-four. Micah was driving to Frankfort, meeting the rest of the Save the Mountains group at the capitol. She'd stay with a friend overnight and pick me up the next morning.

We dropped Joshua off at Jonah's house first. "Okay, Baby, call me if you need anything," I said. "Call me first, and if you can't get me, then call Nana."

"But Nana's closer."

"Call me first. We don't need to bother Nana. Plus, you'll be fine here." He hugged me tight. I had to let go first. Micah was waiting.

"He'll be fine," Anita put her hands on his shoulders. "Have a great time!" Jonah came out to meet Joshua and they ran off into the back yard. I envied that instant comfort.

"Call me if he needs anything," I told Anita. "He's been a little moody lately. Call me if you think he's upset."

"They'll have a blast, Ava. I hope you do too."

"Thanks. I owe you one," I said.

Micah and I drove off, and once I knew I was too far away to have any control over Joshua's life, I gave into the freedom. We were twenty again, singing our way off key to the city, watching the buildings grow taller as the mountains receded.

28

Meetings

The drive from Iona to Lexington was one Micah and I had made a hundred times as teenagers. She made the trip once even before she had a license, since her sister taught her to drive. She had an old gold Pinto her uncle fixed up for her that we'd driven there so many times, it could just about make the trip by itself. Gas was cheap then. Most people our age stayed in Iona on the weekends, drinking around bonfires started from discarded dozer tires on the flattened tops of strip jobs, going to the ball games. We did that too, but once we knew people at UK, once we had tickets to UK basketball games in the cathedral of Rupp Arena, we'd go up for a game, go to the mall, hear a band play, drink beer at fraternity parties we hadn't been invited to. It didn't matter as long as you looked cute and could pass for eighteen. Micah knew how to get us in anywhere. Collis would pile in with us sometimes, but usually, it was just Micah and me. We worked a lot of hours, me at the Save A Lot and Micah at Cullen's, to finance those trips. We bought ourselves some freedom, but the best part of leaving for a few days was always coming home, seeing that first swell of mountains around Camden, the narrowing of the road toward Iona, twisting and turning until it pushed us off onto Main Street. At least that's how I remembered it in high school. I felt like I owned the whole damn place. Or at least I owned half and Micah owned the other half. That was before my dad lost his job selling mine equipment and my parents moved away, before Collis and I married.

Micah dropped me off in downtown Lexington on her way to the Capitol. "Give em hell!" I hugged her, then shut the door to her Toyota, a world away and years beyond the old gold Pinto.

"You too," she honked as she drove off and stuck her hand out the window to wave. Micah still had another thirty-minute drive to get to Frankfort. Dwight and the others would meet her there. This time, it wasn't a protest. Save the Mountains was on the governor's agenda. He had agreed to at least consider regulating how the coal companies dealt with wastewater and overburden. Micah was ready to convince him that this wouldn't kill all his coal company backing, but elections cost a lot of money. All she had to offer was truth.

I sat in the coffee shop in the lobby of the towering, tempered glass Radisson Hotel, where I was supposed to meet Jason. Two men sat at another table in dark business suits, crisp papers spread across the table with just enough room for their coffee cups to perch on the edges. I held my cup in both hands to warm them.

"Can I get you anything else?" the waitress asked.

"No, thanks," I said. I waited for almost an hour, getting jittery from the coffee, watching cars pass outside the tinted windows. I read the paper. Then I gave in and ordered a piece of pecan pie. Now, Jason was an hour and seven minutes late. I tried his phone, but it kept going straight to message. Finally, my phone rang.

"Mama," Joshua said. His voice was quiet, a little unsure, like he had snuck away to call me in private and was afraid he'd get caught.

"Hey, Sweetie."

"When are you gonna be home?"

"I'll be home tomorrow night, Baby. What's wrong?"

"I just miss you." If I had my car, I would have driven straight back to Iona right then, but I didn't. I couldn't.

"I miss you too, Baby, but you'll have fun with Jonah. I promise nothing bad will happen to me or to Nana. Or to you."

"Can I go with you next time you go to Lexington?"

"Sure. We can go for a few days over Spring Break."

"You promise you'll be back tomorrow?"

"I'll be back tomorrow night."

"I love you," he said.

"Love you too." I hung up just as Jason walked up to the table, looking rushed, shaking his head in apology.

"Sorry," he said. "I had an interview I couldn't cut short, one of the miners' families. It was the only time they could all get together before his funeral. I almost got a ticket trying to get here." He slid into the booth beside me. I guess I had no real way of keeping track of him, or who he was with, or when he was telling the truth. I decided not to worry about it yet.

"Well, you're here now," I said. "Surely you can think of a way to make it up to me?" He took my hand and kissed it. I paid for my coffee as quickly as I could. We could eat later.

We checked in and didn't leave the room. This time, I didn't think of Collis whenever Jason and I touched. I was getting better at keeping my life with Collis stored in its own vault now, contained, so I could keep going. This time, when Collis did slip into my mind, or when some touch to my shoulder or hip triggered one of my million memories of him, I told him to go away, that I'd talk to him later. He usually obliged. Now, when I touched Jason, I thought of Jason, the solid curve of his shoulders, the shallow dip of his belly button, his long, narrow body warming mine. He held on to me tight and took his time, deliberate, starting with kisses across my collarbone and working his way down. He didn't seem to mind the rounded belly I couldn't seem to get rid of after Joshua, the full curve of my hips. I felt like he'd protect me from all the awful things our world offered. It had been a long time since I had felt this close to anyone, even Collis. I lay my head on Jason's shoulder, leaned my body sideways against his.

"You want to go get some dinner?" he said.

"I hear there's a great Thai place around the corner."

"That sounds perfect. Let me grab a shower."

I folded myself down into the pile of white sheets and looked out at the lights of the city. Maybe the world could go on. When my phone rang, I expected Joshua. "Hey?" I said, sitting up with my back against the headboard.

"Well, hello Mrs. Maynard. You are still going by Mrs. Maynard aren't you?"

"Who is this?" I sat up.

"I think you know."

"What do you want from me, Johnny?" I asked.

"Oh, I was just checking in. A neighborly call. Thought I'd keep an eye on things for you while you shacked up in Lexington. Everything's fine here at home, just fine. Looks like your boy's enjoying the movie. I could go in the house if I wanted. Anita would let me."

"Don't call me again!" I said. But he had already hung up. By the time Jason got out of the shower, I was dressed and on the phone to Anita.

"Anita, is Joshua there? Is he safe?"

"Ava?"

"Yes. I just need to know that Joshua's safe."

"Calm down, Ava. He's fine. They're just in here watching a movie and eating pizza. What's wrong?"

"Johnny Roberts called. He's watching Joshua. He said so."

"What are you talking about? Why would Johnny Roberts be calling you? You're not in some kind of trouble, are you?"

"No, nothing like that. Collis worked with him. And I helped his niece. He can't get to her through me. He said he could see inside your house. That you would let him in."

"Ava, nobody has been anywhere near here. I've been here alone with the boys all night. And I surely wouldn't let him in."

I sat down on the edge of the bed and steadied my breath, "Ok, ok. He called to scare me, I guess. I hate that it worked. You promise you'll call me if anything at all happens?"

"I promise I will," Anita said. "I swear I'll call if I even have a bad feeling. Do you want to talk to Joshua?"

I could hear Joshua in the space behind her, shouting, "Hi, Mama!"

"No, let him watch the movie. I can let that man get to me." I was sure Johnny Roberts really could see Joshua and Jonah whenever he wanted to. Either he, or one of the guys who worked for him could be right outside the window, watching every scene of the movie the boys were watching. He might even be able to see Joshua chew his popcorn or laugh. I was sure he had his reasons to want to keep me afraid, but I wasn't sure why he wanted to right now.

I couldn't relax, all through dinner. My head was really in Iona. I couldn't even escape it when we went to see an art movie at the Kentucky Theater, with its red-velvet-covered seats and its gold-painted filigree opera boxes. There was nothing like any of this at home.

"You okay?" Jason handed me the popcorn.

"What if he is watching Joshua? What if something happens while I'm here?"

"Johnny Roberts is not going to take a chance like that. Kidnapping? Child endangerment? That's a road even he doesn't want to go down. He has enough trouble already.

"But what if…"

"If you want to leave now, I'll drive you all the way home."

"No, I'm fine." I took a handful of popcorn, stuffed it in my mouth so I didn't have to speak, and handed it back to him. Then I took a sip of my Coke. I didn't know how to quit worrying. I could only think of Joshua, how if anything ever happened to him, I would just give up. There would be nothing left of me worth keeping. The grief I had been trying to tamp down was planning to engulf me in a dark wave any minute. I had to be ready to push it back.

"If Johnny Roberts was really going to do something, he wouldn't call to tell you about it." Jason put his arm around me.

"That doesn't make me feel any better," I tried to stare at the screen calmly, so Jason would stop trying to put me at ease. Nothing he said was helping. It only made me more tense. We were watching a classic French movie, *Children of Paradise*. Neither one of us spoke French, but Jason was absorbed in trying to figure out what the actors were saying. Instead of reading the subtitles so I could understand it, I let my mind wander back to Iona, where I hoped Joshua was sleeping soundly. I hoped Johnny Roberts was far away from there, and I hoped he got caught at whatever horrible thing he was doing. I hoped he had left Brianna and her baby alone. I hoped he died a lonely death in some cold prison. I was holding on to the armrests, as if I would fly out of my seat if I let go.

Jason put his hand on top of mine. "I'm with you," he said. "You're safe."

29

The Long Road

Jason had to be at a hearing for the mine foreman in Charleston by nine, so he got up to leave before the sun was up. It was a three-hour drive from Lexington. He moved quietly through the room, but I woke anyway. I could feel his legs untangle from mine, his warmth evaporate from the bed. "I don't want you to go," I said.

"Go back to sleep. I didn't mean to disturb you." He came over and tucked me tightly into the covers, then kissed my hair, as if I were a child. I wiggled out and sat up in bed. We were on the sixteenth floor of the hotel, and I could see the lightening sky out the window, the first rays of sunshine glinting off the tall glass buildings.

"I can't sleep anymore."

"I'll be back in Iona at the end of the week," he said. "By then, I should be able to write this article and stay home for a while."

"You think?" I said.

"I sure hope so." He kissed me on the lips this time and slipped out the door into the quiet hallway. It almost seemed as if he had never really been there.

I showered, dressed, and was on my way back down to the coffee shop when Micah called. "How did it go?" I asked. "Did the governor put a moratorium on Mountaintop Removal? Did you convince him of the evil of his ways? Did Dwight raise his voice?"

"No, no, and Lord, no," she said. "You know how this state works. Those coal company guys are stuffing hundred-dollar bills into everybody's pockets. Except anybody who actually lives in the mountains, of course. I told them I hope they burned in hell or at least choked to death on coal sludge."

"You did not!"

"No, I didn't, but I wanted to. I don't think the governor has ever even been to Hensley County, let alone to a place like Hawkins Creek. I don't know how those Coal executives put their red ties on in the morning without feeling like they ought to use them to hang themselves."

"Micah…"

"I did get them to create a committee to investigate the higher cancer rates in children at Hawkins Creek, and I did get the governor to call for enforcement of the inspection regulations publicly. Actually, Dwight helped with that. He just looks too holy for them to say no to. They have no problem saying no to a heathen like me."

"Well, come get me, Heathen," I said. "Take me back to the prisoning hills as fast as you can."

In the car, I told Micah about Johnny's call. If Collis had been dealing for him, what had happened in the end? I wondered if Collis had feared for his life, or if he thought the life he had would spiral further and further down into the earth until it just wasn't worth living. I wondered if he had been alone in that mine, or if someone like Johnny had been there to make sure he did what he set out to do.

"You want answers you can never have," Micah said. "You've got to let him rest. What would it change to know?"

"Everything." I turned away from her and looked out the window. Suicide was a chosen death, even a desired death. The kind of death Micah knew was one she could blame on cruel fate, a tragic loss of somebody who was fully alive. I had to blame Collis or myself.

Micah and I were both silent for the rest of the drive until we crossed the town line. A worn painted wooden sign that was sponsored by the local Coca-Cola bottling plant said, "Welcome to Iona, jewel of the mountains. Home to 2,138 friendly people and one grouch!" It was a tradition in high school to try to hit the sign with a beer can as you drove past. That explained the pile of aging empty cans below it, some of the chipped paint. I hoped by the time Joshua got to high school, the number would be down by two.

"I think their numbers are way off," Micah said.

"Definitely," I said. "They might even want to flip them."

Joshua came running out to meet us as we drove up the steep curving driveway to Anita's house. Jonah came up behind Joshua, chasing him. "Got you!" he said. As they wrestled to the ground, Jonah said, "Hey, Mrs. Maynard!"

"Careful!" I said.

Micah looked at me like I was crazy. "You think they're going to listen to you right now?" she said. "That's what boys do." That's exactly what Collis would have said, but it hurt me to see Joshua in any kind of pain, even for play.

I got out of the car and walked up to the door just as Anita started to open it. "Hey, Ava," she said. "You all made good time." There was a small white car I didn't recognize as Anita's or Jake's parked next to the front door. A man in his early twenties came to the door. He was short and compact, with a buzz cut and a mustache. He looked familiar, but I couldn't place him. "This is Tim West," Anita said. "He works at the clinic with me now."

He extended his hand and I shook it. "Pleased to meet you, Mrs. Maynard," he said. "I've got to get back to work."

"Okay," she said. "I'll check on that for you this afternoon. Call me if there's any trouble with the computer."

"I don't think I'll have any trouble. I just wanted to make sure I set it up right, thanks. Y'all take care." He waved to all of us and took off.

I gathered up Joshua's things and finally got him settled down enough to sit in the car. He and Micah started talking about the movie. Sometimes she acted exactly like a kid, which was good, because I didn't remember anything about what it was like to be Joshua's age. I felt like I was a hundred.

"I really appreciate you keeping him." I went back to Anita, "Sorry I got scared. I'm not sure what I need to worry about anymore, what kind of risks are real. I didn't know Iona would follow me wherever I go."

"No, it's alright. I didn't want to tell you last night, but Johnny Roberts's Uncle Thomas lives halfway down the hill. I keep an eye on him though. And if he gives me any trouble, I've got a few people I can call down at City Hall. I got a patrol car to come up here, just to make a show last night."

"You should have told me. I'd have come home last night."

"He wasn't in danger."

"We're all in danger," I said.

"I know plenty of people in this town. You and Joshua are safe. I'm safe. I'll promise you that," she said.

I didn't want to hear anybody's promises. I wanted to live in a boring place, a place where nobody had to worry about pill-heads coming out of the woods to get their children, or rivers of sludge crashing down on their houses. It had been so beautiful once, but the beauty didn't stand a chance against all it was fighting.

30

Highwall

I was walking toward the Foreign Foods aisle at the Save A Lot, looking for some kind of curry. It was probably hopeless to wish for in Iona, where pasta was still stocked in the Foreign Food aisle, but I kept thinking about the Pad Thai Jason and I had eaten in Lexington, and how I'd like to try to recreate it, or at least try to recreate that evening with him. All of that seemed continents away. Maybe I could find a teriyaki marinade. I could work with that. I wasn't really paying attention to anything in the Personal Care aisle, but I had to go through it to get to Foreign Foods. I was pushing my cart forward, thinking about dinner, and there was Brianna with a curly headed baby boy, maybe a year old, sitting in the seat of her cart, making up his own baby language.

"Hi, Ava," she said. My face must have shown my surprise. Brianna grinned. She had a jump on me this time.

"Brianna? What are you doing in Iona? Are you okay?"

"I'm good. Don't put that in your mouth!" she said to the baby. He was biting on the cart handle. When she pulled him off, he looked like he would cry. "Oh, stop it," she said. "That'll make you sick. It's nasty. Nas-ty!" She pulled him out of the cart and perched him on her slim hip. His bottom lip puckered.

"Dat," he said, pointing toward the cart handle.

"No!" Brianna said.

I waved at him and smiled, trying to distract him. He had Brianna's face, but somebody else's huge brown eyes. "Who's this handsome fella?"

"This is Tyler. Wave hi to Mrs. Ava, Tyler." Tyler waved and grinned so his few new teeth showed. "I told you I'd get him back. Thanks. They told me you signed the papers. I know you didn't have to. I hope you didn't catch too much shit for that."

"No," I said. "I was happy to do it. He's a sweet baby. He looks like you."

"Thanks," she said. "Everybody says he looks like his daddy, or worse, Uncle Johnny. I think he looks just like my baby pictures, but prettier."

"He's beautiful," I said. "How long are you all here for?" I was hoping she would say just a week or two. It wasn't safe for her to be here, or for me to help her stay.

"For good. I'm still trying to get my Granny's house. For now, we're out on West's Branch with Tyler's daddy. I heard you met him, Tim West? We're back together. I think we might could make it work."

"Tim West? I met him up at Anita's. He didn't tell me who he was."

"Well, we go back and forth, you know. But right now, we're together."

"It sounds like things are working out," I said.

"I hope so. If I could get a job, things would be better. Tim's mom said she'd keep Tyler for us while I work. She's so happy to have her baby back. Tim's working at the clinic with Dr. Anita. He got his phlebotomy degree in Ohio; he's good with a needle. Johnny got him the job. I'm still not speaking to Johnny, but he can help Tim out. I'll take that, as long as he stays away from me and Tyler."

I wasn't as optimistic as Brianna, but I didn't tell her that. Maybe it was possible for her life to work out here. Maybe Johnny wouldn't push her down a dark road. "Come see me if you need anything," I said. "I hope it works out with the house. Be careful."

"I will. Don't worry. And you come see me if you need anything," Brianna said. "I got some favors to repay you. You never know what I could do for you." The baby was pulling at her platinum ponytail now.

"Thanks," I said, though I worried about what Brianna might be able to do for me. She was just over the edge of a cliff herself. We might pull each other back down.

"Stop it, Tyler!" she said. "Toddlers are mean."

"Yeah, it's a good thing they're cute," I said. I tried to resist asking for what I really wanted to know, but maybe she could do something for me. "Brianna, you'll let me know if you find out any more, won't you?" I asked. "About Collis, I mean."

"I will. I definitely will. Far as I can tell right now, he had small time habits, nothing that could get Johnny's attention. I mean, if you're not pulling your weight financially, Johnny don't even bother. Maybe it was more to do with the mines. You know all the Macy foremen are in on Johnny's game. At least most of them. He don't really give them a choice."

"You just let me know. Whatever you find out, I'm ready to know it."

Brianna studied me as if to gauge for herself whether I could handle the truth. She was so old inside that young body, but every now and then she slipped up and showed that she wasn't as hard-shelled as she wanted to be. I craved the truth now and prayed it really could set me free.

Brianna might make it, I thought. She was strong and smart, but people like Johnny could use that baby against her to make her go back to the life she had run from. She might want to go back. The baby squealed and reached toward the cart again. "Looks like Tyler's getting restless," I said.

"He's gonna wear me out. Aren't you?" she said to Tyler and he grinned. He loved the sound of her voice. She put him back into the cart and pushed him down the aisle.

I never did find the curry, and now I didn't even really want it anymore. I wanted something I knew. I hoped Brianna was right, that she would get a job, get the house, and stay out of trouble. I hoped she would live to see Tyler grow up, live to be an old, old woman. I hoped the house would still be standing as long as she was. Still, I couldn't help seeing the mesmerizing shine of trouble ahead, and it looked to me like she was running straight back for it. I wondered what kind of help Tim West brought with him, but I doubted he was any count. I couldn't be the one to save Brianna, though. I'd be lucky to save myself.

31

The Clinic

I woke up in the middle of the night, heart racing, mind spinning so fast I had to sit up in bed to still it. I stared out the window until it looked lighter outside than inside the room. If I read, that would get my mind off things, but turning on the light meant I was giving in to being awake. Tonight, I decided to leave the light off. Joshua slept quietly next to me. He'd slipped in beside me after I had fallen asleep. I didn't mind; he needed the comfort of his mama's warmth as much as I needed him to need me. I wanted to keep him safe from nightmares. Sleep wouldn't come back to me, though, no matter how much I willed it.

Through the window next to the bed, I could see the streetlights that lit the way to Main Street. I could also see a warmer, flickering light too, thick smoke. I gently slipped my body away from Joshua's. He didn't wake. I covered him up, so he'd stay warm without me, then walked out to the porch where I could smell the fire and maybe get a better view. It wasn't a trash-burning fire, the smell of leaves and plastics. It was bigger than that. The acrid odor of burning wood and electrical wire filled the street. I went back in and threw on some jeans, then locked Joshua in. He would be all right for a few minutes, sleeping as soundly as he was. I had to see what was happening. Several neighbors were up too, out on their porches, craning their necks to try to see down Main Street a few blocks away.

I walked wordlessly with a few of them toward Main, almost at a jog, to see the Health Clinic burning with steady flames. They were bright white and orange, and they shot up to the second floor, breaching the windows. This fire was lit with some kind of fuel, not by accident. It was hungry. Fire trucks gathered, lining Main Street from as far away as Hubbard. Their red lights flashed off the sides of buildings. There was an ambulance sitting in the parking lot, lit up, but nobody was in it.

Anita was standing too close to the building, her face reddened by the heat, talking to a policeman I didn't know. She was in blue flannel pajamas, and she was crying. The policeman pulled her away from the building, toward the street, where several of us were standing. "Anita!" I called, waving her over.

"Oh, Ava!" she walked to me, and I hugged her. "I never thought Johnny would go this far. You know he had been pressuring me to write prescriptions for him? He finds ways to get what he wants. You try to do right in this town and look what happens," she said. She nodded toward the fire and tears started flowing for both of us. "I should have just done it. I've worked so hard for this. So hard."

"What about Jonah?" I asked. "Is he okay?"

"Yeah, he's safe. I sent him to my mother's in Knoxville. Jake took him down there as soon as I got the call. I may have to leave here, Ava. I might... this is no kind of life."

"You can't give in," I said. "You can't give up all your work."

"Can't I?" she said. "What's really left here for our boys? You left. That was the smartest thing you ever did. You know our kids will get caught up in this mess, whether they want to or not. Look at it." She pointed toward the smoldering clinic. The plastic sign that said Stone Health Care had melted into a warped wave.

I didn't say anything. She might be able to leave and start somewhere else. She had only been here for twenty years. Her family was in Pennsylvania. I tried to leave and the mountains had called me back. They weren't done with me yet. Now Collis was part of the mountains, part of the rock and dirt. The poem Gabe had recited to me burned in my mind. "Being of these hills / I cannot pass beyond."

We stood in silence for a while and watched while firemen carted singed exam tables out into the street. They had subdued the flames. The fire had started in the pharmacy. It was mainly smoke and water damage they were worried about now. It was hard to tell what, if anything, could be saved. Pale gray smoke continued to billow into the sky. Some flames kicked back up and refused to die. We had to walk back to the corner to breathe better. I held on to Anita until the policemen asked if she would come with them to file a report. She let go of my hand and followed them to the squad car. "Thanks, Ava," she said. "I really appreciate you."

"I'm so sorry," I said. "I'm glad you and Jonah are safe." After she was gone, I stood and watched the building smoke and spark.

Johnny Roberts had been arrested in high school for setting fire to an abandoned house on Paint Creek. Nobody was hurt, as far as anyone could tell, the place was a hazard to anyone walking around it, whole walls fallen in and the roof sagged in the middle, so he got off pretty easy. He argued that he was only doing the county a favor, training to be a volunteer fireman. Some people thought that was a reasonable excuse. He had enough money to make them see it that way. At the time, he was still a juvenile, seventeen, so he ended up with community service hours at the clinic. Anita was interning there at the time and didn't think he was beyond reform like everyone else. They had some sort of odd respect between them. She thought Johnny deserved the benefit of the doubt. She thought he'd had a tough row to hoe, but as far as I could see, it was no rougher than anybody's in a fifty-mile radius.

Now, Anita was certain that this was Johnny's personal message to her. The fire had started in the pharmacy. If Johnny had done this, or one of his lackeys had done it for him, it made me wonder what all Collis had done in his service. Once, when we had gone hiking with the boys, Anita told me that Collis had hinted to her when he'd come in for a check-up that he needed more pain pills.

"Everybody around here does that though, Ava. That doesn't mean they get them, or that they deal them. Collis had a legitimate need," she told me. "He didn't push it like a lot of them do." Who did he push, I wondered.

Some kinds of pain were handed down, from generation to generation. Some wounds would never be healed. The mountains could be moved and vanished, but not without consequences. Some people only knew to fight destruction with destruction, devastation with fire.

I made my way back home, quickening my step, worried the whole time that Joshua would be missing when I got there, or that the house would be in flames. But Joshua was sleeping peacefully in my bed, his chest evenly rising and falling. I slid back into bed beside him but couldn't go to sleep. The heavy smell of smoke permeated everything.

32

Lady Knights

It was the last game of the regional high school tournament and the gym was packed. We were all trying to forget about the clinic fire, to find some sort of normal again. Basketball was the steadiest thing in our world. Sometimes it was the only thing people around here felt proud of. I wouldn't travel for basketball, though many people would. They lived for it, and they didn't discriminate boys' or girls'. They went with the winners, and the Lady Knights always dominated. The boys' team never had as much stamina or power. I liked to think that was because mountain women were tough, but it was probably because they'd always had good coaching, and once they built a reputation as state champions year after year, little feeder leagues sprang up. I was on a team in elementary school, but I never could stay focused on who had the ball when I was right down in the middle of things. I liked to be up above it, observing. Micah was a star guard until she quit during our junior year.

"I've got more important things to do than play ball," she had said. She'd been to visit Berea College and met up with some activists there. They arranged her a summer service internship. I stayed home that summer and started dating Collis. Micah and I diverged then, like branches of a river, but we never lost touch completely. I was grateful for that.

After this Regional game, the Lady Knights would move on to the state tournament in Lexington, we hoped, or if we were unlucky, the Hubbard Lady Tigers would, and we wouldn't hear the end of it for another year. There was a full house on both sides of the court. The Hubbard girls could hold their own, especially the Bogen girl, who was almost six feet tall and played center.

I promised Joshua we would go to the game, even though I could barely breathe in the Hensley County gym. The room created its own humidity, its own tropical weather. The walls were coated with condensation and sweat, a strange rain. That many bodies huddled together could do that, even when there was still a chill outside in the early spring air. The TV weathermen still called for hard frosts at least three nights that week. We were in redbud winter. The fuchsia blooms on spindly tree branches dotted the woods. After they bloomed, the old folks said, we'd go back to cold weather for a week or two. Then we'd have dogwood winter and blackberry winter. The old people were right about some things; they believed in cycles. They learned to be patient.

Joshua pulled me along through thickets of bodies packed into the gym, and I pulled Jonah behind me. We were on the orange side of the gym, a sea of green and gold filled the other side. We held hands so we wouldn't lose each other in the waves. I wasn't tall enough to see above the crowd. Joshua was even shorter, but a little kid could get through places where a grown up could not. We ended up at the mid-court line, about halfway up the bleachers.

"How's this, Mama?" Joshua was proud of himself for leading us to a good spot. We settled in on the narrow wooden bleachers behind two wide ladies who were short enough to see over. Joshua liked taking care of me, making things work out right.

"These are perfect seats, Baby," I said.

"Mama, don't call me Baby," he said. "I'm almost ten."

"Sorry," I said. "Habit."

"Man, these are the best seats in the house!" Jonah said. Anita had gone to Knoxville to sort things out with the insurance company. She still hadn't decided what to do, but she didn't want to keep Jonah out of school any longer. Her life was filled with paperwork. She rented a trailer to set up a temporary clinic in the shopping center on the bypass. There was a line out the door, starting at seven in the morning when she opened. There was no other place for people to go to get care, unless they went to the ED at Hensley County regional, and that wasn't on a sliding scale.

I had Jonah for the weekend, and it was a good distraction to follow two nine-year-old boys around. They were in love with basketball, with this gym. The place was alive, no doubt about it. People around Iona clung to basketball for the hope that it brought. It could get a kid to college. He or she could become a teacher and come back with a state job, or go off for a while, make a living, and bring some of that back to their mamas and daddies. They would always have a place here, and like migratory birds, they were expected to come back to nest here, at least for a while, to keep the whole process going and save what was left.

I hadn't been a good player, despite my time in little league, but that didn't matter. Most of the people in the gym had never made a shot. Some of the most rabid fans had never even tried. For as long as the game was going, we had no choice but to focus on it instead of all our problems. The band drowned out any thoughts we had with their Michael Jackson medley. We might win or we might lose, but we would be there the whole time, riding the wave of emotion, humming the chorus to Billie Jean. Sometimes, watching a girl make the shot, my arms involuntarily mimicked her motion. When we cheered and chanted during the free throws, we had real power to make a ball go in the basket or bounce off the rim.

Growing up in Kentucky, you had to know the game. It was the one thing we had dominated nationally for decades, and it seemed to belong to us. The University of Kentucky players came from around the world now, but they used to come from the mountains. We still felt responsible for their greatness. Games like this one, in high school gyms around the state, could make a difference, start a star's career.

Gabe was down a few rows from us with his wife and his two younger daughters. I waved to him. He shouted, "Hey Joshua!" and Joshua waved too. Gabe's oldest, a sophomore, was on the team, even though she was a bench warmer. The whole family glowed in Lady Knights orange T-shirts.

Melanie Holbrook got the tip off. She was sturdy and tall, at least 5 foot 10. Her dad was in my high school class. Her mother was from Virginia, just over the mountain. Melanie could pull the ball out of the air before anyone else could reach it. Five minutes in, we were ahead by six and my heart was racing. I screamed as if my life depended on this win. Everything else receded. The reverberating hum of the crowd became backbeat. Each basket counted. I would have forgotten the boys were with me, except they reached up to high five me every now and then or leaned out over the next row to yell louder. The teams traded the lead back and forth, but when the buzzer sounded, we were behind by four. There was a girl on Hubbard's team who was being recruited for the big colleges, Tennessee, Texas, Connecticut. She already had 23 points.

Half time brought some relief. I saved our seats while the boys cruised the hallways, looking for friends, feeling grown. They knew at least half of the people in the stands. "Can we get some popcorn and Cokes?" Joshua asked.

"Sure. Here's some money. Don't lose it." I handed him a twenty and told him to bring back the change. "Bring me a water too," I said.

I watched Joshua and Jonah weave through the stands, which had thinned as people made their way to the bathroom or concessions. Some went outside to smoke or get some air. I kept track of Joshua's blue UK baseball cap in the sea of orange. Jonah's buzzed blond head was easy to lose in this crowd. By the exit door, to the left of the goal, I saw another pair I recognized, Brianna and Johnny. He had a trial coming up for the clinic fire, but he still wanted to be seen and known. If people lost sight of him, they might think fear had shifted, that they didn't need to worry about him any longer. They might even think they had power over him and his people, but they'd be wrong. Here he was, shaggy blond hair tucked into a Macy Energy cap, orange Lady Knights T-shirt stretched over his big belly. Brianna wore all black. I could tell from my spot in the stands she'd rimmed her eyes with thick black eyeliner. They popped out of her thin pale face. I didn't see the baby with her. Hopefully, he was safe with her mother-in-law. I was trying to watch the boys make their way to the concessions without panicking. I couldn't yell and draw attention to myself. I didn't want Johnny to know he had control over me. He was holding on to Brianna's arm. She didn't look upset, but even from here I could tell his grip was too tight. Johnny was leading her into the stands. He had probably taken her outside for a smoke; he couldn't let her go alone. Maybe he had to have a talk with her, tell her he could bring her down with him. Maybe it was a quiet threat. The boys were carried along with the wave of the crowd. *Please God, don't let them come close to Johnny. Don't let him see them. Send them to the right of the basket. Please. Collis? Please.* They flowed to the right with the crowd and out the door, into the hallway where the concessions were set up. I could breathe. I was standing now. I watched Johnny and Brianna cross through the bleachers and leave the building through the doors underneath the opposite goal.

"Ava!" Gabe shouted, motioning for me to come down to his row. Maybe I'd have a better view of where the boys went from there. I made my way to Gabe and Carol, hugged them both. I couldn't tell them I was terrified.

"I bet the boys are having a ball," Carol said. Without his gray hair, Gabe could have been in college, loose jeans, Knights T-shirt, cap on backward. Carol looked decidedly adult in her orange polo shirt and white cardigan. She got a wash and set at the Beautiful Image every week, as if she was my mother's age. She was the head of the Ladies' Auxiliary at church, but she had stopped pushing me to join after Collis died.

"Those boys are in heaven," I said. "Anything for basketball. They're at that age. Can you all see where they went?" I hoped they were on their way back to the seats. I kept sneaking glances across the bleachers as we talked.

"Oh, I wouldn't worry. They're probably at the concession stand with all the kids from school," Carol said.

"That Joshua's built like a point guard," Gabe said. "He could take after his Daddy that way. Collis was quick as lightning. Had a pretty good jumper too."

"He did, didn't he?" Collis had been something on the court.

His arms were long and muscled. He could jump to his own height, it seemed. "He never should have quit," I said.

I still didn't see the boys. What if Johnny and Brianna had lured them outside?

"You okay, Ava?"

"Just trying to see where the boys went. Maybe I should go after them."

"They'll be fine," Gabe said. "Let them have a little freedom. They know more than half the people in this gym."

"Guess you're right," I said.

"Why did Collis quit?" Gabe asked. I tried to focus on the conversation, but images of Johnny and Brianna pulling the boys into the back seat of a car flashed in my head.

"Collis? His daddy died. Alice always said it was Black Lung, but they ruled it pneumonia."

"That's right. I remember now. He was so proud of that boy."

"I wish he'd stuck with basketball, but he said he wasn't big enough to get recruited. Maybe if he had been, things would have been different," I said. "I think Joshua might take after my dad height-wise. He might have a shot at it." I looked for Joshua's cap, Jonah's blonde head, but saw neither. Gabe turned to watch the girls warming up for the second half. He didn't want to be responsible for me slipping down into sadness in the middle of the Hensley County High gym.

"Hey, did you see my Heather out there?" he asked. "She got a couple of minutes. She can give Rochelle Adams a rest every now and then. I wish they'd put her in a little more, let her prove herself."

"I'm sure they will," I said, scanning the crowd. I finally saw Joshua's blue cap, Jonah behind him, bumping into people, excusing themselves down the narrow bleacher aisles, sprinkling a trail of dropped popcorn along the way. I breathed. "I better give those two a hand," I said, pointing to the boys. Gabe nodded and patted me on the back. I inched past Gabe and Carol, made my way to the boys and rescued what was left of the popcorn, then took a deeper breath.

We sat back down as the buzzer sounded. The announcer, Tommy Mattis, had his own heating and air business, and he was telling the crowd that climate control was an affordable way to upgrade your home, comfortable as a mountain breeze. The gym had cooled considerably, with people moving back and forth and the air coming in from outside, but now they sealed it tight again, the girls took their places on the court, and the room began to hum like a hive.

33

Fill

A week later, Joshua and I went back to Alice's for Sunday dinner. We were trying to create a new routine that included all three of us. We were reclaiming each other. "Y'all grab a plate before it gets cold," Alice said. We walked in the door and hung our coats up. Joshua played with the dogs. The radio was turned up too loud to the country gospel station. "Here, let me turn this mess down," Alice said. "I like a little background noise when I'm cooking." Joshua reached for a dinner roll.

"Wash your hands first," I said to Joshua. "This looks delicious!"

"Well, it's not much, but I did get some good-looking salad greens from the garden, and I think my pie's gonna turn out."

"It smells wonderful," I said. Alice served a feast that could have fed ten people, but it was just us three. It seemed the more she loved someone, the more she cooked. I was beginning to understand that she loved us more than I could ever imagine, Joshua and me, not just Collis. Still, it felt strange to be back at the same table we had lost ourselves around a few months before. I could only vaguely remember the clumps of the days right after Collis died, but I remembered where we each had sat at the table, and how we had tried to feed each other. Now, we were trying to find a way to forgive each other for things we didn't do, or hadn't told each other, or couldn't even say. "Pass the potatoes, please," I said.

Alice baked a whole chicken. We had green beans, mashed potatoes, dinner rolls, and the tender butter lettuce from her garden. Joshua piled his plate high with food I knew he could never finish, but I didn't say anything. It would make Alice proud to see him fill his plate with what she had cooked. "It's been too long since y'all came over for dinner," she said

"I ate here after school last week," Joshua said. He was still coming and going between our houses, and that seemed to work.

"Yes, but I mean both of you and a real sit-down dinner. We should do this more often."

"We should," I said. "Why don't you come over to the house next time and I'll cook. I think I still might remember how."

"All right," Alice said. "Tell me when."

I missed Alice's cooking and her company and I was afraid I'd lose the past completely without her. I think she was afraid she'd lose who she was without me too. Together, we might try to move forward. "I've been thinking," she said. "What if Joshua started spending every other weekend with me? Then you could get out more. You must want to do something? Maybe you and Micah could go to that Mexican place. I hear they have dancing every Saturday night."

I tucked into my potatoes and nodded. I didn't want to talk to Alice about getting out. Next she'd want to know if I was dating. I wasn't about to tell her about Jason. She might even encourage me to, tell me it was okay, and I wasn't ready for that. I already had to lie to my mother whenever she called. She hadn't given up on the idea of us coming to Indiana, but now she suspected there was a man keeping me here. She even mentioned a few "handsome neighbors" who had moved into her subdivision. I liked spending time with Jason, but wasn't in a hurry to claim anyone, or let anyone claim me.

"Can I switch out weekends, Mama?" Joshua said. "I miss staying at Nana's. I could stay in Daddy's room." The way he talked about it made it seem like Collis had been gone forever. Why did everybody want me to forget what happened, to be healed already? Alice's heart was long since honeycombed with sorrows. She must understand that some holes weren't meant to be filled. Joshua was young. I had to remember that, and also not let him forget who he was, who Collis was.

"That sounds like a good idea," I said. "And I can make you all dinner when you bring Joshua home. I don't know about the Mexican place, but I guess Micah and I could go to the movies or something."

"That'd be fine," Alice said. I hadn't really thought about her loneliness before. We were the only family she had left, and I'm sure she saw Collis in Joshua's wide face just like I did. I bet, like me, she saw Collis when Joshua ran, lean and compact like a deer, or bit his lips when he concentrated.

"What did you say about a pie?" I asked.

"Derby pie," she said. "Smells like it might be done. Let me get it out to cool."

34

Bust

We'd had a little slow down at the office for about a week. I don't mean we were bored, but we didn't have a constant flow of clients like usual. Gabe said it was because of springtime. Winter brought people in needing heat, food, a place to stay. Some just came into the office to warm up before they went back to the small homeless camp hidden in the woods behind the Save A Lot. The warm weather didn't mean they were better off now, it just meant people were out more, maybe setting out pot plants way up on hillsides, maybe putting in real gardens at a relative's house. I only saw a couple of food stamp and WIC clients in the morning.

There was a job I was looking at applying for in Lexington at a drug rehab center, but I hadn't yet sent in an application. I didn't want to go back to Children and Family Services. I couldn't imagine sitting at that same desk thinking of Collis every day, with no friends or family around. I'd have to find Joshua a new school too. I was sure they would dread seeing him coming at Little River Elementary as much as he would dread going. The desire to leave was beginning to gnaw at me again, even though I loved this time of year in the mountains. In the mornings, I could almost smell the cold rock mixing with the green onion smell of new grass. The oily smoke from coal stoves burning was gone. I was having a harder and harder time imagining what our new home in Lexington would look like. Maybe we would try Knoxville instead, go the whole opposite direction, get out of the state. I could feel myself quietly letting roots down again, and that made me nervous. As it was, I'd have to dig Joshua out, kicking and screaming.

Gabe stopped by my desk, "Ava, I got a call from the state boys." He came into my cubicle and sat down in my client chair. He waited a minute for me to respond.

"About what?" I stopped typing the email I had started.

"Well, you heard about that big bust on Route 23?"

"Yeah, twenty-two arrests?"

Gabe lowered his voice until it was almost paternal. "They got that girl you're working with, Brianna Roberts. This thing goes through all the pharmacies, Stone Healthcare, down to the shoppers and dealers, like her."

I sat back in my chair. "Well, damn. Damn… Are you sure it was her?" I knew better than to trust an addict, but somehow, I thought she was the one I could fix. She had the same spark Micah had, the same fearlessness, but it was all turned in the wrong direction.

Gabe nodded. "Her uncle was in on it. I hear he was the head of the whole operation. Caught them on the way up to Ohio."

"What about her baby?"

"The daddy's got him. They're still in the county. I think he's trying to make her bail." Gabe looked weary, like he ought to quit this job before he stopped caring. I was way too upset about this to be professional. I just wanted to be able to save somebody, anybody. I thought I could put Brianna on the right track, or maybe she could help me find my way. I wasn't helping either of us. "There's somebody else they picked up," Gabe said. He looked up at me, then down at the dingy gray industrial carpet.

"Who?" My voice had become thin.

"Your friend Anita," Gabe said.

I sat back from the desk and covered my face with my hands. Maybe if I hid, the tears wouldn't come. "Oh, Gabe."

"I figured it'd be better to hear it from me than from everybody gossiping in town."

"And Jonah? Who's taking care of him?"

"He's with the boyfriend. He's putting up her bail."

What would I tell Joshua? Why couldn't we have a regular life, where we didn't know any criminals? Where we didn't have to worry about the mountains crumbling and the whole town sinking down with them? Iona was raw and worn, barely recognizable as the place Collis and I grew up loving. Some of the people I had grown up with had shriveled up, their eyes deep dark gaps in their faces by the time they were thirty, but still, I couldn't let the damn place go. I wanted to fix it, somehow reclaim it to what it used to be, the land and the people.

"I never figured Anita for this." I should have been beyond surprise now, but I was shocked. She was so close to us, but I didn't want to see. "It makes sense, I guess, the clinic fire, the boyfriends, but still…"

"People get desperate," Gabe said. "They get a lot of pressure."

"I'll never understand putting your life or your child's life at stake. She put my child's life at stake too! That's not desperate, it's just selfish." I felt shaky, so I grabbed my purse and jacket. "I'll be back. I got to walk this out."

"Okay," Gabe said. "I'll see what else I can find out. You can't go convicting people before you give them a trial. Innocent until proven guilty, Ava."

"Oh, yeah. They're all innocent," I said. "I'm just sure of it." When would the loss stop? When would we ever gain? I stomped out past Kayla, who looked confused. "I'll be back in an hour or so," I said. "Gabe knows."

"Okay. You all right?"

I didn't respond, just shook my head and pushed forward. I should have taken an umbrella, should have taken my sweater too. It wasn't yet warm. It just looked warm through windows, another lie. I walked fast, past the clinic, past Cullen's. I couldn't handle all the talk I'd hear in there. For all I knew, the gossipers would draw Joshua and me into it, convict us too. After all, we spent a lot of time with Anita and Jonah. Deana knew I had a soft spot for Brianna. The sky was blue with puffy white clouds, but every now and then, there was a quick shower. Even the weather couldn't be trusted. The old folks said that's when the Devil was beating his wife; he's happy and she's sad. The sky couldn't make up its mind who to side with. I ran through the light rain toward Nobles. I needed to see Anna. I only saw her once since I fixed the screen door, to buy some enamel paint for the front door, and she hadn't mentioned reading my cards. I needed her again now. I wasn't sure who was lying and who was telling the truth. I figured it did me no good to ask the living. Maybe the dead would know.

The stores on either side of Nobles were closed with butcher paper covering the windows. I couldn't see inside. This had happened since Joshua and I came back. The storefront on the right had been Countywide Insurance Company. There was a sign painted on the window that said they moved to the shopping center out on the bypass. The other side had been a hair salon, The Beautiful Image. My mother used to get her hair set there every week. I wondered what I could hold onto in the chaos of this place.

Anna Noble was an anchor. The fact that she was sitting at the counter, reading the paper, head bent so her white bob hung a little over her glasses, calmed me. "I guess you're reading about the bust," I said.

"What else is in the paper today?" She folded the front page of the Mountain Lion in half and whacked it on the worn wooden counter. "What can I help you with, Ava?"

"Well, I was wondering if you'd read for me."

"I can't guarantee you'll find out what you want to know," Anna said.

"Please."

She slid off the stool behind the counter and motioned for me to come with her. "Come on back," she said. She laid the cards out on the table in a wide fan, collected them again, handed them to me. "Shuffle and cut." I did and she laid out the cross. She shrugged then placed another layer of cards on top of the first. "Ain't much to see here today, Ava."

"Anything about traveling? Anything about health?" Anna's glasses slid down her nose and she looked at me from above them.

"I don't see people moving. Just the earth. Dozers and such, but that's probably just because of the noise up there on the mountain. Sorry, Honey. Maybe the paper can tell you more than I can." The spirits hadn't answered my questions. Not one.

"Thanks for trying," I said. The bell on the door rang and a man came into the store, holding a rubber gasket.

"Customers," Anna walked back to the counter and I slipped toward the door. "How can I help you?" she asked.

35

The Lion

Jason had been working a lot, or at least gone a lot, and now here was his name on the byline of the bust article in the paper Anna gave me. It made me wonder if there was anything else he was keeping from me, anything else he knew that he wasn't allowed to tell. I walked down to the park at the end of Main Street to find a private place to read. The sun was shining now and there was a plump girl with chin-length brown hair, not more than twenty, swinging her toddler on the swing set. She pushed the baby up until it looked like his feet were above the mountains in the distance, and he laughed until he got out of breath. Then she caught him and did it again. I didn't know the girl, but I probably knew her family.

I opened the paper to the article. There his name was, right under the headline, "Twenty-two Busted on Twenty-three." Jason had been back and forth to West Virginia a lot to write about Macy, but he didn't tell me this was coming. Maybe he didn't trust me. Maybe I didn't trust him either. For the most part, I could walk steadily through the day now. I didn't cry every time I saw a miner anymore. Still, this was the first spring Collis would miss, and I remembered the hikes we took up through the mountains every year. I remembered moving into the house on Zion Creek, and the spring that Joshua was born. This didn't leave much room in my head or heart for Jason. But here he was again, working his way in.

I read the article:

Twenty-two people were charged in Hensley County with trafficking in narcotics when two vehicles were pulled over for a routine traffic stop on US Route 23. Police say there was drug paraphernalia in both vehicles, which provided probable cause for a further search. Troopers recovered twenty small bags of marijuana, 354 grams of suspected crack cocaine, and 2,000 80-milligram Oxycontin pills.

"We're working to combat it," Sgt. James Chittenden said. "We're working with the U.S. Attorney's office and trying to target the bigger dealers. It seems like we take one person down and others are there to take their place."

Abused and illegal drugs "are the scourge of this county," said Hensley County Prosecuting Attorney J.B. Connor. "Some of these people have $200 or $300 a day habits. They steal from their family and friends or shoplift to get money for drugs. U.S. 23 is the pipeline for a lot of the illegal drugs. They'll get a dollar per milligram," Conley said. "One 80-milligram of Oxycontin will sell for $80. Sometimes drug dealers will stay in addicts' homes and set up shop."

Sgt. Jim Smith of the highway patrol said making traffic stops that uncover caches of illegal drugs is more and more common. "Our focus is to remove drugs from the highway."

I took the rest of the day off to hide in my bed and figure out what I was going to tell Joshua. Jason had left me three messages, asking me to call him as soon as I could. Usually, I waited a day to get back to him. I didn't want to seem overeager, but this time I called back immediately. Maybe he had some good news.

"Ava, hey. I was wondering when I was going to hear from you," he said.

"I'm a mess. You know that."

"We're all some kind of mess," he said. "I'll be in town now for a few weeks. They want me to follow up on this bust. Maybe I could see you."

"Maybe. But, Jason? I read your article. Why didn't you tell me?"

"I couldn't let anybody know about the bust before it happened, Ava. I had to protect my sources. You have to understand that."

I wondered if he would always have to keep things from me. "I want to know everything you know," I said. "I want to know about Brianna and Anita. Is it true? Did they really do it? Can you tell me what you know now?"

"I don't know, Ava. It doesn't look good. It looks like they're both on Johnny Roberts's payroll. They both made bail, though."

"But it can't be true about Anita. I know her. Joshua's stayed with her. She's not that type of person, Jason. She's really not." It was too much to think that Joshua had been in danger, and that Jonah lived in danger every day. I believed Anita about the fire. I believed she was resisting Johnny's pressure. Why cave now, after the insurance company had settled?

"With that much money to be made, people get greedy. She might be using too." Jason said.

"Wouldn't I have been able to tell that? Wouldn't it have shown?"

"Maybe. She's a doctor, maybe she knows how to cover it up."

"And Brianna? Are you sure he wasn't forcing her to do this?"

"She was driving the truck when they got pulled over. Johnny knows better than to do that himself. It doesn't look good for her. Not when you add it to the old charges she had. Whether she wanted to do it or not, she was there."

"Why does it feel like the whole town is rotten?"

"It's not. I'm not. There are plenty of people doing good. They just get drowned out by the bad news. I wish I didn't have to write it."

"Well, thanks for letting me know." I wasn't sure what else I should say, so I started to say goodbye.

"Don't go," Jason said. "I'd really like to see you again." I could imagine how sincere he looked. I could imagine the warmth of his skin.

"I'm thinking about it. Probably too much. Ghosts, you know. I do miss you, though," I said.

"You could have dinner with me next week. I'll tell you everything I know."

"Okay. But don't expect much. I'm really not right."

"You're alright, Ava. Or you will be."

The next morning, I drove up the hill to Anita's house because I figured you ought to ask someone directly what the hell they were thinking whenever you thought they were doing something crazy. I'd be able to tell in her eyes if she was lying. She was still one of the only friends I had here, and if she'd let me, I'd take Jonah home with me and keep him as long as she needed me to. He was definitely innocent. A man was standing at the front door of their house, like a sentry. At first, I thought it was Anita's boyfriend, but when I got closer, I could see it was Tim West, clean and taut in a tight white T-shirt and jeans. He walked up to the car. I rolled down my window.

"Hey, Ava."

"Hey, Tim. You standing guard?"

"You could say that, I guess," he said.

"Well, I'm just here to see Anita. Thought I might take Jonah off her hands for a day or two. Is she here?" Tim was right up at my driver's side window, blocking my view of the house, but I thought I saw someone draw the shades in the living room.

"She is. But she said if you came up here to tell you she's okay. She said to tell you she's not guilty, but she can't talk to you. For your own protection. Said you'd know what she meant."

"What about Jonah? Is he safe?"

"He's at his Grandma's in Knoxville."

"And your family? How's Brianna?"

"She's alright. She's staying out at her Grandma's place. My cousin's watching out for her and the baby. They're innocent, Ava. It was a set up."

I wasn't sure what to believe. Part of me wanted to drive out there and check on Brianna, give her one more chance. The other part wanted to finally admit there was no saving her or her baby, that it never was a thing I could have done. I had to learn the difference between the way the world was and the way I wanted it to be.

"What about Johnny? Won't he find her out there?"

"He's on the run out of state, last I heard. But I've got Brianna safe from him. Don't you worry. I know people from Florida to Michigan looking for that man. He won't be able to show his face for a while."

I did worry, but it was clear I had gotten all Tim was going to give me.

"Well, tell Anita I came by," I said.

"Will do," he said.

I turned around in the tight space of the driveway and inched back down the hill. All I wanted to do then was pick Joshua up early from school and take him to Micah's where we might have a hope of staying safe and sane. I'd find out what happened in a trial, eventually, but I wasn't sure if I'd ever find the answers.

36

Aquifer

I took the day off and began going through each room of the house, culling. I had to be ready to go, if and when I got the guts to. I had to lighten our load. Like me, Joshua didn't want to believe the news about Anita. He loved her and Jonah. He didn't know how to make sense of this place either. I took vacation days and let Joshua stay home from school and play video games for a few days, while I filled boxes with knick-knacks and bags with clothes. Some of it was ours, but some of it was stuff people had brought to us when we first came back. It's funny how I'd already attached myself to those things, like the wedding ring quilt Gabe and Carol gave us. Carol made them to sell at craft fairs, and they were beautiful, hand stitched. I spread that across my bed, and the clean geometry of intertwined circles made a constellation of ordered stars. I threw T-shirts and jeans people had brought by for Joshua into the box. He'd already outgrown most of the jeans. Alice had taken him to Belk's at the mall last weekend to get new clothes for school. When I had four boxes full, I loaded them into the trunk.

"Come on, Joshua," I said. "We have to take these to the church." The Baptist church had a clothing ministry.

"Do I have to go?" he asked. I could hear the ping and flourish of his video game when he made a point. "I'm almost at the next level."

"Turn it off now, or I will, and you won't get to save your level," I said.

"You're mean," he said.

"I know it. But I'll take you to Micah's after we drop off the boxes."

"I've got fifteen more seconds." I waited and watched as he shot computer darts at computer balloons with ridiculous accuracy. When the clock ran out, there was trumpeting. "Yes!" he said.

He chattered about the game all the way to the church, then on to Micah's. In spite of all that had happened, he still sounded like a kid who had worlds that belonged to him.

"Here, scatter this feed around the yard over there," Micah said to Joshua. We showed up when she was feeding the chickens. I packed enough clothes to stay for a few days. Gabe understood. Micah's wasn't far, but it was far enough that I wouldn't have to hear gossip about the bust everywhere I went. I wouldn't have to see all those looks, wondering if I had gone bad too. Joshua took the feed and tossed it toward the chicken coop in big handfuls. "Don't just throw it at them," Micah told him. "Shake it out so it's spread out. Broadcast it." Joshua walked slowly now, shook his open palm full of feed over the ground and let it slide through his fingers onto the dirt. "There you go!" she said.

"I'm thinking getting out in the country is the way to go," I said. "You know, we could join you out here and make our own compound, go off the grid."

"Having chickens is not off the grid. And living out here sure won't get you away from the craziness."

"So, I'm supposed to accept my lot and wait until the last addict dies or goes to jail? And what about Anita? I don't want to believe she was in on it. Was she?"

"Look, Ava, at least there was a bust. At least it'll slow Johnny Roberts and the others like him down. And we'll have to wait for the truth about Anita and the rest. I don't know any more than you do. Everybody makes their own choices."

"So, there's nothing we can actually do?"

"Well, not for the people, but maybe for the land. You can either lie low and let things get taken from you, or you can stand up and fight as hard as you can. That's the only part that's up to you."

"I guess you're right." I decided right then I would rather be full of fire and get a little burned, like Micah, than sink down into the muck and get stuck, like Anita and Brianna.

"I'm setting up a sit-in for Thursday. Ever sat in front of a bulldozer?"

"Not lately."

"Would you? I need numbers to make an impact. I need people who aren't afraid to get arrested."

At this point, I figured I didn't have much left to lose, in jail or out. Except Joshua. "I want to, Micah, but Joshua..." He had scattered all his feed and was now stalking Micah's ancient, fat, striped cat, which wanted nothing to do with him. I couldn't do anything that would worry him any more or make him think I would ever leave him.

"It's okay... I figured. That's why I didn't ask you before. What about Alice? You think she'd do it?"

I hadn't thought of Alice as an activist with her tiny frame and quiet voice. But maybe she could be. "She might."

"Well, call her. And Jason. What about him?"

"To sit in?"

"No. To cover it for the paper. There's nothing more powerful than words and a camera."

I could ask him for that. I was sure he would. "I'll call him, but I want to do something too."

"We'll need you to get us all out of jail, to make calls, all of that. I already thought of that," she said.

I knew my answer meant more than just this protest. It was like gardening, you want to be around to see the fruit grow. I had to at least try to bring some good back. I wanted to be part of something as tall as the mountains and deep as the last seam of coal. I wanted evidence of my life, Collis's life, and Joshua's life to be marked here years and years from now. I wanted to be a fighter. I wanted to be, for once, exactly who I was. "Ok, I'm in."

I hadn't felt like this in years. Definitely not since before Collis lost his job. It was not only that I was unafraid, it was that I was really looking forward to something, that I wanted to stand up for something even though I figured we'd lose. I wanted Joshua to have the beauty and protection of these mountains when he was grown. At least to have a chance at making it better. I wanted him to get grown and to thrive, rather than just survive. I wanted to give him back everything I could that had gone missing from our lives. I wanted to stay. Living in these mountains was a war. I finally felt brave enough to take a side.

37

Sit Down and Stand

Jason and Frankie, the Mountain Lion's photographer, pulled up in his beat-up red Toyota pickup. Jason said no matter where in the world you look that people are in trouble and struggling, war zones, refugee camps, remote villages, you'll find a bunch of beat-up Toyota pick-ups carrying them around. Other cars were parked on the edges of Micah's steep gravel driveway. Some trucks were even out by the small barn. Micah's eclectic collection of protestors wandered out of their vehicles toward the house, stepping carefully around the garden in the dark.

"Glad you all made it." I greeted everyone on the front porch. "You're early. Come on in and get some coffee." Daylight wasn't even close. By the time the sun actually rose, we'd be up on the top of the mountain, sitting in the middle of a dirt road, deep in a wide dozer rut, ready to get run over. At least some of us would.

Micah was in organizer mode. She had coffee and donuts for the twenty or so people who had gathered at her house. Of course, Dwight was there. It felt more like a party than a protest. "Morning, Ava," he said. "You ready?" Even Dwight seemed a little nervous. His cheerfulness couldn't mask everything.

"I guess so. But I'm not getting arrested. I'm just bailing you all out." I had Joshua to look out for and our future, all of this would show up in the news. It would definitely be front page of the Lion. I wasn't ready for that. Yet.

"You never know what'll happen," Dwight said. "Them company guys can be hard to take. But the bunch of us can give 'em hell, at least for a little while. I'll tell you what, it'll keep you alive living down here."

I'd only ever thought of the way this place wore me down, wore the mountains down, but Dwight was right, in a way. If you didn't get pulled down into the darkness, you spent your life trying to pull the whole place back up to mountain height, and that took strength. Dwight started organizing the motley bunch in a choir practice of sorts. For me, it was way too early for singing, but they were happy to sing a cappella versions of "This Little Light of Mine" and "We Shall Not Be Moved." I refilled their coffee.

Joshua was sleeping in the back bedroom that used to be Micah's when she was a kid. I slipped into the room and kissed him on the cheek to wake him, but he only rolled over.

"Time to wake up," I whispered. Then a little louder, "You don't want to miss the whole thing, do you?" He sat up in bed, hair matted to one side, eyes still not fully open.

"Let's go, Mama. I'm ready," he said.

Dwight drove us all up the gravel road behind Micah's house in the church van, and a few cars followed. Alice was there, too. She seemed lit up by being with the group, a little more present in her body, a little more color in her cheeks. Micah had a way of persuading people to come along and join her cause. It was a talent. But people felt a wave of destruction coming their way even before Micah organized this protest, and they had a natural urge to push against it. There had been a big decline in coal company profits in the last quarter, so companies were looking for new sources of income, places they might extract some gas after they'd blasted out all the coal. The big monster was insatiable. Blasting away this mountaintop to get at the coal and gas would destroy not only the land, but the water and the integrity of everything and everyone that sat below it. Saving the mountain and the whole of Cattle Island was way more than wanting to exist. It was living.

The protestors assembled in rows just behind the yellow "Do Not Cross" tape, which was strung between two trees. There was a "No Trespassing" sign, too. I made sure Joshua didn't cross it. People were standing around, nervously chatting. At first sound of a dozer coming up the hill, the plan was to link arms and sit down. They were not supposed to resist, but they didn't have to help anybody carry them off, either. Collis used to say I was like a cat. I could adjust my weight to hold me to the ground when I didn't want to be moved. I was always pulled to the earth. I belonged to it and it to me.

"You're more solid than you look," Collis said.

"I'm full of the element of surprise," I told him. That always made him smile.

Some of the people gathered looked solid too, some were heavy, but some, like Alice, looked like they might blow away, or be easily carried off. Joshua and I waited by the long white van. As the sun lightened everything, we could see the thick green of Cattle Island, Straight Creek flowing clear beside it, and down on the winding road, a giant yellow dozer barreling in our direction. It was so loud, we had trouble hearing each other. Everybody linked hands.

Jason was driving Frankie's truck just ahead of the dozer, and Frankie was standing in the bed of the truck, braced against the cab, shooting pictures one after the other, in what sounded like strings of Morse code. When they made it to the top, they both stopped. The dozer driver was some man I didn't recognize, but Dwight and some of the others knew him as Jimmy Calvert. He kept the motor running. It seemed to shake the land already. I could feel the vibrations under my feet. If the mountaintop removal began as scheduled, Micah and her neighbors would feel blasts shake the earth and crack the foundations of their houses every day.

"You can't destroy my home!" Micah yelled at Jimmy Calvert, but he wasn't listening. He was calling for police and company backup on his cell phone. It was as if we were just a few flies on his food that needed to be swatted away. He would likely win this battle eventually. We knew that, but it wouldn't be the last one.

Dwight started off "We Shall Not Be Moved" in call and response style, and the group fell in. Alice belted it out as loud as she could. I sang quietly on my side of the line, my hands on

Joshua's shoulders. The top of his head now reached my collarbone. How long before he'd be my height? Collis's?

Jimmy Calvert was off the phone now. "People need jobs around here, you know. People need power. What else did God put the coal and gas here for? You crazy tree-huggers need to get out of the way before we have to haul you off to jail. You got to let a man do his work."

Dwight just sang louder. "We shall not be, we shall not be moved!" It was more of a shout or proclamation now than a song. Jimmy Calvert shrugged and climbed back into the dozer to wait for reinforcements. He rolled the windows up tight, but I was sure he could still hear us singing.

"Come on, Mama. We should be on that side!" Joshua said, tugging at my arm and pointing across the yellow tape.

I looked at Jason, leaning against the truck typing notes into a laptop, each movement of his hands across the keyboard quick and sure. He was confident of his words, of what he wanted to tell the world. "Jason," I said. He looked up from his notes. "Will you bail us out?"

"Every time," he said.

Joshua and I stepped across the yellow tape. Micah reached out and took Joshua's hand, guiding him carefully beside her. It felt like Collis was nearby, watching proudly. We sat down with Alice in between us, both of us solid enough to hold her to the earth, to hold the whole mountain in place.

———

Acknowledgements

This novel has taken its time to get into the world, and I'm grateful to the many people who have guided me along the way. Thanks to Erin Chandler and Emily Wilhoit at Rabbit House Press, for your belief in the book and your dedication in producing it. Merci beaucoup to Laurie Smithwick for so many things, including this amazing cover and years of artistic friendship.

Thank you to the many brilliant friends who gave me feedback and encouragement, including Heather Mallory, Adam Sobsey, Kathy Pories, Julia Ridley Smith, Amy Rowland, and Laura Van Prooyen. Thanks to Michael Parker and Judy Goldman, writers I admire, for reading the manuscript and writing kind words. Thank you to the Virginia Center for the Creative Arts, Hambidge, and the Sewanee Writers' Conference for supporting my work over the years.

Yeep! to the commune, and thanks for the enormous support and joy you bring. Thanks to Michelle Goodman for her excellent counsel. Thanks to the Tacombi Writing Group and Writing Space for keeping me motivated. Thanks to Mimi McLaughlin, Kelly Colliver, and Pam Pecchio, longtime friends who keep me laughing. Thanks to Kay Collier McLaughlin, for a lifetime of guidance. Thanks to Justine Richardson, Tom Hansell, Katie Dollarhide, and all my friends from Appalshop, who know about loving the mountains. Thanks to my family near and far: Wagners, Whetstones, Durbins, and Zilbersteins. Most of all, thanks to Jack Henry, Cole, and Jeff, who inspire me.